?

BY

DUTCH

Published by DC Bookdiva Publications
Copyright © 2012 by Dutch

No part of this book may be reproduced, stored in or introduced into a retrieval system, or transmitted, in any form or by any means (electronic, mechanical, photocopying, recordings or otherwise), without prior written permission of both the copyright owner and the publisher of this book; except in the case of brief questions embodied in critical articles and reviews.

ISBN-10: 9780984611058
ISBN-13: 0984611053
Library of Congress Control Number:

Sale of this book without a front cover may be unauthorized. If this book is without a cover, it may have been reported to the publisher as "unsold" or "destroyed" and neither the author(s) nor the publisher may have received payment for it.

Publisher's Note

This is a work of fiction. Any names historical events, real people, living and dead, or the locales are intended only to give the fiction a setting in historic reality. Other names, characters, places, businesses and incidents are either the product of the author's imagination or are used fictiously, and their resemblance, if any, to real life counterparts is entirely coincidental.

Edited by: Jenell Talley

DC BOOKDIVA PRESENTS

DUTCH

DC Bookdiva Publications
#245 4401-A Connecticut Ave
NW, Washington, DC 20008
www.dcbookdiva.com
facebook.com/thedcbookdiva
twitter.com/dcbookdiva

Scan and follow us everywhere!

CHAPTER 1

1989

"Yo, God, I'm sayin' (sniff) we eatin' (sniff-sniff), but we ain't eatin' eatin', you know what I'm sayin', B?" YaYa said, between sniffs of heroin. He held the wax paper carefully between his heavily jeweled fingers, using his pinkie nail to powder his nose. "Now, Fell and them? They out West Virginia gettin' they weight up."

"I hear you, God," Shameeq replied, smoking a blunt and pushing his cocaine-white kitted Benz 190 down Market Street.

"And not only Fell," YaYa added, "Beeb and them down South, Ak up in Connecticut, Mel Kwon out in Ohio ... I'm tellin' you, God, we need to migrate! Get the fuck up outta Newark and fuckin' *feast*," YaYa said, thumbing his nose as he sat back in the plush piped interior and lit a cigarette.

Shameeq looked over at his man, shearling coated up and truck jewelry'd down, looking like a dark-skin version of Rakim. If it wasn't for the system banging out the truck, every time YaYa moved it would've sounded like slave chains clanking together. He had on that much jewelry. They were barely twenty and already heavy hitters. Shameeq handed him the blunt, chuckling. "We ain't eatin'. How you sound, B? Avon doin' five of them things a week, 17th Ave doin' eight on a bad week, not to mention—"

"I ain't say we wasn't eatin.' I said we wasn't EATIN' EATIN'," YaYa replied, his eyelids getting droopy.

Shameeq sucked his teeth. “Stop playin’. Word is bond, Ya, if you was stackin’ yo’ shit instead of putting it around your neck and up your nose, you’d be EATIN’ EATIN’, B,” Shameeq argued, even though he was damn near as jeweled up as YaYa.

“Fuck that, I’m a muhfuckin’ Don,” YaYa replied, going into a dope lean.

“Whatever, B.”

Shameeq pulled over and double-parked in front of Ali’s jewelry store to pick up the nugget bracelet Ali was fixing for him. He threw on the hazard lights and hopped out into the frigid early morning air.

Downtown Newark seemed to stay crowded on Saturdays, even in the coldest weather. Shameeq was on his way in the store when a brand-new burgundy Acura Legend coupe at the light caught his eye. The system was pumping “Like This” so loud it drowned out Shameeq’s system. His eyes followed the car as it made a left on Halsey Street. He glanced at the driver, and his eyes got big as plates.

“Oh, shit!” he cursed, jogging back to the car. He snatched the door open and got in so quickly, his entrance made YaYa snap out of his dope nod and snatch the pistol from his waist.

“Meeq, the fuck wrong wit’ you?” YaYa growled, mad he disturbed his nod.

Shameeq threw the car in drive and pulled out, making a right on Halsey in pursuit of the coupe.

“I just seen KG bitch ass,” Shameeq gritted.

“From Elizabeth?”

“I know this muhfucka ain’t buy no new whip wit’ my paper,” Shameeq growled. He had to run the next light to keep up with the Acura. When they reached the end of Halsey, Shameeq flashed his lights until the Acura pulled over.

Both cars double-parked, then Shameeq hopped out and stepped up to the driver's side window as KG lowered it.

"Sha—,"

"Yo, B, this you?" Shameeq asked angrily. He had already peeped the temporary license plate in the back window. "Please tell me you ain't buy no new whip!" Shameeq's hand rested under his Giants hoodie.

KG thought seriously about just pulling off, but the look in Shameeq's eyes seemed to dare him to do just that.

"Yo, yo, Sha, word to mother, I was comin' to see you. I just been—" KG began explaining, talking so fast the words tumbled out over each other. Shameeq opened the door.

"Get out," he told KG calmly. KG hesitated, so Shameeq repeated it more firmly. "Yo! Get the fuck out!"

KG got out slowly, watching Shameeq's hands.

"Yo, Sha, this word to mother, B, I was coming to see you—"

"When?" Shameeq demanded, cutting him off. "After you spent my shit up?! I ain't seen you in two months. Now all of a sudden you was comin' to see me?!" Shameeq blazed him, getting angrier with every word. KG could see it building in him, so he quickened his plea.

"I got like two on me now."

"Two?!" Shameeq echoed, spit flying out of his mouth and lightly sprinkling KG's face. "Two?! You owe me seventeen, nigga, not two!!"

"I- know."

"You tryin' to play me, B?!"

"No, Meeq, never that."

"Huh?!"

"Sha, word to mother!"

"Fuck your mother. Gimme the keys," Shameeq demanded, looking around, scanning for the police.

"Sha, man, I swear I'ma—"

Smack!

Shameeq cut off KG's weak pleas by smacking the shit out of him.

"Yo, B, chill!" KG hollered, holding his face.

"You think I'm fuckin' playin'?!" Shameeq hissed, hooking KG with a vicious left that crumpled him against the trunk of the car. He stood KG up and went in his pockets. "Punk muhfucka, you gonna disrespect me like that, huh?! You think shit is sweet?! Shut up; don't say shit. You disgust me," Shameeq barked while he beat KG's ass and pocketed his money.

"Yo, Sha, you dead wrong for that, God," YaYa yelled from the car, laughing.

"Come on, Shameeq, man, don't do it like that. I swear I'ma get yo' money, yo," KG mumbled as his lip swelled.

Shameeq smirked. "Then get it. But until then, the Ac' me, B."

He shoved KG off the car and got in under the wheel. It was then that he realized there was a chick in the car. He looked at her as he closed the door. "Yo, your man owes me money. You part of the payment or something?"

She sucked her teeth and said, "Picture that."

"Then get the fuck out!"

"Hmph! And freeze? Please. Somebody takin' me home," she sassed, then crossed her arms over her breasts.

Shameeq looked shorty over. She was a fly, chinky-eyed cinnamon bun with mad attitude. Her hair was cut like Anita Baker, and she wore two sets of bamboo earrings. Her name was written across one pair.

"Okay, Nikki," Shameeq shrugged, reading her earrings. He pulled off, watching KG standing in the street behind him.

"Whatever ... Drama," she replied, smirking.

He looked at her.

"Yo, who is Drama?" he asked, playing stupid.

Everybody in the streets called him Drama except his crew. He would answer to it, but he never called himself by it.

"Who don't know Drama?" she replied, thinking, Wit' your fine ass.

She was holding her composure, but on the inside, her stomach was doing backflips and semis. With his Egyptian-bronze skin tone, hazel eyes, wavy hair and dimples, every ghetto chick wanted his type of drama in her life. He was 6'1", bowlegged, and his swagger gave chicks chills.

"So, you fuck wit' clowns like that?" he asked, looking through KG's tape collection.

"No," she answered quickly.

"I can't tell. All them bags back there. You must be one of them bitches that juice nigguhs, huh?" he said, popping in 3XDope's "Funky Dividends."

"Like I need a man to take care of me," she replied dismissively. "All that's for his son, which he too sorry to provide for. Shit, the only reason he in town is 'cause I threatened to take his ass to court," she explained.

"In town? Where he was at?" Shameeq's ears perked up.

"Virginia."

"Doing what?"

"What you think?"

Shameeq's mind went back to what YaYa was talking about earlier.

"That's why you nor I seen him. He owed me too," Nikki chuckled.

Shameeq looked at Nikki. She was a dime, no question, but she ran her mouth and had no loyalty to a man she had a child with. Still, he could tell she was open on him, so he planned on making fucking KG's baby mama part of KG's payment. But first he had to fuck with her head.

"Where you live?" he asked.

"Brick Towers."

At the next block he pulled over in front of the bus stop. She looked at him confusedly.

"What? You thought I was takin' you home? Picture that. I got shit to do," he said, holding a smirk.

"Like you can't take me a few more blocks, Drama. Brick Towers ain't that far," she snapped.

"Yeah, well, I ain't goin' that way," he answered, looking at his Movado, then glancing in the rearview. "Here comes the bus now. You betta hurry up."

She eyed him to see if he was serious, then sucked her teeth. She reached in the back for the bags, but Shameeq stopped her.

"What you doin', yo? Didn't I tell you he owed me dough?"

"What's my baby's clothes got to do wit' that?" Nikki probed.

"Like I ain't got a son," Shameeq lied, but she kept reaching. He jerked her arm. "Fuck, you deaf? That shit mine. Now beat it. Your bus is coming," he said, bopping his head to the music.

Nikki was close to tears.

"That's foul, Drama. Word is bond, that's foul," she said, but Shameeq turned up the radio and started rapping along with E.S.T.

Nikki got out. She pulled her earmuffs out of her pocket and put them on her ears. Shameeq pulled off, then headed straight for the bus stop on the corner of Elizabeth and High streets, where he knew she'd get off. He knew with her good looks she was used to dudes fawning over her every whim. So he decided to put down the demonstration so she knew it was all about him, not her.

A few minutes later, the bus pulled up and Nikki got off. Shameeq blew the horn, then pulled up beside her. Nikki rolled her eyes and kept walking. Shameeq lowered the passenger window, smiling.

"Ay, yo, Nikki, my fault, yo. I ain't mean to flip on you like that. I was just mad at your man."

She ignored him and kept walking, so he rolled at a creep beside her.

"Come on, get in. I know it's cold out there, " he said, holding back his laughter.

"I'm fine," she replied, but he could damn near hear her teeth chattering.

"At least come get yo' baby's clothes," he offered.

"Keep it."

He slammed on the brakes and barked, "Ay, yo, Nikki, bring yo' ass here! I ain't tryin' to have all that attitude, word up! I said I apologize 'cause I like you, but if it's like that, fuck it then!"

Nikki's ears perked up when he told her he liked her, so when Shameeq began to pull off, Nikki called out, "Drama! Hold up!"

She pranced over to the car and got in.

"So this mean you accept my apology?" he grinned.

She gave him the eye. "Maybe. And like I told you, he *ain't* my man!!"

Fifteen minutes later, Shameeq was nine inches deep in Nikki's guts. She straddled him as he reclined on the couch, riding him like a thoroughbred. Her firm C-cup–sized breasts bounced with every stroke, and the gushy sounds of sloppy sex filled the room, punctuated by her screams of passion.

"Yeeessss, Drama, ohhhh, right there! Fuck this pussy," she moaned, grinding her hips into him and biting her bottom lip.

Shameeq grabbed her around the back, then laid her on the floor. He cocked her legs up over his shoulders, then started long dicking her like he was trying to knock the bottom out.

"Drama ... oooohhh, " she gasped, clawing at the floor trying to squirm away from the dick, but she was pinned beneath him helplessly. "Ahhhh, baby, I--I feel it in m--m--my stomach," she squealed, eyes rolled up in the back of her head.

"Take this dick, bitch," he growled. "Tell me you want Drama in your life!" Shameeq slid in as deep as he could go, grinding her spot until her body shook with her fourth orgasm.

"Oh, I doooo ... I do, I do. I want Drama in my life! I wanna have your baby," she moaned.

Picture that, he thought being careful not to bust the condom. Shorty definitely had the type of pussy that a man would rush home to, but she played herself by giving it up too quickly. Shameeq fucked her three more times, then fell asleep. Shorty woke him up, washed him, fed him and then fucked him again. She wanted him to know the pussy was his when he wanted it. He already knew that because his dick game was crazy.

By the time he left, it was after nine. He drove around to his spot on Avon, laughing with his workers about the whole incident with KG and his baby moms. But little did he know the joke would soon be on him. A black Monte Carlo SS had been sitting in the cut waiting for him to come through. They knew his crew was too deep to try anything right then, so they waited. They had been paid to do the job right. They followed him to YaYa's block on 17th Avenue but couldn't make their move. Once he left YaYa and hit Irving Turner Boulevard, they finally got their chance.

He pulled up to the light pumping "Ain't No Half Steppin'" by Big Daddy Kane. The SS pulled up beside him on the passenger's side. An Uzi sub-machine gun was stuck out the window. The only thing that saved Shameeq's life was the light turning green and him pulling off a split second before the Uzi began to spit. That split second made all the difference because the shots that burst through the window aimed for his head penetrated the headrest, making Shameeq duck and mash the gas.

"What the fuck?!" he barked, but the only answer was a shower of bullets.

The staccato sound of the automatic fire filled his ears as he desperately tried to weave in and out of traffic to stay low. The Acura was fast, but it was no match for the SS. They tried to pull up beside Shameeq, but he veered hard to the right, trying to ram the nose of the SS into a parked car. The screeching sound of metal on metal rang out, and shooting sparks danced across the hood of the SS head as the driver fought to maintain control. He had the better car, but Shameeq had the better driving skills.

Shameeq aimed his Beretta through the back window and opened fire on the SS. Then he made a hard left, momentarily losing them. The SS came up behind him and bumped the rear. They accelerated, trying to push the Acura into the next busy intersection. Shameeq turned completely around in the seat and took aim straight at the driver. He shot out the windshield of the SS, causing the driver and shooter to take cover. He used the opportunity to speed up, then throw up the emergency brakes, fishtailing the Acura. That made the SS slam into the rear flank of the Acura, causing the air bags to explode in the driver's and shooter's faces. The driver's head jerked back. Blood was everywhere.

In a second, Shameeq was out of the car and pumping shot after shot at the driver. The passenger, still discombobulated by the accident, stumbled out of the passenger's side and took off in a drunken sprint. Shameeq let off one more round before his clip was empty.

"Shit!" he cursed, then sprinted off in the opposite direction as the sounds of approaching sirens blared in the distance.

Not knowing who or what was waiting for him at his crib, Shameeq took a cab up to Vailsburg, where his twin sister, Egypt, lived. She greeted him at the door with a hug. He peered over her shoulder at the dude sitting on the couch, broke the embrace and said, "Yo, B, you gotta bounce."

"Excuse you?" Egypt quipped, one eyebrow raised.

Shameeq ignored her, grabbed the dude's coat and put it in his lap. "She'll call you later."

"Shameeq!" Egypt yelled. Dude looked at Shameeq, then at Egypt, confused.

"Yo, B, I'm the one talkin' to you, not her. Family crisis, and I ain't tryin' to repeat myself," Shameeq said calmly, eyeing dude.

When Egypt heard him say family crisis, she sighed and said, "Jerome, let me call you later, okay? Let me speak wit' my brother."

There was no denying Shameeq was her brother they looked just alike, to their long eyelashes and thick eyebrows, although Egypt's were slightly arched. She was slim and flat chested, but her hips and ass more than compensated. At six feet even and bowlegged just like her brother, the only thing distinctly different about them was the fact that Egypt wore long, skinny salon locs. No extensions; it was all her own hair.

The dude grabbed his coat. "Yeah, a'ight," he said, eyeing Shameeq hard, but Shameeq had his back to him, talking on Egypt's cordless.

"I'll call you," Egypt whispered, giving dude a kiss on the lips.

She closed the door just as Shameeq hung up the phone and sat down.

"Ohhhh! This better be good! Bustin' up my groove, and I was about to get me some," Egypt fumed with a smirk. She tied two of her dreads around the rest to make a ponytail.

"Watch yo' mouth," Shameeq warned. "Don't make me chase dude down and smash his ass, yo. I'm already heated; don't make it worse."

"Whatever, Shameeq."

"I know whatever. Wait until you get married," he huffed.

"Too late," she giggled, going into the kitchen. "Now, what's this crisis, or you just here cock blockin'?"

"Muhfuckas tried to kill me."

The sound of silverware hitting the floor was all you heard as Egypt rushed back in the room.

"What?! Who?! When?! Are you—" she rattled off, coming over to check his face, but he swatted her hand away.

"I'm a'ight. Damn, mother hen, I said *tried*."

Egypt stood back with her hands on her hips.

"So what we gonna do?"

"We? *We* ain't doin' shit," he replied.

"Oh, so you gonna play me lame now? Hell no Shameeq! You all I got yo. You think I'm just gonna stand by and let these punk muhfuckas take that?!" She was so vexed, she was close to tears, but she had murder in her heart.

"See, that's why we ain't doin' shit. Look at you 'bout to cry and shit. What you gonna do, huh?" He pointed his fingers like a gun, shaking like he was scared. "You shot at my brother, boo-hoo, I'ma kill you," he chuckled.

"Fuck you, Shameeq," Egypt hissed and stormed into the kitchen.

"Yeah, that's right, you in the best place for a woman," he yelled, although he knew his sister wasn't the average female.

They had grown up parentless since they were eleven, after their mother killed their father, then killed herself. She had found him in the bed with another woman. They refused to be split up by the system, so they took to the streets and either hustled or starved. When crack hit Newark around '85, they used the opportunity to come up. They never looked back. It was him and her against the world, taking trips to New York, posted up on the corners and handling any beefs that came their way.

When YaYa came home from Caldwell, he and Shameeq took their hammer game to the next level, earning them the name Drama Squad and Shameeq the name Drama. They stayed in some shit because none of them had a cool head, all three live wires. They were young, black and reckless, getting paper and making a name for themselves in the street. As shit got heated, Shameeq made Egypt fall back, get her G.E.D, then go to community college. She was in her second year, studying business management.

Despite his jokes, Shameeq knew Egypt was serious because she loved him to death and she was no stranger to putting in work.

YaYa got there in no time with Trello and Casper. Both were fifteen and hungry to be made in the Drama Squad. Trello was a short, brown-skin dude who weighed a buck fifty soaking wet, but his Uzi weighed a ton, and his hammer game made him a beast.

They called him Casper because he was albino. Red eyes and a deadly temper, he had hands so nice that he was a two-time Golden Gloves champion. He had a promising career awaiting him in the ring, but the streets had a hold of him and wouldn't let go.

Shameeq explained the scenario to YaYa, and they both came to the same conclusion.

"KG," YaYa surmised.

"I feel like that too," Shameeq concurred.

"Yo, I told you you was dead wrong, B. You can't play a dude like that in front of his bitch," YaYa said.

"Shameeq, I know this ain't over no pussy," Egypt remarked, knowing her brother. "That shit gonna be the death of you."

"Don't mark me like that, girl. And I told you dude owed me money!"

"But you fucked her, though, didn't you?" Egypt inquired, knowing she was right because Shameeq didn't answer. "Trick."

"Watch yo' mouth."

"But yo, B ... yo, it might not be KG," Trello added. "It might be them dudes on Renner still in they feelings 'cause we housed they block."

"Or that kid off 20th Street," Casper added.

"Drama," Egypt smirked, shaking her head at her brother. The streets had named him well.

"So what up? Word to mother, B, somebody gotta bleed, rightly or wrongly," YaYa growled, ready to set it.

"Indeed, indeed. So yo, first thing in the morning, we gonna snatch that bitch up!" Shameeq exclaimed.

"What bitch?" Casper asked.

"KG baby moms. If dude did do it, I know exactly how to find out," Shameeq smirked.

CHAPTER 2

The next morning, the Drama Squad waited on the corner of West Kinney and High Street in a brown conversion van, watching for Nikki. She had told Shameeq she worked at the Marriott on 1st and 9th streets. So he knew she'd be coming out any minute. She came out of the building, bundled up in a pink goose parka and matching earmuffs. The wind whipped furiously around her as she trekked to the bus stop.

"There she go," Shameeq said from the passenger's seat.

YaYa pulled off, making a U-turn so he could come up beside her. Nikki didn't notice the van until it was too late. Casper threw the sliding door open, then he and Trello jumped out. He cuffed her mouth and snatched her inside the van so fast she didn't have time to scream until she was lying in the back of the van.

"Shut the fuck up!" Shameeq growled, backhanding Nikki. He didn't try to hurt her; he just wanted her to know shit was serious.

"Dra--Dra, what did I do?" Nikki sobbed, holding her reddened face.

"You know what you did, bitch! You set me up for your man so he could kill me!" he yelled in her face.

"Noooo! I didn't," Nikki protested, but Shameeq grabbed her by the throat.

"Bitch ... don't ... lie," he seethed, his hazel eyes a crimson red.

"No—I mean—argh," she gagged, "I--I don't know! No!"

"What you mean you don't know, huh?! You must know somethin' if you know it's somethin' not to know!!" Shameeq grilled her, relaxing his grip on her throat.

"No, Drama, no! I meant I don't know what you're talking about! I swear!" she cried, but Shameeq just eyed her without answering. She continued.

"K--KG, he called me flippin', askin' me why I didn't get out wit' him and where you take me."

"And what you tell him?!"

"I told him you dropped me at the bus stop, that's it," she stressed.

Shameeq snorted. "You expect me to believe that shit?!" he hissed.

"I swear on my mother, Drama!"

"So you sayin' you ain't know he did it?" Shameeq's tone lowered, but he was still skeptical.

"No," she sobbed. "I would never do something like that to you, Drama," she vowed, leaning up and hugging his neck hard.

He winked his eye at Casper and Trello, then untangled her arms from around his neck. "Naw, yo, I can't trust that shit, yo. I can't trust you!"

"You can, baby, you can trust me," Nikki replied quickly, looking him in the eyes and willing him her heart.

"I can trust you? You sure?"

She nodded, then hugged him again.

"Then I need you to do something for me," he began.

Nikki wiped her eyes with the back of her hand and answered like she was down for whatever. "What?"

"I need you to call KG. Don't ask him about shit, just go at him and clown him about me takin' his whip. A'ight?" Shameeq instructed her.

"That's it?"

"Yeah."

"What if … what if he did it?" Nikki asked timidly.

"What you think?" he replied. She could already see KG's blood in his eyes.

"Word is bond, Drama. KG ain't much, but he all I got. I--I don't care either, but if—who's gonna do for me and my son?" Nikki inquired, hoping this show of loyalty would bond her to him.

He smiled and caressed her face.

"You won't have to worry no more, Nikki, I got you," he promised.

She nodded and kissed the palm of his hand.

??????

Shameeq and Nikki waited in her apartment. It took a while for KG to finally call back after paging him repeatedly. When he did call, Shameeq picked up the kitchen phone; Nikki had the cordless.

"'Bout time," Nikki huffed, the sassiness back in her voice. "What, you was fuckin' some bitch?"

"I ain't got time for that shit, Nikki. Fuck you want?" KG spat back.

"You ain't got time?? I could be callin' you 'cause yo' son is sick! What you mean you ain't got time?!" Nikki winked at Shameeq, knowing she was doing her job. He smiled back, but he was thinking, Scandalous bitch.

"What … do … you … want?" KG repeated, gritting his teeth.

"I need some money."

"I just took yo' ass shoppin' yester—" KG tried to say.

"And I *told* you that dude who took your car wouldn't let me get my shit!" she replied.

"Ain't nobody take *shit* from me! I gave that bitch muhfucka that shit," he exclaimed.

"I can't tell. But *anyway*, what you gonna do? Because yo' son still need clothes. It ain't his fault you got stripped," she giggled.

"Bitch, you think that shit cute?! His faggot ass had a gun, that's the *only* reason I ain't beat his ass! But trust me, after what I sent at his ass last night, I *bet* you he respect KG now!" he boasted, not knowing he had just signed his own death warrant trying to save face with a chick who didn't give a fuck about him.

Shameeq was fuming. He pressed mute on the receiver and whispered, "Get him over here."

Nikki nodded.

"Whatever. Just when you comin'?"

KG sucked his teeth.

"I'm about to bounce. I'll wire it to you."

"Oh, hell no, Kevin! That's that bullshit! The last time you said that, I ain't get shit. But fuck it, I see how you wanna play. Monday morning, I will be up in Essex County—"

"You a triflin' bitch, you know that!" KG spat. "I'll be through there."

"When?"

"Later." He hung up.

"Beep him again," Shameeq ordered. He wanted KG right then.

Nikki did as she was told. She beeped him three times back to back. KG called back, vexed.

"Bitch, didn't I say later?!"

He wanted to strangle Nikki's ass, but he was ready to get back to VA, and he damn sure didn't need a child-support warrant hanging over his head.

"And I gotta go to work now! Just come gimme the money so you can go back to your lil' hoes!" she replied.

"Have yo' ass downstairs when I get there. I ain't climbin' all them damn steps!" KG roared, then hung up.

"So ... wh--what you gonna do, Drama?" she asked nervously. "What if he don't come up?"

"He will," he assured her.

"And then?" she probed.

"Nikki."

"Yes?"

"You talk too much. I told you, I got you," Shameeq answered, peeping around the curtain like Malcolm X, gloc in hand. He could see the front side of Brick Towers, nine stories below. Down the block, YaYa had the van parked.

As they waited, Nikki debated several times whether or not to break the silence. She finally got up the nerve and said, "Drama."

He looked at his watch, then at her.

"I ... I love you," she blurted out before she lost the nerve.

"You what?" he snickered.

She came over to him.

"You probably think I'm foul 'cause I'm doin' this to KG and he my baby father ... but I really do have feelings for you. You ain't like all these nigguhs out here; you different. Just give me the chance to show you I'm different too," she vowed, never losing eye contact.

Nikki felt that by being willing to commit an act of murder with him, it was the ultimate show of loyalty. Drama would see she was a down-ass chick and take her under his wing.

Shameeq pulled her close, then kissed her forehead, nose and lips.

"So you want Drama in your life like that, boo?"

Nikki smiled seductively and bit her bottom lip.

"And other places too," she replied, grabbing his dick.

Shameeq eyed her body and thought about a quickie, but one glance out the window killed that thought.

"He here."

Nikki looked. KG was driving his old black '88 Seville with the beige rag. She looked up at Shameeq questioningly.

"Just chill," he told her, eyes trained on the car.

They could hear him blow his horn and the faint thump of his system.

"He's not comin' up," she surmised.

Shameeq stayed vigilant.

KG blew the horn several more times, then began to pull off. Nikki was about to breathe easy, thinking he was leaving, but KG made a U-turn and parked across the street. He hopped out and crossed the street. He kept his head on swivel, looking back and forth. He kept his hand tucked under his Avirex coat as he disappeared inside the building.

Nikki's knees got weak knowing what was about to go down. Shameeq peeped her expression as he cupped her chin in his hand and said, "Everything is cool, ok? I got you."

Nikki nodded.

"You wit' me now. Walk like a champion," he winked.

Nikki's eyes lit up with her smile.

"I'm good, baby," she assured him, although her stomach was in knots.

"When you let him in, turn back and walk over to the couch, a'ight? I'll take care of the rest."

Shameeq got in the closet by the door. Nikki stood in the middle of the room, hoping it would all be over soon. The knock on the door made her jump.

"Nikki! Open the fuckin' door!" KG demanded.

She took a deep breath, drawing her last ounce of sass, then barked, "Boy, wait! Knockin' on the door like you the police!"

She unlocked all the locks and opened the door. She turned and walked to the couch like Shameeq had instructed her. "Just let me get my coat!"

"Didn't I tell you be downstairs?!" KG fumed. He felt safer now that he was in her apartment.

KG came deeper into the apartment, allowing Shameeq to ease out of the closet and put the gun to the back of KG's head.

"What up, B? Remember me?" Shameeq hissed like a cobra ready to strike.

KG froze up and damn near shit a brick.

"Sha?" he gulped, in a voice so high pitched he sounded like a mouse.

He held his hands where Shameeq could see them. Shameeq reached around and took the pistol off his waist, then spun KG around to face him.

"Surprise, nigguh," Shameeq smirked.

"Man, my word, I got yo' money!" KG confessed.

"Keep that shit, dude. This about that shit last night!"

"What sh—" KG began, but Shameeq smacked the shit out of him with his own gun. KG fell flat on the floor. Shameeq continued to pistol whip him.

"Muhfucka, you tried to body me?! Huh?! Bitch-ass nigguh, you missed!" Shameeq huffed, then put the gun to his forehead.

"Sha, I swear I don't know what you talkin' about," KG lied, his whole mouth swollen and several teeth lost on the floor.

"I'ma ask you one time and one time only, B, Do you want to live?"

KG nodded vigorously.

"Where the otha muhfucka? I bodied one of them faggots, but I want 'em both or word is bond, I'll body you here and now," Shameeq gritted, cocking back the hammer.

KG quickly weighed his options. Any hope of survival was enough for a coward because a spineless nigguh can fit in the smallest places.

"You tell me, K, and I'll give you a pass because a dead nigguh can't pay me my paper. But if you lie ..."

"Shameeq, he a cat from Grafton Avenue. Cat named Hameef. He 'posed to beep me so I can give him his money," KG blurted out.

"What code he usin'?"

"111."

Shameeq knew KG was telling him the truth because he was too scared to lie. He took KG's beeper off his pants, checked the numbers, then clipped it on his own belt. He stood up, looked down into KG's mangled face in disgust, then raised the gun.

"Sha, nooooo!!" KG pleaded, throwing up his arms like they were bulletproof and could protect his face.

Pop!!! Pop!!! Pop!!!

Shameeq killed him with three in the head. Nikki had been watching in horror, but seeing KG's head explode all over the dirty brown carpet was too much. She grabbed her mouth and her stomach then sprinted to the bathroom. Vomit erupted from her gut and leaked through her fingers. Shameeq followed her into the bathroom.

"You okay, boo?" Shameeq asked.

She nodded but didn't take her head out of the toilet. He put the gun to the back of her head and pulled the trigger.

"Told you, boo ... I got you," Shameeq laughed.

CHAPTER 3

"Where the fuck is 757?" Shameeq asked, looking at KG's beeper. Him, YaYa and Egypt were sitting in his living room. It had been two days since KG's murder, and he was still waiting for the 111 code to come up because he wanted dude that bad.

"Ay," Shameeq said, mushing YaYa's leg, disturbing his dope nod.

"Wake yo' ass up. What area code is 757?"

YaYa scratched his face, eyes still closed.

"Fuck outta here," he mumbled.

"Virginia," Egypt told him, lighting up a Newport and plopping down on the couch next to him.

"How you know?"

"You asked, didn't you? Why you ask if you ain't want an answer?" she quipped, blowing cigarette smoke in his direction. Shameeq waved it off with a frown because he hated cigarette smoke.

"I'm sayin', whoever it is, they been blowin' KG up," Shameeq remarked, flicking through the numbers on the beeper readout.

"So call," Egypt shrugged.

Shameeq contemplated the suggestion momentarily, then grabbed the cordless phone off of the coffee table. He chose a number, then dialed. As it rung, he pulled the blunt from behind his ear, then leaned over on Egypt to get a light.

"Yo, who this?" the voice on the other end asked gruffly.

"Who this? You beeped me?" Shameeq answered.

Catching the Jersey accent, the voice probed, "KG? That you?"

"Naw, this..." Shameeq inhaled the blunt, "this his cousin. KG sleep right now," he said, chuckling at his own joke.

"Oh, well, yo, stic, tell him to call Blue when he get up."

"What up, though? I'm holdin' it down right now," Shameeq explained.

"That's cool, stic, but I'd rather speak to KG. Nuttin' personal, just business."

Click.

Even though YaYa was nodding, he was still coherent.

"What he say?" YaYa asked.

"He said he want KG to call him. He ain't wanna say," Shameeq replied, blowing the weed smoke at Egypt. She waved it off. She hated weed.

"At least he on point, B," YaYa remarked hoarsely. "I'm tellin' you, B, the shit is clear. KG was goin' O.T. and flippin' our shit. Them dudes blowin' him up because they thirsty. Probably ain't nobody down there to connect wit'. That's our future right there, B. Word!"

Shameeq sat back contemplating YaYa's words. For the past couple of days, he'd seen the same numbers come up over and over, and he was starting to see the potential. Newark was getting more and more crowded every day. Street beefs were sparking wars. Crews spent more time beefing over blocks than getting money on them. The Drama Squad was well-known and respected, but respect carried no weight with the hungry. Anybody could get it. Every day your rep was made, and every day it was tested, either to be upheld or crushed.

But the South had promise. New territory with no roots. You could be one place one day and another the next. Money could flow like water, and Shameeq was beginning to see the logic in making the move out of town.

"I agree wit' YaYa," Egypt said, crushing her cigarette in the ashtray. "We need to at least check it out."

"Ay, yo, Egypt, you been on this we shit a lot lately. *We* don't include you because you stayin' here," he stressed, pointing to the floor.

"Shameeq, I'm tired of this college shit," she whined. "I ain't cut for that shit. Square-ass dudes and dizzy-ass broads. Fuck that! If it's money to be made, I'ma be there," she stated, looking her brother in the eye.

"Egypt, get that shit out your head, a'ight? We already talked about this—" he began.

"No, *you* talked about it! Get off that bullshit, Sha! You know half these bitch-made nigguhs ain't got the heart *I* got!" she bragged.

Shameeq leaned forward on the couch.

"You think that shit matter?! Fuck heart, B. I ain't got nothing to prove! You think I wanna be the nigguh muhfuckas be talkin' about like, 'Drama was doin' it, Shameeq was doin' it. That nigguh had heart?!' And I be somewhere dead or doin' dinosaur numbers?! Fuck that," Shameeq spat.

Egypt sucked her teeth. "Yeah, I hear you talkin', but that ain't got shit to do wit' it," she retorted.

"It got everything to do with it because one of us gotta know they world—the square-ass dudes and dizzy broads—'cause they the ones that grow old and die happy," he explained.

"Well, *you* go to school, and I'll go to VA," Egypt chuckled.

Shameeq playfully mushed her head. "Fuck outta here and go do your homework. Fuckin' square," he joked.

CHAPTER 4

Present Day 1994

The square concrete room smelled of stale tobacco and cheap cologne. The type it seemed all police wore. Brut mixed with musty Old Spice. The room was filled with smoke that wafted up and around the one light above the desk where he sat. A two-way mirror was on his left. The kind witnesses came to look through and point people out in lineups. But he knew there were no witnesses behind the glass because there was no need. He had come to point himself out. To point the finger on the Drama Squad's career.

Mullins, a gray-haired DEA agent sat in front of him, coatless, sleeves rolled up and damp spots under both armpits. Behind Mullins stood Agent Jacobs and the freckled-faced, Opie-looking agent McGrady. They all watched him through eyes that shined with victory. After all this time, the Drama Squad was finally about to be brought down by one of its own.

"So you're telling me KG, aka Kevin Graves, was murdered in 1989?" Mullins probed skeptically. Mullins looked at the manila folder in front of him, then rifled through a few pages. "But our *other* informant said KG was the leader of the Drama Squad at least until 1991."

He laughed and blew out a stream of smoke toward the ceiling.

"That's what the Squad wanted people to think," he said, then leaned his elbows on the table. "Like I said, his murder was what brought the Squad down here in the first place. Cats already knew KG. They thought he was running the show, so we let em' run with that. KG a leader?" he chuckled. "Naw, your little snitches got it wrong."

"Well, that's what you're here for. To tell it right ... *snitch,"* McGrady smirked with a racist gleam in his eye. "I can't wait 'til the rest of your crew finds out what you're doing. There won't be a federal pen you'll survive in. Then you'll come crawling to us to protect you from your own. Isn't justice ... poetic?"

He tensed at McGrady's every word. He wanted to lash out, but he knew McGrady was right. If he did this, he'd become the pariah of the game. The lowest form of existence known to the streets. A rat, a stool pigeon, a snitch. The whole Squad's life was in his hands. Dudes who called him family. Dudes who had pledged to be loyal to the team just as he had. But there he sat, and from the D.E.A's point of view, he was on their team. Despite his annoyances, he had to smile because justice would truly be poetic.

"Something funny?" Mullins asked.

"McGrady, tell me ... how did you feel when you found out you were different than all the other little boys in the sandbox?" he asked, inhaling his cigarette, then breaking into a fit of coughs.

McGrady's ears turned beet red.

"You callin' me a fag, you spineless piece of shit?! We'll see who's the fag when your asshole is bleedin' in Lewisburg!"

"McGrady!" Mullins barked, looking over his shoulder slightly. When he felt McGrady had calmed, he turned back around and pointed at him. "And *you.* This is not a game! We've got you bastards with conspiracy to distribute cocaine, money laundering, and so many counts of murder we stopped counting!" Mullins huffed, letting it sink in. He added, "Now, I'm going to check into this KG thing along with everything else you tell me. And if you lie even *once,* big or small, the possibility of any deal is off the table! Understand?"

He held his hands palms up and shrugged. From the look of his hands, McGrady could tell he had never worked a day in his life. The thought disgusted him.

"A deal's a deal. I give you what you want and you give me what I want. Fair exchange ain't no robbery," he winked. "So what do you want to know?"

"Everything. From the beginning," Jacobs answered. Jacobs wasn't feeling him at all. Jacobs had been the agent most familiar with the Drama Squad. He knew every ranking member. Jacobs had watched them. Studied them. But there was something in his gut, something he couldn't place, that told him something wasn't right.

"The beginning?" he echoed, putting out his cigarette in the ashtray.

"Listen closely, 'til your attention's undivided because the story I'm 'bout to tell will twist you up if you ain't sharp. But by the time I'm through ... it'll all be clear," he smiled.

"So? We're waiting," McGrady sighed.

"The Squad in VA really started ringin' bells with the New York beef," he began, lighting another cigarette.

"What New York beef?"

"Yo, it went down like this ... "

April 1989

Shameeq, YaYa and Trello had been in Virginia six months, but shit wasn't as sweet as YaYa had made O.T. seem. Instead of finding VA thirsty for up-top work, they found the seven cities teaming with already established crews. Some were local, but most were from New York; a few were from Jersey. If it hadn't been for a few spots in Norfolk, Virginia Beach and Portsmouth that they inherited from KG, shit would've really been tight.

Shameeq had to admit that KG's name did carry a little weight, so he knew he had made the right decision letting people assume KG was the boss. He rode the "Yo, KG makin' moves, so he sent us" type of line. This way, if cats started givin' up names, they'd put it on a dead man instead of him. But that was something he found out wouldn't likely happen because KG had some real soldiers on his team.

Blue out of VA Beach was a big fat nigguh, but the only thing soft about him was his belly. Blue could sit down and eat a whole chicken to the head, and his appetite for the game was just as large. Montez out of Norfolk was a tall, lanky kid who resembled

Chris Tucker. He was quick with the jokes, but even quicker with that pistol. And Lil' B from Portsmouth. They used to call him Lil' Bulldog but shortened it to Lil' B. He was short, but solidly built like the pit bulls he loved to fight. All of them were young, no more than 19, and all of them were thoroughbreds.

They were feeling the Drama Squad too, more than they were feeling KG. Mainly because KG tried to keep them hungry, giving them petty percentages while he G'd off with the lion's share. But they saw the Drama Squad as being in the same boat as them: nigguhs on the come up, not nigguhs who had made it. Shameeq purposely painted this picture. The Drama Squad left the jewels and expensive whips back in the Bricks with Casper and Egypt. They came down in Timberlands and Carhartt, pushing three used Volkswagen Jettas, which really made an impression on the VA cats. They were used to out-of-towners coming down there trying to shine like the city was theirs.

Some tried that gorilla shit like they were real killers when, in fact, most were flunkies for larger dudes back home, or they had been run out of the tri-state area and couldn't eat up top anymore. Dudes like that became statistics and pushed the murder rate in seven cities, Richmond and DC to a new high between '89-'92. But the Drama Squad would be different. Real recognized real, and when it came to breaking bread, Shameeq made sure the VA cats ate lovely. He could afford to since he was making almost four times as much as he did in Newark off each brick of coke.

The downside was he was moving fewer bricks than he did in Newark. And when it came to weight, he couldn't fuck with the prices the New York crews were giving. What they were pushing them for in VA, he was paying for up top! Shameeq felt like he was just spinning his wheels, and the shit was beginning to frustrate him.

"Ay, yo, look at this shit," Shameeq spat, referring to the piles of money on the table. He, YaYa and Trello were counting the money, sitting in their apartment on Lake Edwards Drive. "Trello, what's the count?"

Trello continued to count, coming across a fake twenty-dollar bill. It was really a one-dollar bill with twenty-dollar bill ends taped to it. "What the fuck? Damn."

Shameeq snatched the bill from him. "This is like the third one of these shits, B! Either the fiends takin' them dudes fast or them muhfuckas think we slow. Ya, you don't check this shit when you pick it up?"

YaYa, cigarette tucked in the corner of his mouth, rubber banded the loose money into g-stacks, answered, "Man, I ain't tryin' to hear that shit. You check 'em."

"Well, you take it then," Shameeq retorted, tossing the bill at YaYa, who tossed it on the floor.

Trello leaned back and lit the blunt with a gun shaped lighter. "That's sixty-eight right there, yo."

"What we got at the other spots?"

"Forty-eight from Blue, plus he on his way wit' twenty. We got like thirty-nine wit' Montez, and I ain't holler at Lil' B yet," Trello ran down to him. Trello offered the blunt to YaYa playfully. He already knew YaYa didn't smoke weed. Shameeq took the blunt.

"We come all the way down here for *this*?" Trello asked. "We might as well go home."

"Fuck no," Shameeq responded. He wasn't about to let the situation beat him.

"Fucking right we ain't goin' back," YaYa sneered. "This shit is sweet, word to mother. We just need mo' spots, and we need to push them New York muhfuckas back the fuck up top. I hate fuckin' New Yorkers."

"Push em' back wit' what?" Shameeq wanted to know.

"Let the wolves out, B," YaYa replied.

"How the fuck we gonna feed em'? Wit' this?" Shameeq countered, gesturing to the money on the table.

"Wolves feed themselves."

"True," Shameeq agreed.

"I don't know about you Sha, but I'm ready to get on some '86 shit, B, and lay them clowns down! Remember that, B?

Muhfuckas see us comin' and hold they breath," YaYa laughed, slapping Shameeq a pound shake.

Someone knocked at the door.

"Who that?" Trello yelled, gripping the burner.

"Blue!"

Trello stood up, adjusting the sag in his jeans as he went to answer the door. Blue entered, carrying two things: a knapsack filled with money and a bucket full of KFC chicken.

"What up, stic?" Blue greeted him, breathing hard. He had the fat-dude syndrome—always breathing audibly. He handed Trello the knapsack as they went into the kitchen.

"Drama, Ya, how you?" Blue said, dapping them both before sitting down.

Trello handed Drama the money.

"Yo, I know it took a little longer to move that last package, but yo, them fiends on that sky-blue New York dope. They say that shit mind blowin'!"

"Sky blue?" Trello asked confusedly.

"Food coloring," YaYa schooled him. "Nigguhs do that so you can distinguish they shit."

"Do it make it better?" Blue questioned, eyebrows raised.

Shameeq shook his head. "Naw, just a gimmick."

"Well, yo, tell your man we could get a lot of nigguhs to fuck wit' us, but that food coloring got them fiends fucked up. Tell KG his shit decent, but he need a better connect, " Blue suggested.

"I got–I mean K got the best connect in Manhattan, B," Shameeq bragged.

"Yeah, well, tell him check Brooklyn, Queens, something," Blue chuckled, biting into a chicken leg. "Them New Yorkers killin' us, stic," he added with a mouthful of chicken.

YaYa slapped the table.

"Like the fuck I said, B! Let the wolves out!"

"So they can blow the spot?" Shameeq was itching to get it too, but he knew Virginia wasn't Jersey. Too many murders, and the police would be everywhere, making it too hot to make money.

They needed a way to remove the competition quietly, or at least anonymously. He inhaled the Cohiba and a smile crossed his face.

"What?" YaYa asked, now grinning. He knew whenever Shameeq smiled like that, shit was about to get diabolical.

"Ya, you said take it back to '86? Remember how we used to rob them Uptown nigguhs?" Shameeq quizzed.

The memory made YaYa laugh. "Do I? Stick them nigguhs hollerin' Brooklyn! Shit, them nigguhs still probably think it was BK!"

YaYa and Shameeq broke up with laughter. Blue looked at Trello, thinking he knew what they were talking about, but Trello just shrugged his shoulders.

Shameeq turned to them. "Look, we gonna shut them nigguhs down, but it ain't gonna be us!"

"Who's it gonna be then?" Blue wanted to know.

"Brooklyn!" YaYa hollered, holding his gun in the air.

Blue was confused, so Shameeq broke it down.

"We gonna hit the Uptown spots hollerin' BK and hit the BK spots hollerin' Uptown."

Blue stopped chewing, then started nodding. "Okay, okay, kill two birds wit' one stone. Yeah, I like that."

"Word," Trello chimed in.

"Finally, B, that Drama Squad shit," YaYa remarked.

"Who?" Blue asked.

"Nothin," Shameeq smirked. "Let's go get at family."

??????

"Nigguh, you best to give that mutt to yo' bitch," Lil' B laughed, "'cause that ain't no pit, that's a *pitiful!"*

Lil' B was in Tidewater projects, where he was born, raised and respected. He and a few of his boys were clowning another cat about his dog. The pit looked official, but Lil' B knew dogs like the back of his hand. He already knew that the pit didn't come from a strong bloodline.

"Pitiful my ass, nigguh. Put yo' money where yo' mouth is," the cat shot back.

"You ain't said nuthin' but a word, Stic. What you wanna lose?" B asked.

"Twenty-five hunnid."

Lil' B grabbed his nuts. "When and where, nigguh? I'm there!"

The Drama Squad pulled up with Blue in his blue '82 Cadillac Seville. They got out just as the dude with the dog walked away. Lil' B walked over and greeted them with pounds and hugs.

"What up, yo? I was just about to beep you," Lil' B told Drama.

"You finished?" Drama questioned.

"Yeah, shit correct."

"Bet," Shameeq replied, then added, "but yo, nigguhs 'bout to put in some serious work. You down, B?"

"Work like what?" Lil' B probed.

Shameeq ran the game plan down to him. Lil' B dug the idea, but he asked, "You talk to KG about this?"

Shameeq gritted his teeth. He needed to camouflage, but he was getting tired of hearing KG's name. He started to reply, but Blue quipped, "For what? It's on us to hold this shit down. Besides, we 'bout to make him rich."

"Yeah, and hot if them New York cats find out. 'Cause it's war," Lil' B countered.

"Let me find out you scared," Blue chuckled.

Lil' B skeet spit, "Nigguh, only thing I'm scared of is being black and broke in this white man's world. Hell no, I ain't scared!"

"Then strap up," YaYa told him.

"You ain't said nothin' but a word, stic. Hold up," B answered, then jogged off to his apartment.

Montez felt the same way when they got to his spot in Norfolk. He was having the biggest problem moving his packages because Norfolk seemed to be infested with up-top crews, big and small. For that reason, he had the biggest beef with up-top cats, but he also had the biggest arsenal to match.

"My nigguh," Montez stressed, slamming his fist into his palm, "I been waitin' to get busy on these up-top clowns! No offense to y'all nigguhs, Drama, but a lot of them cats act like they can't get it!"

Shameeq chuckled.

"No doubt, B, I understand. So what up, you got guns?"

Montez flashed his gold-fronted smile.

"Do I? Yo, stic, follow me."

Montez lead them to the back room. He unlocked the padlock and turned on the light. What YaYa saw made his eyes bulge like a kid at Christmas. "Word up, B! This is what the fuck I'm talkin' about!"

Montez had wall-to-wall guns, literally. Like a collector, he had his shit mounted on three of the four walls as well as spread out on a large wooden table. SK-47s, AK-47s, tech nines, an assortment of Uzis, riot pumps, Mac 11s and too many handguns to name.

"Damn, Tez, fuck you waitin' on, World War III?" Trello joked.

"Naw, nigguh, the revolution! When we rid the streets of all the suckas!"

"I love you, B," YaYa told Montez as he took a SK-47 down off of the wall. YaYa had a love for guns, so he was like a kid in a candy store.

Blue grabbed two Uzis, kissed them both and remarked, "This me here."

"You?" Montez echoed. "My nigguh, you ain't 'bout to get me locked up!"

"Fuck you talkin' 'bout Tez?" Blue growled.

"Muhfucka, while we in there getting money and the dope, you'll be done grabbed the refrigerator talkin' 'bout, 'Grab the other end! We can't leave the food!'" Montez joked, and the whole crew laughed.

"Nigguh fuck yo' black ass!" Blue chuckled.

"Black?!" Tez echoed. "You so black they call you blue! Lips lookin' like the red rubber band around collard greens!" Montez cracked, then puckered his lips. Lil' B was in tears.

"I ain't fuckin' wit' you Tez," Blue smirked.

"I know!"

Shameeq laughed then said, "Keepin' it real though, yo, this ain't no robbery; this is a homicide."

He looked around the room to make sure he was heard. Montez grabbed his riot pump and said, "Is there any other way to do a robbery?"

YaYa was loving Montez more and more!

??????

For the next two weeks, they meticulously planned their robbery spree. There were three main Brooklyn crews that were loosely connected and had the most drug spots in the seven cities. Two Harlem crews were strong as well, so the Drama Squad focused on these five crews. They scouted many spots, but some were more heavily armed or were less lucrative. They ended up choosing seven spots that belonged to the BK cats and three to the Uptown crew. The Drama Squad broke up into two clicks for the robbery spree. Shameeq ran one, and YaYa ran the other. Montez, Blue and Lil' B enlisted eight thorough ass dudes. Six were from VA and two, Montez's cousins, were from DC. The plan was to hit all ten spots, each crew hitting five spots apiece, all in one night.

"These nigguhs won't know what hit 'em," Shameeq sneered, squinting from the blunt that smoldered in his mouth while he loaded the AK-47.

"We in and out, leavin' nothin' but bodies and a story to tell, B." Montez snickered. YaYa nodded in agreement, then threw his head back and howled like a wolf. "Let the wolves out!"

The crew broke up with laughter. Montez, always the funny one, cracked jokes the whole night while they prepared for their mission. But make no mistake, his murder game was about to become legendary.

The first place Shameeq's team hit was a Brooklyn spot set up in the Bowling Green projects in the Tidewater section of Norfolk. The BK dudes had a few VA cats pitching for them, but they controlled the apartment. Shameeq already knew the drill. Three dudes held the crib down, housing the money and keeping the block workers supplied with the product. Fiends hurried to and fro, on foot and in cars, to get a blast of that New York blue cocaine. Shameeq, Lil' B and two of Lil' B's henchmen sat in the old, beat-up Ford LTD peeping the scene. Blue sat behind the steering wheel with an Uzi in his lap. Blunt smoke filled the car as the team prepared to set it off.

"Y'all nigguhs ready? Anybody not, speak now 'cause I ain't havin' no bitchin' up," Shameeq warned, sliding on a pair of leather golf gloves.

"We ain't new to this, we true to this, stic," Lil' B boasted, tucking a .44 bulldog in his waist and gripping the riot pump.

"Say no more then, B. Let's make a move," Shameeq winked, pulling the Jason mask over his face. He grabbed the SK-47 and opened the door. They were all wearing Jason-style hockey masks as they hopped out of the car and approached the apartment. Blue stayed low in the car and kept it running.

From inside the apartment, they could hear the sounds of Rakim's "Let the Rhythm Hit 'Em". They waited in the cut for fifteen minutes, until one of the workers came for another pack. When he did, Lil' B yoked him up while Shameeq put the nine under his chin.

"Live or die?" Shameeq gritted.

"Huh?" the worker stuttered before getting smacked.

"Live or die??! Shameeq repeated in a low growl.

"L-l-live!"

"Knock on the door," Shameeq instructed him.

Lil' B took the worker to the door. Shameeq's team stood on both sides of the door, guns aimed at the worker. He knocked.

"Who?"

"It's me!" he said, his voice cracking.

"Me who?!" the Brooklyn accent retorted. He peeped through the peephole and opened the door. "Yo, kid, I told—"

That's all he got out before he caught the butt end of Shameeq's SK-47 in the mouth. The dude fell to the floor, and Lil' B shoved the worker inside. Another dude on the couch strapped with a nine didn't hesitate to shoot, hitting the worker.

"Arrgghh!" he screamed out in agony as Lil' B used his body as a shield long enough to return fire and blow the dude off of the couch. The third BK cat came out the back, firing wildly, but Shameeq cut him down with the SK.

The worker and dude who opened the door both lay on the floor groaning. Shameeq wasted no time. He bent down and snatched the BK cat off the floor.

"You got that, son, you got that," Brooklyn conceded, bloody mouth and all.

"Nigguh, this ain't no robbery, this a warning! Y'all BK nigguhs is over! Uptown run this shit from now on, you got that?!" Shameeq hissed in his face.

"Yeah, yo, I hear you," he replied like he wasn't fazed by the threat.

Boom!

The bullet entered Brooklyn's groin area, causing him to collapse in agony to the floor.

"You hear me now?!" Shameeq taunted.

"Yeah, yeah, son—arrrgghh!" Brooklyn screamed because Shameeq stepped on the fresh gun wound.

"Say it then! Uptown run this shit!"

"Up—arrgghh—okay, okay! Uptown ... run this shhhhiittt!" Brooklyn grimaced until Shameeq removed his foot.

"You got beef, you know where to find us!" Shameeq announced, then punctuated the statement by killing the worker with two to the dome. The blast from the SK-47 point-blank range guaranteed the young boy's funeral would be closed casket.

Shameeq and his team exited without taking anything but lives.

??????

Meanwhile in Virginia Beach, YaYa wasn't letting them off so easy. He, Montez, a VA cat named Red and Montez's DC cousins, Twon and L, had caught one of the Harlem spots slipping lovely. They caught them with two duffle bags full of money, which they later found out was over a hundred thousand, along with six kilos of crack.

YaYa had the three Harlem cats and two college chicks lying face down in the living room.

"Fuck y'all Uptown nigguhs thought?! We ain't let you breathe in the city, fuck make you think we was gonna let y'all breathe down here?" YaYa barked with the Uzi pointed at the victims.

"Yo, G, you got what you came for—" one of the Harlem cats began, but Montez let the nine spit twice and painted the floor with his brains. The chicks screamed hysterically, so Montez blew the light-skin broad's brains out too. The other chick trembled in shock.

"Anybody else got somethin' to say?!" YaYa stressed, but everyone stayed silent.

"We see *any* of y'all Uptown faggots again, it'll be the same thing!" YaYa vowed. "BK run VA muhfuckas!"

YaYa squeezed the trigger and killed the heavyset Harlemnite in the middle, leaving one dude and the chick. On his way out he started to kill the other chick, but Montez stopped him.

"Naw, naw, naw, stic, not her. Look at that ass, stic," Montez said. "Don't waste no ass like that!"

YaYa smirked under the mask. On his way out, he hollered, "BK, son!"

By the end of the night, Hampton, Newport News, Norfolk, and VA Beach had all made the front page. The Drama Squad had murdered twelve people, injured seven and made off with close to half a million dollars along with ten kilos of crack and cocaine. They had also sparked a war that would have the streets in the seven cities as hot as firecrackers.

CHAPTER 5

Present Day 1994

"YaYa Mitchell!" the burley U.S. marshal called out from the front of the pod.

YaYa was sitting in the dayroom with Blue and Rivera. He turned in the direction of the voice.

"What?!" he snapped.

"Come with us. They want you downstairs again," the marshal informed him.

YaYa stood up. "For what? I already said what I got to say: nothin'!" he barked, loud enough for the whole pod to hear him. When you're locked up and the police want to talk to you, you never want to give the impression that you want to talk to them ... even if you really do.

"Yeah, well, they said they need to see you again."

"Pssst," YaYa blew out impatiently as he got up from the table. The marshal burst the door and escorted YaYa out of the pod.

Rivera looked at Blue. Blue waited for him to speak, but when he didn't, he asked, "What?"

"Yo ... what up wit' that?" Rivera asked.

"What up wit' what?" Blue answered.

"Didn't he just come from downstairs?" Rivera questioned suspiciously.

"And?" Blue emphasized.

"I'm just sayin', yo."

"Sayin' what?" Blue quizzed.

Rivera shrugged.

"I'm just sayin', the marshals questioned me once. They questioned you once, right?"

"Get to the point, stic. You tryin' to say my man might be flippin'?" Blue probed, aggravated. Even though all three were arrested together, Rivera wasn't an original member of the Drama Squad, so Blue didn't think it was his place to imply such a thing, not knowing YaYa like that.

"Yo, Blue, in situations like this, who else can flip if it ain't your man?" Rivera shot back. Inside, Blue acknowledged his point. "All I know is somebody talkin', and all I know is it ain't me," Rivera concluded then walked away from the table.

The D.E.A. knew about shit in detail, stuff only muhfuckas involved or part of the team would know. And he too wondered why YaYa was going to see the agents again. Deep in his heart, he felt YaYa was too real to flip. He had known YaYa for years, put in work with him, so he could personally attest to the fact that YaYa's gangster was solid. But his rational side told him that Rivera was right. In situations like this, only those who knew could tell, and those who knew were those closest to you. And YaYa definitely knew it all. He was the Drama Squad's second in command. If he did flip, he would take them all down. Blue didn't know what to make of this. But one thing was for sure: Someone was talking. He just hoped it wasn't YaYa.

Three marshals escorted YaYa down the hallway in silence. All you could hear was the slight rattling of the keys on their hips and the solid connection their spit shine boots made with the linoleum. YaYa looked at the sterile white walls, contemplating his situation. After all the years of sex, money and murder, his life had been reduced to this. He never thought he'd see the inside of another prison even though every day since his release years ago he had lived a life of crime. Not that he didn't think he'd ever get caught, but he had vowed to hold court in the streets if he was ever faced with such a situation. But the D.E.A. had caught him, Blue and Rivera slipping ... badly. Even quitting heroin cold turkey wasn't as bad as the wrenching feeling in his gut about that. Coulda, shoulda, woulda dominated his thoughts and he contemplated what freedom meant to him and what he would do to achieve it.

"Ay, yo, y'all ain't give me a chance to piss," YaYa hissed.

"Save it," one marshal told him, then turned to him with a smirk and added, "unless you have a problem holding water?"

"Fuck you, cracka. Take me to the bathroom."

The agent was prepared to say no, but another agent made a head gesture letting his partner know to take YaYa to the bathroom.

??????

"My bad, fellas, but that shit just ran through me," he said, after coming from the bathroom. He sat back down then added, "Church's do me the same way. Mullins, you know Church's Chicken, don't you?"

Mullins glared at him.

"Nigguhs and nigguh food give me heartburn."

He threw his head back and laughed.

"Come on, Mullins, you look like the type of cracka that loves the taste of dark meat," he said, then paused and added, "you know, when nobody's lookin." He winked.

"You talk real glib for somebody on their way to a cell," Jacobs remarked, scrutinizing him.

He shrugged.

"It feels good to clear my conscience, you know? Maybe you guys should try it, because we've all got skeletons!"

Mullins picked the recorder up, pressed rewind and then played back his last words: "We sparked the war, and them dumb nigguhs played right into our hands."

Mullins stopped the tape, then hit record.

"Let's get this over with. I'm tired of looking at your face," Mullins sneered.

"So let me get this right," Jacobs began, rubbing his chin, "that series of killings that ravaged Virginia in '89 wasn't really Harlem and Brooklyn transplants?"

He shook his head.

"Naw it was them, they just didn't *start* it. We did."

"By 'we,' you mean Drama Squad?" McGrady probed.

"Naw ... KG."

"You just said KG was killed in New Jersey," Jacobs reminded him.

He sighed.

"He was. I'm sayin', when them New York jokers found out what really happened, we was still rollin' wit' that KG the boss shit. So to them, it was KG's crew, which was really Drama Squad."

McGrady still didn't understand, but Mullins understood fully.

"And when they found out, that's when you killed Donald Baron?"

"Naw. That came later."

??????

June 1989

Sincere pulled his black-on-black convertible Saab into the parking lot of Military Circle Mall. The sounds of Sade's "Sweetest Taboo" played at a tolerable level as he scanned the lot. He drove slowly, tilting his shades down so he could see more clearly. He spotted the smoke-gray Jag with five-star rims on it parked near the rear of the parking lot. Mark and Gutta sat in the Jag awaiting his arrival.

Sincere pulled into the space next to the Jag, then all three got out and greeted one another.

"Peace, God," Mark greeted Sincere.

"Peace," Sincere replied, adjusting the pants of his silk suit. "Gutta, what up, son?"

"Chillin, Sin," Gutta answered, stone-faced.

They were all from East New York, but Gutta didn't really like Sincere. He dressed like a Harlem nigguh, and any reminder of Harlem was a problem for Gutta. Especially at the time when so many lives had been claimed because of the beef that flared out of nowhere.

"Yo, how Don? He beat that case yet?" Mark asked.

Sincere grinned.

"He lounging, dude. They still got him under no bail on the Island, but it's only a matter of time. Ain't no witnesses left to testify," Sincere said with a devilish grin. "But what's going on down here, son? Nigguhs up top sayin' y'all turnin' VA into the Wild Wild West and makin' it hard to get cake."

Gutta shifted in his stance, rocking back and forth with one hand gripping his wrist, waist level. He looked like a ball of energy ready to explode at any time.

"And it's gonna stay wild until we run these bitch-ass Uptown nigguhs the fuck outta VA, and when I see 'em back home, it's still on!" Gutta vowed, biting his bottom lip.

Mark shook his head.

"About a month ago, like five of our spots got hit. The muhfuckas ran up in there reppin' Uptown and saying BK couldn't eat in VA anymore, so—"

"So we fuckin' murdered them faggots! Who the fuck these nigguhs think—" Gutta started ranting, but Sincere shut him down.

"Yo, Gutta, where your manners? Let the man finish."

Gutta gritted his teeth but stayed quiet.

"Go 'head, Mark."

"Yo, so like Gutta said, it was crazy retaliation ... from both sides," Mark said.

"Both sides?" Sincere echoed.

"Yeah, them Uptown nigguhs saying' we set it on *them*!" Mark shook his head. "Sayin' we ran up in they spot masked up the same way they ran up in our spots yellin' the same shit!"

Sincere snickered, knowing his people. "Well, did we?"

"Not us. Maybe some other BK nigguhs down here, but none of ours. I don't know what's going on, God. All I know is once bodies started dropping, nigguhs ain't ask no questions," Mark informed him.

"Word is bond, God, they killed Gut, Mousey, Chill from Flatbush, Prime," Gutta said, using his fingers to keep count. "They killed family, and that shit is unacceptable!"

Sincere nodded as he listened. It had been a minute since he had been on the block pitchin' hand to hand, but he still had the heart of a soldier. That's why Don Baron had him in charge while he was on Riker's Island. Sincere was in charge of distribution in four states: Pennsylvania, Maryland, North Carolina and Virginia. Mark was in charge of Virginia, getting the weight all over the state to the different spots they controlled. Gutta ran the crew out of Norfolk. He was one of many block lieutenants, but since Norfolk was their biggest operation in the seven cities, Gutta was the strongest—and the wildest. Mark feared Gutta, and Gutta hated Sincere, but Don Baron kept them all in check.

"Gutta, run it to me in detail. Don't leave shit out," Sincere instructed him.

Gutta hadn't been at any of the spots that night, but he had heard the story over and over from different cats so much it was like he had been there. "They was wearin' masks. Jason-type shit and ski masks. Muhfuckas had AKs, ow-wops, the whole nine! Half the spots they ain't even robbed, but in all spots they was screamin' that Uptown shit and murderin' family!" Gutta explained.

"You say they were wearin' masks?" Sincere asked.

"Indeed," Gutta answered.

"Reppin' Uptown?"

"Word."

"And it wasn't all robberies, just all one message ... to both sides?" Sincere quizzed, turning to Mark.

"Yeah, yo, as far as I know."

Sincere shook his head.

"Shit don't sound right, yo. On this muscle, it sound like all this shit been for nothing."

"Nothin'?!" Gutta echoed. "They killed my people! *Your* people!"

"Exactly!" Sincere emphasized. "Whoever did it knew if you shed blood, muhfuckas wouldn't stop and think. Check it ... what's the greatest trick of the devil?" he quizzed, but when neither said anything, he answered his own question. "To make sure the original man think he don't exist! This shit was a calculated attack," Sincere concluded cryptically.

"Calculated?" Mark echoed.

"Look, I'ma be in VA for a minute, at least until Don get out. So until then, tell our peoples to parlay, Gutta. Til—"

"Paylay?! The fuck you—"

Sincere grilled him and barked, "Yo, son, don't ever cut my wisdom again! I said parlay, and that's what the fuck I meant! Par-the fuck-lay!"

"Pssst," Gutta blew out air, then got back in the Jag.

Sincere turned to Mark.

"Whoever did it, we'll find 'em. Trust me. And when we do, we gonna make examples of 'em in the worst way! But for now, cooler heads have to take over. You got one, Mark?" Sincere asked intensely.

"Got what?"

"A cool head."

"No doubt, God, no doubt," Mark assured him.

"Then leave them Richmond nigguhs alone too," Sincere told him. "Don said them nigguhs ain't playin' fair, so chill."

"Naw, son, I can handle it. I'm only messin' wit' one cat. Cat named Rivera out of BX. He solid, yo," Mark replied.

"Whether he is or not, son, Don said chill, a'ight? He might be the only one *you* messin' wit', but who *he* messin' wit'? Remember, it only takes one, you know?" Sincere jeweled him.

"Yeah, yo, whatever you say," Mark agreed reluctantly.

Sincere studied him a moment longer, then said, "All money ain't good money, son, remember that."

With that, Sincere got back in the Saab and bounced.

With the New York cats trying to figure out what was going on, and the police keeping it too hot in their areas to make money, the Drama Squad started to expand and capitalize. They opened up more spots, catching the traffic too scared to venture into the war zones the New York–dominated areas had become.

Blue, Lil' B and Montez thought Drama was a genius, which drew them closer to him, and seeing him put in work made them more loyal. But one question continued to arise.

"Yo, what up wit' KG? I beeped that nigguh but got no answer. Did you tell him what I said?" Blue asked one day while they were all bagging up and packaging the dope.

YaYa, Montez and Lil' B sat around the table as well, while Shameeq smoked a blunt, leaning against the stove. Trello had just made a run to Jersey and had come back with the coke, supposedly from KG. Trello looked at Shameeq.

"Ay, yo, let me ask you something," Shameeq began. "How you meet KG?"

"At the Greekfest in '88," Blue told him. "Really, it was Tez that cut into him first, and he turned him on to me and B."

Shameeq nodded and blew a stream of smoke in the air.

"Okay. So I'm sayin', is that yo' man like that, or was it just business?" Shameeq probed.

Lil' B shrugged.

"I mean, stic a'ight. He tried to run with some slick shit one time, and I checked him. But other than that, he cool. Why?"

"Because he tried me like that too," Shameeq smirked, inhaling the blunt, "so I kilt him!"

Montez looked up at Shameeq. Because Shameeq was smiling, Montez took it as a joke.

"Nigguh, stop playin' and pass the blunt."

Shameeq took one last pull, then tossed it to Montez. He caught it, then blew the ashes out of his hand. YaYa looked at Montez.

"He ain't jokin,' B," YaYa confirmed. "That joker worked for us."

Lil' B looked at Blue, Blue looked at Montez, and Montez looked at Trello. The room was silent. YaYa eased his hand closer to the burner on his waist without anybody noticing.

"When?" Blue questioned.

Shameeq broke down the whole situation with KG and how that made him want to come down to VA.

"Remember that time you beeped KG and his cousin answered the phone?" Shameeq reminded him.

"Yeah."

"That was me, B."

Blue smiled and shook his head.

"When I met you, I thought that was you, but all y'all up-top cats sound alike," he chuckled.

"For real, though, stic," Lil' B began, "I ain't wanna say nothin' because I thought the nigguh was yo' man, but the nigguh was some straight bullshit."

All three of them had stories about KG not being a real nigguh, so Shameeq knew it had been in their hearts the whole time.

"The reason I'm tellin' y'all is because shit 'bout to get live. Once them NY nigguhs get back to business, they gonna notice how loud our names ringing," Shameeq warned them.

"And they comin'," YaYa added.

"So I wanted us all to keep it real wit' one another, you know what I'm sayin'? Because I see y'all as my nigguhs for real, and we about to lock shit *down*," Shameeq told them.

"My nigguh, let's make it happen then," Montez said.

"Let them nigguhs know, yo, we got it. Straight up, I brought fifty more bricks that we lettin' go for sixteen," Shameeq explained. "I want nigguhs to know they can eat wit' us even though I'ma take a loss on this run."

Shameeq knew he'd take a loss, but he looked at it as an investment. Besides, with the money he got out of the lick, it was basically New York's money he was spending.

"Word, B, we gotta build a strong team because them New York jokers gonna definitely catch feelings," YaYa surmised.

"Especially if they ever find out it was really us that set that whole beef off," Lil' B snickered.

"Find out how?" Shameeq chuckled. "Them dumb muhfuckas'll never figure that shit out."

But for once, Shameeq was wrong.

CHAPTER 6

Chuck was a crackhead. Plain and simple. There was no shame in his game. If someone wanted to buy it, he would steal it. He had even stolen the air conditioner out of a local church's window. His Jones was that sacrilegious. Everybody in Lake Edwards knew Chuck. He had been a mechanic in his former life, but once Scotty got him, his occupation became crack. Chuck used his car to facilitate his jack moves, and he was quick to rent it out to anyone with a twenty piece of crack or more.

That's how Black knew.

Black was a Virginia cat who pushed packages for the New Yorkers. He was only a block hustler, but he was known to go hard for the paper. He had been out that night when the Drama Squad robbed the spot in Bowling Green projects. He saw the black LTD backfire and pull off, but that's not what let him know the car in the parking lot was the same car. It was the "Baby on Board" sign in the back window and the way the bumper had been "nigguh rigged" with electrical tape and a chain to stay attached to the car. He remembered it distinctly, and now he was staring at it from the front seat of his Nissan Sentra.

Black had come to pick up a chick he was fucking who worked at Red and White but once he saw the car, his mission became finding out who was driving that car. A few minutes later, Chuck emerged from the store, looking around nervously and walking fast. Under his old-ass Member's Only jacket was a bulge that engorged his entire waist. He held the bulge like he had a baby in his stomach, but it was in fact a bunch of steaks. Black watched him with amusement, wondering how he even made it out of the store until he saw Chuck approach the LTD and pop the trunk. Black grabbed his pistol, tucked it, then hopped out and yelled, "Yo, old coon! Old coon! Let me holla at cha."

Chuck turned around, wide-eyed, just knowing he had been caught.

"Be easy, brah," Black smiled as he approached, "I ain't the po-po. I'm just tryin' to see what you trying to get off," he lied, like the spider to the fly.

Chuck looked around, then pulled out a steak.

"Naw, naw," Black told him, "don't do it out here. Get in the car."

Chuck was so hungry for a blast, he did it without hesitation. He got in under the wheel, while Black got in on the passenger's side. As soon as he was in the car, Black backhanded Chuck against the door, then whipped out his pistol and put it under Chuck's chin.

"Man, you can have 'em! Go 'head take 'em!" Chuck squeaked, scared to death.

"Nigguh, fuck them steaks! You 'bout to die for that shit you did out in Bowling Green!" Black vowed.

Chuck had done dirt everywhere, so he thought quickly about what he could've done in Bowling Green serious enough to die for. "It wasn't me!"

Black slapped him with the pistol, then looked around to make sure no one was looking.

"Stop fuckin' lyin'! This your car, ain't it?!"

"No!"

Smack!

"Yes!"

"Then who was wit' you when you robbed our spot in Bowling Green?!" Black demanded.

"Please, young blood, listen! I ain't no stick-up kid! Only guns I have is the ones I steal to sell! I ain't never stuck up no crack spot!" Chuck swore truthfully.

It was obvious to Black that Chuck wasn't the type to carry off a robbery-homicide, but the fact remained that this was the car of whoever did it.

"Who you rent this shit out to then?" Black probed, leaning back but keeping the pistol aimed at Chuck.

Chuck thought hard because he rented the car out a lot, especially to young boys too young to drive, who usually wanted to joy ride. He thought and thought until he remembered Blue renting the car one night a while back. He knew they were up to no good because they were toting enough ammo to rob an armored truck. He had forgotten all about it until the smacks from the pistol refreshed his memory. He knew it had to be them, and if it wasn't, they were damn sure about to wear it.

"Th--this fat dude! Big fat dude got a lot of young boys workin' for him and be messin' wit' some up-North dudes! I think they from Jersey, but I know his name KG," Chuck snitched.

"KG?" Black echoed, vaguely remembering the name. "Where they be at?"

"I knew 'em from LE," Chuck replied.

"Lake Edwards? I heard 'bout some cats out there 'posed to be holdin' too," he thought aloud, then said to Chuck, "A'ight, let's go. You gonna show 'em to me."

"Show 'em?! Man, I can't—"

Smack!

Vroom! Chuck followed instructions and pulled out.

Chuck pulled onto the strip in Lake Edwards. Black kept the gun pressed into his side. Various crackheads tried to shout Chuck down, and a few young boys motioned to him that they had dope, but other than that, the block was clear.

"You see 'em?" Black asked, eyes peeled.

Chuck shook his head.

"Keep lookin'."

They drove past the Lake Edwards Apartments. Chuck noticed Shameeq talking to a chick by his Jetta.

"That's him! That's the dude KG!" Chuck exclaimed. He didn't know Shameeq and had never seen KG, but he knew KG was the leader, so he automatically assumed Shameeq was KG.

"Slow down," Black said, getting a look at Shameeq. "Turn around."

Black had death in his eyes and ambition in his heart. Black knew if he killed KG, the New York cats would love him for it and he would surely get bumped up a notch or two on the totem pole.

Chuck read Black's intentions in his eyes and wanted no part of a drive-by shooting, especially since he felt that Black would probably kill him too, because he would be a potential witness. Chuck stopped the car.

"What you stop for?!" Black barked. "Turn around and go back!"

"I thought you said—"

Smack!

Chuck was getting woozy from all the blows. He U-turned in the middle of the street, but he had to wait until a beer delivery truck went by. Black saw the Jetta pulling off too quickly. Then Shameeq disappeared around the corner.

"Fuck!" Black cursed, smacking the dashboard. Chuck silently mouthed a prayer and vowed in his heart never to rent his car out again.

"Take me back to the store," Black mumbled, deep in thought.

Even though Shameeq had gotten away, Black still had the answer to the million-dollar question. "KG," he repeated to himself.

??????

"KG? Who the fuck is KG?" Sincere asked as he whipped the Saab down Virginia Beach Blvd. The sounds of Soul II Soul's "Keep on Movin'" pumped loudly.

Gutta was sunk low in the passenger's seat, arm hanging out the drop.

"This bitch-ass nigguh from fuckin' Jersey! A fuckin' nobody! I can't *believe* he'd try some shit like this, son! Word to God son, word to God, his whole team gonna be statistics when I see 'em!" Gutta growled.

"Didn't I tell you the whole shit was a setup?" Sincere said.

"Yeah, well, he gonna wish he never set that shit up, son!" Gutta was amped to set it.

Sincere stopped at the light.

"Word, son, I know you ready for war, but be easy. We can't handle it like that."

Gutta looked at him, wide-eyed.

"Fuck you mean we ain't gonna handle it like that?! Fuck that, *I'ma* handle it *just* like that!" Gutta retorted.

Sincere eye checked Gutta coldly.

"Yo, Gutta, what the fuck I just say?" he asked calmly, but his voice took on a deadly whisper.

"That's that bullshit, Sin, and you know it! We can't let no shit like that go, son! Fuck no! Justice must be dealt with the swiftness!" Gutta barked.

Sincere understood Gutta's point because he had come up just like Gutta. He respected his anger, but this was business, and Gutta was taking it too personal. The light turned green, and he pulled off.

"Did I say it wouldn't get handled? I said not like *that.* Y'all had this shit on fire and it's just getting back to normal. You think we gonna run out lookin' for this nigguh and blow the spot all over again?" Sincere stressed. "Fuck no! We here to get money, son, period, point blank."

Gutta didn't respond.

"Right?" Sincere repeated.

"But family got killed, God. I—"

"Son, I raised Gut, God bless the dead. You don't think I feel that shit, huh? But this is the path we chose, and muhfuckas get killed. Muhfuckas get locked up. Gut knew that, just like Mousey and them. Tomorrow it could be you or me, but once we gone, we gone. Muhfuckas gonna remember us, just like we remember Gut, but we can't make decision for the dead, God. We gotta make decisions for the living, the true and living. This shit is business, son, straight up," Sincere schooled him.

Gutta just turned his head and looked out the drop.

"Trust me," Sincere continued, "it *will* get handled, just not on that rah-rah shit, a'ight?"

"I hear you, son," Gutta replied, unconvinced.

Sincere pulled into the parking lot of an expensive-looking apartment complex. He parked and got out. "Yo, Gutta, come wit' me. I wanna show you something."

Sincere knocked on the door, and a moment later a cute brown-skin girl answered. She was all bubbly as she let Sincere and Gutta into the living room. Gutta watched her jiggly ass disappear in the back, then his eyes fell on the couch, then on the man on the couch. A big smile spread across Gutta's face.

"Yo, Don?! What up, son?! When you get out?!" Gutta said as Don stood to greet him with a hug. He loved Don because he was a true Brooklyn head in his eyes. Don had come up hard in Red Hook, and even though he was already a millionaire at twenty-five, he was still known to put in his own work if a nigguh got him fucked up. The body he had just beat was a result of a dude who had smacked his sister at the infamous Love People Nightclub. Don was average height and looked like a light-skin version of Jam Master Jay, and he had bulked up during his stint on the Island.

"Yesterday," Don lied. He had really been in VA a week, but no one in the crew knew except Sincere. Despite the fact that he had heavy operations in several states, no one knew how important VA was to his empire, so he had to come down and check shit out for himself.

"Sincere told me what was up down here, yo, and he told me you was troopin' it like a soldier," Don told Gutta.

Gutta's chest swelled being acknowledged by Don.

"You know me, Don. I rep BK to the fullest," Gutta boasted.

"Indeed, indeed," Don replied as he sat and gestured for Gutta to do the same. "So, yo, tell me ... what's going on?"

Gutta started to explain the situation, but a gorgeous light-skin chick came over and brought Don a drink, then perched on the arm of his chair.

"Yo, son ..." Gutta said, his eyes questioning her presence.

"She wit me, son," Don announced proudly as he traced circles on her knee. "This my lawyer, Nya Braswell."

"Among other things," she added as she sipped the drink, eyeing Gutta like she could devour him on the spot.

Not wanting to be disrespectful to Don, Gutta tore his eyes away. But every chance he got, he snuck a peek at the beautiful vision before him. From her manicured toes to her cat-like hazel eyes, every inch of her fought for Gutta's attention as he told Don all he knew. Nya listened to every word. She wasn't concerned with what had happened because she knew Don would handle it. The only thing she would later focus on was the one name: KG.

??????

Present Day 1994

Mullins slid a series of photos in front of him.

"These are some of the members of Don Baron's team that got fed time and ultimately cooperated with the government. Did the Drama Squad deal with any of them?"

He looked over the pictures, then pointed to a picture of Mark.

"You guys dealt with Marcus Freeman? Was he at any time a member of the Drama Squad?" Mullins probed.

"Naw, but he dealt with some people we dealt with," he replied.

"Of Don's crew, did any of them ever join the Drama Squad and/or deal with you?" Mullins continued to dig.

"A lot of us came from Don's crew after he got murdered. Wit' the Squad, it was either roll wit' it or get rolled over," he shrugged.

"What about her?" Jacobs asked, sliding another picture in front of him. He smirked as he looked at the picture.

"Miss Untouchable."

"Not anymore," Mullins mumbled under his breath.

He studied the photograph. It caught her mid-strut, coming down the stairs of the courthouse. Christian Dior sunglasses hid her eyes, and strands of her hair had fallen into her face. She was beautiful. She was poetry in motion, though her beauty wasn't like that of a rose, virtually harmless and innocent, fragile. Her beauty was like the stalk of a panther—which even its prey had to admit was breathtaking—right before she pounced. He slid the picture back to Mullins.

"What about her?"

"Everything," McGrady demanded, slamming his fist on the table, making Mullins flinch. "You okay?" he asked Mullins, peeping his reaction.

"Just answer the damn question," Mullins growled, downing the rest of his coffee like it was scotch.

"Nya Braswell," he started, "best defense attorney in VA. Drug charge? Murder charge? You had the money, Nya made it go away. And if you didn't have money, but you had a soul to sell, she'd take that too." He lit a cigarette. "Humble beginnings, got a prime position in the DA's office straight out of law school. Not even thirty and she made assistant district attorney, but then, out of the blue, she resigned. Went into private practice, specializing in drug and murder cases.

"Now try tellin' us something we don't know," Jacobs remarked.

"Like what?" he answered, looking at Mullins instead of Jacobs.

"Like the fact she was the Drama Squad's drug supplier? That she used her influence with key people to make our cases go away? That's what you wanna know?" McGrady chuckled.

McGrady slid the recorder closer.

"Keep talking!"

He leaned forward on his elbows. "Listen closely ... because this is where it gets deep."

??????

Late June 1989

"Take off your clothes. Both of you."

They stripped with the quickness.

"Take off everything."

They did. Then stood before her.

"Hmmm. Delicious. Do you work out?"

"I just came home from Lorton," the one she was speaking to replied.

Nya sat in the stylish leather recliner with her long, toned, French-vanilla legs crossed seductively. The slit on her skirt rose high enough to let the two men know she wasn't wearing any panties. She never did. Her natural Auburn-tinted hair was hidden under the jet-black wig she wore on occasions such as this, but it was just as long as her natural mane, which fell to the center of her back. Her piercing hazel eyes were camouflaged with emerald contacts. Without the façade, she was the spitting image of Sally Richardson, but tonight, she looked like a young Vanessa Williams. They were in a luxurious suite, high atop the Omni Hotel in Alexandria, Virginia. The picture window gave you a view of Washington, DC.

She picked up the two dudes earlier at a DC nightclub. Tonight she was Lisa. Tonight they were Joe and Jerome, cousins. They all had their own charade going, but the masks would soon come off.

Joe, who said he was fresh out of Lorton, was the shorter of the two. Stocky and built like Tyson. His dick wasn't huge, but it was thick. She preferred width over length. Jerome was taller and slimmer. His dick was less thick, but it was long and slightly curved. They were both horny and both hard as rocks, and their dicks were aimed straight at her. "So what up, yo? Now it's your turn, Lisa. Take off your clothes," Joe crooned, gripping his dick lustfully.

Nya lifted her dress and spread her legs, placing each one over either arm of the chair. The soft pink of her pussy gaped open and filled the room with her fragrance. Both their dicks jumped and quivered. They both started towards her.

"Hold on, fellas. One at a time, but I get to pick who goes first," she drawled, southern accent almost sexy enough to make a man beg.

She looked them over, like she couldn't choose.

"Damn, I want to fuck you both so bad, but I'm not into the ménage à trois," she told them.

"So why you bring us both up here?" Joe asked impatiently. He was ready to fuck.

"Because you *came*, and now that you're here ... we'll play a game. I'm the prize for whoever wins," she cooed.

"Wins what?" Jerome asked.

"The fight," she replied with a giggle.

They looked at each other, dumbfounded. Nya ran her fingers over her pussy lips then slid two inside. "Ssssss ... damn," she said as removed her fingers and licked them. "Don't make me wait. Mmmm ... tastes like strawberries."

Joe didn't hesitate. Cousin or no cousin, grew up together, whatever, he was tapping that. Joe caught Jerome with a left that should've dropped him, but lust kept him on his feet. He upper-cutted the charging Joe, lifting his chin for a clean right cross. But Joe ducked just in time and took it on the forehead.

"You bitch mother—" Joe grunted, wrapping his arms around Jerome and slamming him to the ground.

"Yes," Nya squealed, fingering herself vigorously. She loved to be the cause of the evil that men do.

Jerome tried to flip Joe off him, but Joe had him pinned and proceeded to pummel Jerome's face until he laid motionless.

"And the winner is," she groaned as Joe came over to her, chest heaving like a beast. The sight of blood on his chest sent Nya over the edge, and she came just as Joe plowed into her, making her pussy feel so creamy he almost came himself. He fought back the urge by gritting his teeth. "So you want it rough, bitch?! Huh? Huh?"

"Beat this pu--pussy," she moaned. "Beat it like you just beat him!"

She didn't have to tell him twice. He pinned her legs back until her knees pressed up against her breasts, taking her breath away with every stroke. Joe was so caught up in the moment, he never saw Jerome get up. Never saw him grab the lamp. Never saw him raise it. All he saw was the inside of his eyelids as he fell to the floor.

"He wasn't fuckin' me right anyway," Nya cooed, standing up to bend over, then she guided Jerome's dick inside her ass.

Joe killed Jerome two weeks later and went back to Lorton with life. They were cousins, but after that night, things weren't the same. But to Nya, it was just another night.

Nya woke up the next morning in the oversized bed the way she always did. Alone. She never allowed her trysts to break dawn. She viewed men in her life as play things, toys. Once content, they were to be discarded. She ran her hand over her head and frowned momentarily until she remembered that she still had on the wig. The art of the illusion was her specialty because with Nya, nothing was as it seemed.

Rubbing her legs together underneath the silk sheets, the feel of her own skin turned her on, and her pussy throbbed for her attention. Nya spread her legs, pulling the skin back on her clit and began to massage herself until she dripped. A soft moan escaped from her lips, but before she could explore herself deeper, her beeper buzzed uncontrollably on the nightstand. She wanted to ignore it, but she knew whoever it was, it was concerning her first love: money.

She rolled over reluctantly and checked the number. When she saw it, she sucked her teeth and started to put it back down, but it buzzed again. Same number.

"This better be good, Richard," she mumbled to herself. Nya sat up and put the hotel phone on the bed. She swung her faux mane away from her phone ear and dialed the number. Almost instantly, it was answered.

"Something's come up," the male voice said.

"Hello to you too, Richard. No, you didn't wake me, thanks for caring," she quipped, mocking his abruptness.

"We need to talk ... immediately," Richard answered, ignoring her sarcasm.

"I'm out of town, Richard, can't it—"

"No," he emphasized. "Page me when you're back, and meet me at the usual place," he instructed her, then hung up.

Nya took a deep breath, then hung up. She hated to have her space invaded, but from the sound of Richard's voice, she knew it had to be something.

??????

"It's bad, real bad," Richard told her, as she took a seat opposite him at one of the outside cafés on Colley Street in Norfolk.

Nya looked him over as she sat. He looked more ruffled than he usually did. He was a bails bondsman and a retired Navy officer. On top of that, he was a heavy drinker and chain smoker. His straight white hair receded slightly and always looked uncombed. His bulb-like nose stayed red winter, spring, summer and fall. He would've resembled Santa Claus, but he was thin.

"What could be so bad you had to disturb me?" she replied, waving off the waiter politely.

"This."

He handed her a folded newspaper. The half-page article's headline read: **Drug Bust Nets Thousands**

"So?" she glanced up at him.

"Would you read the friggin' thing?" he shot back, putting out one cigarette and lighting another.

She skimmed the article. The feds had raided a Motel 6 in Richmond and found six kilos of crack, eighty thousand in cash and several automatic weapons. The only thing that caught her eye was the name of one of the individuals arrested: Marcus Freeman.

"Interesting," she remarked, handing him the newspaper.

"Interesting?" he echoed, leaning towards her, voice low. "With the anti-drug abuse act of '88, he could get five years for simple possession of crack!! Nya, he had six keys of the shit! It ain't like the old days. Now the 5K is the only way to avoid a fucking asshole full of time!" Richard whispered hoarsely.

5K refers to a section of the Federal sentencing guidelines that offers a lighter sentences to individuals who provide substantial assistance. Assistance meaning snitch. "I'm a lawyer, Richard. I'm familiar with all of that," Nya answered sourly.

"So are you also a fortune teller? How long you think it'll be before he starts naming names?"

"Not long ... or maybe never."

"Are you willing to take that chance? Do you think your father wants to take that chance?" Richard quizzed her. He knew throwing her father in her face would wipe away her smug little attitude. Nya's smirk disappeared at the mention of her father because he was the only man in her life she couldn't control.

"Chance or no chance, that is our only *choice*. For all we know he's already talking, and the operation is already compromised," Nya retorted, suddenly feeling the need for a drink.

Richard nodded in agreement, inhaling the cigarette.

"I'm cutting Don off for now," he finally announced.

"If you cut him off now and Mark's been busted, what other reason will Don have to be here? Then how will we know what's going on?" she tried to reason.

"You're his lawyer ... among other things," he smirked. "You'll figure out something to keep him around."

Nya smirked.

"You cut him off, then how do you think daddy will take that?"

He smashed his cigarettes in the ashtray. "We've all got a job to do, Nya. You do yours and I'll do mine."

Nya sighed. "Richard, trust me, if Mark turns on Don, and Don wants to turn on anyone, I'll be the first to know. I agree that precautions should be taken, but Don is our biggest money maker. So keep your eyes open, but relax. Never drop the prey for a shadow."

"And if you aren't the first to know?" Richard inquired.

Nya winked. "Then I'll just kill you," she replied.

Richard chuckled because he knew his factor in the equation guaranteed his life—at least for the time being.

"Lawyers are much more expendable," he retorted, lighting another cigarette. "Okay, Nya, we'll do it your way ... for now. Keep the bastard close, and if he even stutters ..." he let his voice trail off and stood up.

"I am my father's daughter, aren't I? And, as they say, the apple doesn't fall far from the tree," she answered.

Especially rotten apples, he thought as he leaned down to kiss her on the cheek. "I'll be in touch."

??????

Nya returned to her office after the meeting with Richard. When she walked in, her secretary, Kim, a blonde paralegal, cautioned her, "Nya, Mr. Baron has been waiting in your office. I told him to just come back—" she tried to apologize, but Nya cut her off.

"It's all right, Kim, I was expecting him."

She stepped into her office to find Don Baron. He stood as she entered. He looked vexed.

"Hello, Don," she greeted him. She started to walk by him, but he pulled her to him firmly.

"Yo, where the fuck was you last night??" Don grilled her.

"Fucking," she shot back truthfully, without missing a beat. "Isn't that what you wanted to hear? Isn't that what your attitude is all about?"

Don gritted his teeth.

"Word is bond, Nya, you got a smart-ass mouth, you know that? Don't make me wire that shit up."

You wouldn't dare, she thought to herself.

Don was a straight killer in the streets. No games, no shorts. Bodies in every state he ever hustled in. But when it came to Nya, she turned his G into straight P: pussy.

"If you must know, I went to a banquet honoring the mayor. It ended so late I decided to stay at the hotel it was held in. Happy?" she lied.

"Wit' who?" he questioned.

"Alone."

He eyed her momentarily, then replied, "Next time say that shit instead of fuckin' playin' wit' me," he replied, letting her arm go.

Nya smiled to herself. Tell a person the truth, they think it's a lie. Lie, and they take it for the truth. She sat at her desk, taking off her frames.

"Look, Don, if you came to give me attitude, maybe you should go. I've had a long day."

He sighed as he sat back in the chair.

"Naw, boo, it ain't like that. Shit just been crazy. I tried to call you last night on some professional and personal shit."

"Oh?" she replied, folding her hands on the desk. "You aren't in any kind of trouble, are you?"

Don sat down in the chair, pinching his nose. "Honestly, I don't know. It depends on this kid Mark. You remember him?"

"Vaguely," she lied. She knew his whole crew. "What about him?"

"Kid got bagged up in Richmond yesterday."

"Is it serious?"

He looked at her. "Six kilos serious, yo," he said as he stood up, aggravated. "I told that muhfucka to leave them dudes the fuck alone! Now look at his ass," he said, more to himself than to her. "We can talk in here, right?"

"Of course. You know lawyer-client conversations are confidential," Nya replied.

It's like this, Nya: I'ma need you to take his case, get the nigguh a bond," he told her.

"I don't know, Don," she said, shaking her head. "I don't know if even I can pull that off."

"Whatever it cost, Nya, I don't give a fuck! I want his ass out in the streets. After that, don't worry about the case because he won't make it to his first court date," he said, looking out at the view of the bay.

Nya got up and stood close to him.

"Don't say any more. As your lawyer, I can't be privy to anything ... premeditated. But I will tell you this: How will it look for your lawyer to take this case and, as you said, something happens? It's too much of a trail. Anyone with two eyes can follow. So the feds'll start looking at you anyway. It defeats the purpose."

He nodded, pinching his lip pensively.

"True, indeed."

"Don't worry, I know a few excellent attorneys in Richmond. It shouldn't be hard to get one for the right price," Nya told him.

"Yeah, baby, good lookin'. Check into that right away."

"Just know I'm here for you," she whispered sweetly.

Don pulled her close.

"Here too?" he whispered, letting her feel the bulge in his silk pants.

"Whatever you need," she replied, kissing him deeply and making the bulge harder.

"That's why I love you, boo, straight up. You wit' me 100%, and you ain't no dumb broad. You really do got a nigguh back," he told her, caressing her cheek. "A man got a woman like you in his life, ain't nothing he can't do."

She smiled up at him.

"Tell me truthfully, baby ... can Mark ... hurt you?" she probed.

Don took a deep breath, then answered, "Them feds don't play fair, yo. All he gotta do is breathe my name and I'll have a conspiracy charge."

Nya hugged him tightly, pouring it on thick.

"Oh, Don, I swear I don't want anything to happen to you!"

"Don't worry, ma, ain't nobody in the world gonna take me away from you. I'll do what I gotta do," he explained.

"Would you ever ... cooperate?" she probed.

He pulled away from her.

"Fuck no. I mean, not against my team, yo," Don answered, deep in thought. "But a muhfucka like my connect—yo, his shit sweet, but ... if it's me or him, fuck that cracka."

It was ironic that the same emotions that bonded him to her were the same emotions that had the potential of taking her away. It was clear that if it came down to her or the connect, he'd give up the connect before he gave her up. Which was a problem.

Because she was the connect. He just didn't know that.

It was clear to Nya someone had to go, and she didn't intend on it being her. Don slipped his hand under her skirt and slid two fingers into her wet pussy, making her jump. Don thought it was the sensations of his touch that made her react, but it was really because her pussy was still sore from the beating it took the night before.

"Damn, girl, do you even own a pair of panties?" Don quipped, because it seemed she never had any on.

Nya giggled as she bit Don's ear and licked it. "Hmmmm ... later, baby. Every second is precious. Let me handle Richmond."

Don kissed her. "I love you, Nya. Maybe this shit is a sign, you know? I've had a good run. Maybe it's time to settle down ... me and you."

She laughed hysterically inside, but she remained composed and coolly replied, "Maybe. Now go, or I'll never get anything done."

After Don left, Nya's conniving mind began to spin a web of deceit. Don had to die, there was no question about that. But she knew it wouldn't be easy. He moved like a shadow and had an army of street soldiers at his disposal, so he was seldom unprepared. She knew none of the local crews would do. Most of them were nothing more than forty ounce–guzzling hooligans, unorganized and undisciplined. She didn't want to be involved in any way, so she needed someone to use, someone who could get at Don and make her trouble go away. She thought back to the conversation Gutta and Don had.

"And it wasn't even them Uptown nigguhs. It was a fuckin' Jersey cat name KG."

KG?, Niya asked.

This KG had to be somewhat clever if he could devise a plan like the BK/Uptown beef. He also had to be a killer to murder so many people just to make a point. But could he do it? Would he do it? The second question she quickly dismissed because she felt like there wasn't a man in the world she couldn't control and devour. But she couldn't go to him; she wanted him to come to her. By the time she finished a glass of brandy, she knew just how to do it.

CHAPTER 7

Shameeq got up from the table and headed for the door. Outside, the sun was just beginning to set. He hopped in the Jetta and the sounds of Kool G Rap's "I'm Fly" filled the car.

"That's him, detective. Getting in that Jetta," Dion said from the backseat of the unmarked sedan.

"You sure?" Detective Wallace responded.

Dion hesitated, hating what he was doing, but glad to be free. And soon, his case would be thrown out.

"Yeah, I'm sure. That's Drama, the dude who robbed me," he snitched. Just then a young cat rode by on a bike, so Dion sunk low in his seat.

Wallace nodded, then got on the radio.

"This is Wallace. Unit four move in. The blue Volkswagen Jetta. I repeat, the suspect is in the blue Volkswagen Jetta."

Shameeq looked down for a split second, long enough to adjust the volume and put the car in gear. By the time he looked up, the two police cars skidded to a stop in front of the Jetta, forming a V and blocking him in. Both police officers jumped out, guns drawn.

"Turn the car off and get out *slow!*"

Shameeq was dumfounded. It happened so fast. He mentally went over the car, making sure there were no drugs in the car. He knew that there weren't, but then he remembered the gun under the seat.

"Damn," he cursed, dangling the keys out the window, then dropping them. He opened his car door from the outside and got out, hands raised.

"Is there a problem officer?" he asked in his calmest voice.

The lead officers kept their pistols trained on him as a rookie threw him against the hood. He frisked him roughly and pushed his head against the hot metal hood. He cuffed him, then snatched him upright by the collar of his shirt.

"Yeah, you're the problem! You're under arrest!"

"For what?!"

"Armed robbery," the cop hissed, shoving him towards the car.

"Armed what?! Get the fuck outta here!" Shameeq protested as he got stuffed in the backseat. "This some bullshit!" he yelled as the officer slammed the door in his face.

Another officer searched the Jetta with his flashlight. It didn't take long to find the Snub tucked under the seat.

"Bingo!" the officer yelled, sticking his pen through the loop on the trigger to hold up the gun he found.

Shameeq just sank down in the seat, shaking his head.

??????

Shameeq entered Norfolk County jail escorted by two policemen. Inside, officers bustled back and forth, while a few family members waited anxiously for news about loved ones arrested. What caught his eye, or rather his nose, was the strong smell of fish coming off some scraggy, bearded white man, eyeing him. The white man nodded as Shameeq passed him, heading for the magistrate.

This muhfucka lookin' at me like he know me or something, Shameeq thought, but brushed it off, instead concentrating on his dilemma. He didn't see Detective Wallace enter behind him. He walked up to the bearded man.

"Hello, Bobby. Waitin' on bigger fish, I see," Wallace said, then leaned in closely and whispered, "Tell the bitch we're even now."

Richard nodded as Wallace disappeared in the back room.

Inside the magistrate, the old gray-haired white woman wrote up Shameeq's arrest sheet. He said his name was Jamal Jenkins. She set his bond as a $50,000 unsecured bond. He knew it would be hard to get a bondsman to do his bond because he was from out of town. His mind searched for an answer, but there would be no need. The answer was right in front of his face.

"Excuse me, can you hold up a minute?" Richard asked the officer escorting Shameeq to the back.

"Hey, Ack," the officer greeted him in a heavy Virginian accent. "Catch anything good today? We sure did," he laughed, referring to Shameeq.

Richard looked him up and down.

"Who the fuck is you?" Shameeq hissed.

Richard grinned.

"Well ... I just may be the answer you need. I'm Richard Ackerson. I'm a bondsman."

To Shameeq, he looked like a broke-ass drunk. But if he was a bondsman, he was probably thirsty for money so he could cop his next bottle. Just what Shameeq needed.

"Fifty G's unsecured," Shameeq told him, quickly adding, "but, yo, for my auntie, Seventy-Five Hundred is no problem. She could have it here in no time."

"Fifty G's is a lot of money," Richard replied, in mock contemplation. "Where you from ..." he let his voice trail in that subtle way you do when you're asking someone's name.

"Jamal. Jamal Jenkins. Lake Edwards, yo."

"That's a helluva accent for Lake Edwards," Richard said as he and the officers laughed.

"Naw. I'm from Jersey, but I'm staying with my aunt in Lake Edwards. I'm down here to go to Norfolk State. She's payin' my tuition, which is why I know Seventy-Five Hundred is nothing' to her, especially when I ain't do the crime," Shameeq lied, running his game on the bondsman.

Richard knew it was a game, but he let Shameeq think he was getting over. If the mark think he's a con, then he ends up conning himself.

"How long will it take your auntie to get here?"

"Soon as I call."

"Make the call."

Forty-five minutes after being booked and fingerprinted, Shameeq walked out of the county jail with Richard. A bad-ass redbone named Melody who looked like Salt was waiting in the gold Jetta. She handed Shameeq $7,500, and he gave it to Richard.

"Tell your aunt she's a knockout," Richard quipped.

"Naw, that's her daughter," Shameeq lied.

"Look, it's none of my business whether you did it or not. My concern is that you go to court. Understood?"

"I'll be there," Shameeq assured him.

He handed Shameeq a card.

"What's this?"

"Virginia doesn't play when it comes to guns. Believe me. This card is for Nya Braswell, best lawyer around. She specializes in handling cases like this, and for the right price, she can make it go away," Richard told him, looking Shameeq in the eye. "I'll tell her you'll be calling."

He extended his hand, and Shameeq shook it.

"Yo, I appreciate this."

"And I'll appreciate you being in court," Richard replied, walking away.

Shameeq looked at the card, then stuffed it in his pocket as he got in the car.

"What happened, boo?" Melody asked, trying to touch his face.

He brushed her hand away. "Nothin', yo, just drive. Get me the fuck away from here."

Melody pulled off.

"Shit was crazy, baby. The police said you robbed somebody and they found a gun. They even towed the car. What you wanna do about the car? I know a—" she began, talking nonstop.

"Melody, damn! Shut the fuck up sometimes and let me think!" Shameeq exclaimed, sitting back in the seat. He had already decided what to do with the car. They could have it. He'd have Casper bring down another one. The real issue was the whole chain of events. Shameeq believed everything happened for a reason. There was no such thing as coincidence. He knew the only muhfuckas he robbed were the New Yorkers during the robbery spree, but if he had been arrested for that, robbery would've been the least of his worries.

He didn't know what to think, but he did know he didn't want his name ringing bells with those country-ass cops. The first thing he planned to do was shut down the Lake Edwards operation. Of that, he was sure.

When he got back and talked to the rest of the Squad, Blue commented, "One of these soft-ass nigguhs put shit in the game, stic. They just want us out the way."

"Word, but if you got that chick Braswell, yo' case good as dismissed," Lil' B told him.

Shameeq told himself he would go and pay her a visit first thing in the morning.

??????

Shameeq arrived at Nya's office around one o'clock. He had called earlier that morning and made the appointment. The secretary acted like she had been waiting on his call; she was so accommodating. Shameeq took that as a good sign. If she was as good as Lil' B made her out to be, then he knew he had to have her working for him. The way things were going in the streets, it was only a matter of time before one of the Squad caught a murder charge.

Shameeq stepped in the office doing his best impression of a college dude. He wore a pair of Dockers, Clarks loafers on his feet and a Norfolk State shirt. He had a fresh haircut; his curly 'do was cut close.

He approached the secretary with a bop and cleared his throat.

"I'm here to see Ms. Braswell," he said clearly.

"Whom shall I say is here to see her?" the blonde secretary chimed brightly.

"Jamal Jenkins."

"Please have a seat, Mr. Jenkins. Ms. Braswell will be right with you," she replied, then picked up the phone to announce his arrival. When she finished the short phone call, she told him, "Ms. Braswell will see you now."

Shameeq didn't even have time to sit down. He walked down the short hallway and knocked on the only door marked office.

"Come in, Mr. Jenkins," he heard.

When he came in, the first thing he noticed was the sounds of Sade's "Smooth Operator" playing softly in the office. The mahogany furniture was impeccably designed and matched the burgundy rug and gold-plated accessories. The paintings over the small bar and bookshelf were abstract and matched the decorum. But the most impeccable, most beautiful thing in the room was Nya herself. His eyes landed on her face after a few seconds of checking out the lay of her office, and when he saw her, he thought, Damn! Blue didn't tell me she was fucking gorgeous!

Her long black-brown mane was all pulled to one side and hung down over her right breast. Her tanned vanilla skin gave her a Latin air, while her small nose and lips showed that she was clearly mixed.

Nya looked up from her desk, and her eyes went to his face almost immediately. Her heart sighed like an avid collector's would after eyeing a rare work of art. Her mind said, Damn, almost at the same time his did. His thick eyebrows, green eyes and bronze skin made her pussy wet instantly. Shameeq peeped the lust in her eyes for a split second before she concealed it. He smiled to himself because he was used to that type of reaction from women. Nya saw the lust in his eyes as well and smiled inwardly because she was used to the reaction as well. Both thought of the other, "Got 'em!" But they pretended it was all business.

The game had begun.

Nya stood and extended her hand.

"Hello, Mr. Jenkins. It's a pleasure to meet you."

"The pleasure is all mine," Shameeq replied smoothly, giving her his sexiest smile. He held her hand a pulse longer than necessary for a formal handshake, then slowly released it as he sat down.

He can't be as bad as Dion made him out to be, Nya thought, because he was too fine to look like the killer he really was.

"So, Jamal, what can I do for you?"

"I caught a robbery charge, which is bullshit. I mean—excuse me, which ain't true. I ain't robbed nobody! I'm down here staying with my aunt to go to college at Norfolk State," he spat, running his whole spiel.

"I see," Nya nodded. "Norfolk's a good school. What are you majoring in?" she quizzed, seeing straight through his façade. He may not have looked hard, but his demeanor screamed street.

Shameeq cleared his throat. "Business."

Drug business, she thought to herself.

"Oh, okay. Well, Jamal, I'll be honest with you," she began sitting back in her chair, "Virginia is extremely hard on gun offenses, especially with out-of-towners. So many northerners have come down here with drugs, that the sheriff's office is cracking down hard," she said. She could see his spirit sink.

"But I'm tellin', you Ms. Braswell—"

"Nya. Call me Nya."

Shameeq smiled. "Nya, I'm tellin' you, I ain't robbed nobody! I mean, look at me. Do I look like a thief?" he smirked.

Of hearts, she thought, but she said, "I wouldn't cross the street if I saw you coming my way," she flirted, then glanced at the open folder in front of her. "But according to Donald Baron, you did. Do you know Don Baron?"

Shameeq frowned. "Nah, never heard of 'em in my life."

Nya nodded, looking at Shameeq.

"You know, I believe you; therefore, I'm going to help you."

She picked up the phone, dialed, then waited.

"Yes, this is Nya Braswell. Is Mr. Myers in? Great. Could you put him on for me? Sure." She placed her hand over the receiver. "Classical music. Aargh!" she joked, referring to the music that played while she held on. "Yes, Phillip. How are you? Oh, I'm well. Yes, I got it. Thank you. That was sweet." She winked at Shameeq.

"Listen, I have a Jamal Jenkins here, and he's been charged with robbery with a dangerous weapon. Yes, it was a gun."

Shameeq's heart sank.

"No, it just happened. He just got arrested," she said, letting her voice trail off so Shameeq could fill in the blank.

"Last night," he said, wondering who she was talking to.

"Last night," she repeated. "Anyway, I'm calling as his attorney, hoping maybe we could work something out. Uh-huh I see."

"What up? Who that?" Shameeq whispered.

Nya held up her index finger, signaling him to wait.

"Okay, yes, I'm familiar with that case. I received it pro bono, and you *know* I hate pro bono," she giggled. "I see. So what about my client?"

She smiled at Shameeq and gave him the thumbs-up. "Not a problem. Three years sounds fair. He'll accept. Thanks, Phil, you're a doll."

She hung up.

"Three years?!" Shameeq exclaimed, "I ain't doin—"

"Not you, Mr. Jenkins. That was the District Attorney. He agreed to drop the charge against you as long as I can plea out a case for him. So you're all set, she explained.

"Just like that, huh? So that's how it works?" Shameeq smirked, impressed with the way she handled her business. "What if dude don't plea?"

Nya leaned her arms on the desk. "Oh, he will, Jamal. Believe me, I *always* get what I want."

"I'm sure you do," he commented, thinking, You can damn sure get it too.

"Now that that's over, what are you going to do for me?" Nya flirted, biting her bottom lip subtly.

"What do you want?" he replied.

"Lunch."

"Huh?"

Nya stood up, grabbing her purse. "Lunch. I'm starving."

Shameeq stood up.

"That's it?"

"Believe me, I have very expensive taste and a voracious appetite," she replied, eyeing him like she could devour him on the spot.

Shameeq smiled, thinking he had her right where he wanted her, but he was actually right where she wanted him.

??????

"So, Jamal, tell me ... what's your story?" Nya asked before sipping her glass of Chablis.

They were having lunch at Francois, a very expensive restaurant in the heart of Virginia Beach. Everything about the place smelled of old money. It was the type of place Shameeq had never been exposed to. Nya had standing reservations, which impressed him even more.

"I don't have a story," he replied, cutting his filet mignon.

"Everyone has a story," Nya urged him.

"Then what's yours?" Shameeq countered.

"Veni, vedi, veci," she smirked.

"What?"

"I came, I saw, I conquered. It's Latin," she explained. "So why'd you choose Norfolk State? Did you have a scholarship?"

"Yeah," he lied between bites.

"For what?" Nya probed further.

Shameeq looked up from his plate and met her gaze. He could tell she was trying to get in his head, so he played along.

"Baseball."

"Ohhhh, how big's your bat?" Nya quipped, with a twinkle in her eye.

Shameeq chuckled.

"We still talkin' about baseball?"

Nya sipped her drink.

"You know what I think?"

"What?"

"I don't think you go to college at all. You don't strike me as the college type," Nya surmised.

"No? So how do I strike you then?" Shameeq wanted to know.

"One of those Up-top guys with—how can I say it ... an entrepreneurial spirit. What do you guys call it? Oh yeah, goin' O.T."

Shameeq smirked. He had to admit, Nya was sharp. But he stuck to his story.

"O.T.? Who you been talkin' to? Naw, love. O.T.? Whatever that means, it ain't me. I'm goin' to Norfolk 'cause I wanna be the next Reggie Jackson," he replied.

Nya smiled and shook her head.

"You can't bullshit a bullshitter, Jamal. I'm a lawyer, remember? So I know it's more to you than what meets the eye."

Shameeq shrugged.

"Ain't no mystery, Nya. What you see is what you get."

"I definitely like what I see. It's what I can't see that has me so intrigued."

Always keep 'em guessin', Shameeq mused to himself.

??????

Shameeq drove over to Montez's spot feeling like he had won the lottery. Nya was the type of chick he felt like he should have. She was smart, had paper and was the type of lawyer that he needed on the team. Plus, he just knew she was on his dick.

"I really enjoyed lunch, Jamal," he remembered her saying once they got back to her office. She had kissed him on the cheek, then smoothed away the lipstick on his cheek with her thumb. "*Anything* you need, just call," she had told him.

He couldn't wait to get back and brag to these Virginia nigguhs how he had bagged a broad they could only dream about.

"My word, B, the bitch acted like she wanted to fuck a nigguh right on the table," Shameeq boasted as Montez passed him the blunt.

"Word? Nya Braswell? That bitch high maintenance, stic. That type bitch probably only fuck wit' crackers wit' yachts and shit," Montez commented.

"Yeah, well, she want that Drama in her life now," Shameeq retorted.

"How much she charge you to get the charge dropped?" YaYa wanted to know.

"Lunch, B," Shameeq laughed. "I told you, she on my dick."

"Pimp hard, young man, pimp hard," Montez chuckled, giving Shameeq dap.

"We need a bitch like that on the team 'cause one of these faggot muhfuckas gonna make me catch a case," YaYa grumbled as he counted his money, a cigarette dangling from his mouth.

"It's in the bag, Ya. Don't sweat it," Shameeq assured him.

??????

The next day, Shameeq went to put the icing on the cake. He bought a bouquet of pink roses and went to surprise Nya at her office. He planned on taking her out and laying his game on thick. He knew once he put that dick in her, he'd have her on lock.

"Wait here, B," he told YaYa. "I'll be right back. Let me work this bitch."

Shameeq hopped out the car and went inside the office.

"Nya here?" he asked Kim, the secretary.

"Yes, she's in her office. Jamal, right?" she answered.

"Yeah, Jamal."

Kim asked, "Do you have an appointment to see Ms. Braswell?"

"Naw, just tell her I need to see her."

She called and relayed his message.

"She said that she's very busy. Just make an appointment and she'll see you then."

Shameeq frowned slightly, then replied, "She back there, right?"

"Yes, but—d"

Shameeq started towards her office.

"I wouldn't do that if I were you," Kim called after him, but Shameeq paid her no mind. He figured Nya was just having a bad day, all the more reason to see him.

"It's cool, boss, I got this," he told her.

Shameeq entered Nya's office. She looked up, stone-faced. "Didn't you hear my secretary?"

Shameeq attempted to charm her with his smile.

"Yeah, I heard, boo, but I had a surprise for you," he told her, pulling the roses from behind his back.

Nya just looked at the flowers blandly. "I don't like surprises, first of all. Second, roses are a dime a dozen. You must be crazy if you thought you'd dazzle me with such trash."

"Ay, yo—"

"No, yo, this is a place of business. If you don't have any business with me, then you have no business *here*. Now, unless you have an appointment, then I suggest you leave my office at once. Oh, and by the way, I hate pink."

Nya spat her spiel with such coldness, Shameeq was froze in his spot. It was like she had never seen him before in her life! He had never had a woman flip on him like that.

"Damn, Nya, it's like that?" was all he could say.

"Ms. Braswell. And I said good day," she replied, then returned her attention to the open folder in front of her.

Shameeq turned around to find the secretary with an "I told you so" look on her face. He brushed past her and headed for the door.

When he got to the car, YaYa took one look at his face and cracked, "I think you forgot your face inside."

"Fuck you," Shameeq spat. Realizing he still had the flowers in his hand, he tossed them to the ground with disgust, got in and pulled off, tires skidding.

CHAPTER 8

Present Day 1994

"Look, we're not interested in the boy-meets-girl bullshit," McGrady huffed, eyeing him hard.

"You said you wanted to know everything, didn't you?" he replied calmly, blowing smoke into the air.

"Don't be a smart-ass," Mullins warned him. "You know damn well what we want to know. The facts, names, dates, who did what! We want answers, not a goddamn love story!" Mullins huffed.

He leaned forward on the table and clasped his hands. The cigarette in his mouth made him close one eye against the smoke." Look, I don't like—" He broke up in a fit of coughs. "I don't—yo, could I get some water," he asked, but no one moved. "*Please.* Goddamn."

Mullins reluctantly relented. "Get him a glass of water."

Jacobs brought him a glass. When Jacobs handed him the glass, he noticed that his nails were manicured, and it disgusted him. He hated the whole metrosexual thing.

He sipped the water, then sat the glass down. "Now, where was I? Oh, yeah, I was tryin' to explain the dynamics that caused the whole house of cards to fall. This ain't just a shoot-'em-up, bang-bang type thing; it's a lot of twist to this shit, a'ight? And a lot of it is cause *love* got twisted. Which, as you see, is why I'm sittin' here. We'll get to that now. Keep up, 'cause if you ain't sharp, you'll get lost," he said, then glanced from face to face to make sure they understood.

"Wait a minute, let me get this straight," Jacobs said, pacing the floor. "You said the New York beef was really orchestrated by the Drama Squad, right?"

"Yeah."

"And once Don found out, somehow Braswell heard about it too, so she decided since you guys were already gunning for Baron's crew, why not use it to her advantage," Jacobs surmised.

"Exactly," he confirmed, putting out his cigarette.

"So why did Baron take out the robbery charge?" McGrady asked.

"He didn't," Jacobs answered for him. "Braswell set that up too."

"Bingo! Now I see why you guys get paid the big dollars: You're fucking geniuses," he quipped. "Nya was playin' chess, not checkers, with both sides. The Squad was nobody in her eyes, which was her biggest mistake. She underestimated us," he smiled.

"So how did Drama Squad go from nobody to somebody?" Mullins asked.

"When Egypt came to town."

??????

1989

"Owww ... yessss ... fuck! Right there, right—man, nigga, don't bite it! Oh, yeah, just like that, just like that. I'm—owwww ... I'm about to cummmm," Egypt moaned as her body jerked and spasmed. After the tremors subsided, she breathed a sigh of relief.

"Damn, boo, you getting nice. You practicing on somebody else or somethin?" Egypt joked. She grabbed her Newports off the nightstand and offered him one.

Casper waved it off.

"Come on, Egypt, my dick hard as a rock. You gonna let me hit that?"

Egypt blew smoke out. "For what? I already came."

Casper was pissed.

"That that bullshit, yo. That's the second time you beat me for the head. I ain't doin that shit no more," he vowed.

"That's what you said last time," she giggled.

Before he could respond, a beeper went off.

"Is that me or you?"

"Man, I don't know," Casper replied disgustedly as he walked toward the bathroom.

She checked her beeper, then his. It was neither. She thought for a minute, then looked at the beeper in her purse. When she grabbed it, she saw the number had the code 111.

"Yo, Casp! Casp, come here. It's him!" Egypt exclaimed.

"Him who?" Casper answered from the bathroom.

"Him, nigga, him! The 111 muhfucka! The nigguh that tried to kill Meeq!" she yelled, feeling her blood start to boil.

Casper ran back in the room.

"Word?!"

"Yeah!"

"Gimme the beeper!" he demanded.

"For what?"

"I'ma call him back," Casper said like, duh!

"And say you who?" Egypt questioned. He fell silent. "If he hear a nigguh voice other than KG, he ain't gonna fuck wit' it."

Casper thought about it. "True, indeed. So what we gonna do? We can't just let this nigguh get away."

"Fuck no! I'ma call him," Egypt told him, dialing the number.

"And say what?"

Egypt didn't respond because the phone had started ringing.

"Hello?" the voice answered.

"Somebody beep 555-3714?" Egypt said.

"Naw, you got the wrong number," the dude lied.

"This KG girl. He left the money wit' me," Egypt quickly blurted out, not wanting him to hang up. "He out of town."

No response.

"Hello?" she said.

"What money?" the dude probed.

"If I gotta tell you, then I guess this is the wrong number," Egypt replied.

"Where you at?"

"Where you at?" she shot right back.

"Where you need me to be?" he said.

Egypt thought quickly, then said, "You tell me. I ain't from Newark; I'm from Roselle."

"Roselle?" he said.

She could hear the laughter in his voice. She wanted to rock him all the way to sleep, thinking he was dealing with a soft, suburban girl.

"Yeah, is that a problem?" she said with fake attitude.

"Naw, naw. You know where Grafton Avenue at?"

She knew she had him if he was showing her where he rest his head at. "No. Explain."

He told her what she already knew, then she hung up. Casper tucked his pistol. "So how we gonna do this?"

"I'ma walk up on 'em and give it to him," Egypt replied simply.

"You?!" Casper echoed, wide-eyed. "Hell no! Meeq gonna flip! Ain't—"

"'Meeq ain't here, and if he was, he my brother, not my goddamn daddy. Besides, the nigguh think he meeting a female. You show up and you probably won't get within ten feet. Now, come on, 'cause I'm the one that know where he at, so it's goin' down wit' or without you," Egypt stated firmly, pulling a pistol out of the closet and tucking it in her pants.

Casper shook his head."Meeq gonna flip," he said, then followed her out the door.

Egypt got off the bus across the street from Grafton Avenue projects. She had gotten on the bus a block away because she had told dude she was taking the bus from Roselle. The plan was for Casper to pull up and scoop her up after she blazed the kid up. Egypt looked around for Casper's car but didn't see it. She did see three dudes standing outside the corner store the kid said he'd be in front of.

As she approached, she could tell at least two of the dudes had pistols from the bulges on their waist. Hers was tucked in the small of her back.

"Damn, ma, you lookin' for me?" one of the dudes flirted.

"I don't think my man KG would like that," she replied.

"Who the fuck is KG?" dude asked.

"Chill, B, this business," the other dude with a gun said, then looked at Egypt. "I ain't think you were comin' all the way from Roselle."

"Word, ma, you got any friends?" the unarmed dude quipped.

She ignored him and turned to the mark. "I got that for you."

"Cool, let me get it," he replied.

"Egypt handed him a bulging envelope. While he peeled it open to look inside, she subtly reached for her gun. He looked in the envelope to see it was filled with torn up pieces of paper.

"Yo, what the fuck kinda game—" he began barking on her, but before he could finish the sentence, Egypt had the gun in his face.

"That's from Shameeq, faggot!" she bellowed, then gave him two in the face.

"Bitch!" the other dude exclaimed. It had happened so fast, he was totally off guard, but he tried to reach for his pistol anyway.

Boom!! Boom!! Egypt dropped him with two in the dome. Just as Casper skidded up to the corner, she turned the gun on the third dude.

"Yo, chill! I ain't got nothin' to do with it!" he claimed.

"Too bad," she replied, giving him three in the chest, stopping his heart before he hit the ground.

She backpedaled, then turned around and jumped in the passenger's seat. "Nigguh, drive! And don't stop 'til you hit Virginia!"

??????

Jefferson Avenue in Newport News was crawling with police, along with an ambulance and even a news crew. YaYa and Shameeq drove by casually, only glancing over even though their hearts were racing.

"Yo, who the fuck blew up the spot?" Shameeq asked YaYa as he rounded the corner.

"Who you think? Them muhfuckin' New York nigguhs, B," YaYa replied.

"Fuck you talkin' about, B? How the fuck they know it was us? Shameeq retorted. "Them dumb muhfuckas ain't figured it out."

"Well, this damn sure wasn't any robbery. Somebody killed three of ours. Who the fuck else could it be?" YaYa shot back.

"There go Lil' B. Pull over."

YaYa pulled the Jetta over in front of an old, raggedy house. It was the spot Lil' B used as a stash house. Lil' B was standing out front smoking a cigarette, looking up and down the block through slit eyes. At his feet sat a red-nose pit without a leash.

YaYa and Shameeq walked up. "What the deal, B?" Shameeq asked.

"Shit crazy around here, stic," Lil' B replied, full of energy. "Muhfuckas *really* want a war bringin' that shit to my block!"

"You ain't told us nothin'," YaYa said. "What happened?"

"I don't know 'cause I wasn't there," Lil' B answered, thunking his cigarette to the ground. "But the crackheads said two nigguhs with up-top accents hopped out on my little mans and 'em, talking 'bout the block is closed or they can't serve on the block no more! I don't know, some shit like that. Anyway, my youngins, they pedigree, so they bucked. Fuck you mean?! The heads said they gunned my nigguhs down! Them was lil' nigguhs. The youngest was thirteen! Fuck I'ma tell his mother?!" Lil' B ranted, then skeet spit to his left.

YaYa looked at Shameeq. "Up-top accents," he said, repeating Lil' B's words. "Now who the dumb muhfucka?"

Shameeq's beeper went off. He checked the number, then put it back on his waist.

"Naw, B, I *know* them nigguhs don't know! They just hearing we gettin' money over here, and they tryin' to push up and stop the flow," Shameeq replied.

"I don't give a fuck *why.* I'm just lookin' for who! Them nigguhs want a war, I'll send 'em all back the fuck up top in bags!" Lil' B exclaimed with aggression, which made his pit bull sit up and growl. "Be easy, Menace," he told it, and the pit relaxed his ears.

"Then that's what it is then," Shameeq said as his beeper went off again. He checked it, then sucked his teeth in disgust.

"We don't need an army. Let's go handle it then," Shameeq added as his beeper went off again.

"Yo, whoever keep beepin' you, answer that shit or turn it off. Goddamn!" YaYa spat, irritated.

"Fuckin bitch Nya," Shameeq told him.

"The one that dissed you," YaYa smirked.

"Fuck outta here, nigguh! Ain't no bitch diss me. You see she blowin' me up! Fuck her, though. She can wait. Let's go handle this shit."

??????

The three of them rode out to Virginia Beach. They knew where a few Brooklyn nigguhs were getting money, so they targeted them.

"So how we gonna handle this?" Lil' B asked, driving the rusty hooptie they had rented from a crackhead for the mission. "You want me to pull up and we just blaze them nigguhs drive-by style?"

"Fuck that. That's how little kids get hit. The Squad don't get down like that. We bring it to your goddamn chest!" YaYa barked, loading the banana clip on the Uzi.

"Indeed, B, indeed. So don't even skid up. Park around the corner and be ready to pounce when we done.

"Why the fuck you nigguhs get to have all the fun?" Lil' B complained.

"'Cause, nigguh, you know these streets better than us, stic," Shameeq smirked.

"That's that bullshit, yo" Lil' B twisted up his mouth.

When they got to the block, it was close to midday, so traffic wasn't heavy. Three nigguhs were playing dice, and one was serving the few crack fiends who came through. Lil' B parked around the corner, but when YaYa and Shameeq got out, he got out too.

"Fuck is you doin'?" Shameeq asked.

"Fuck that, them was *my* youngins. I left the shit runnin'," Lil' B replied.

"Just come on," YaYa told him, "but if somebody jump in our shit while we gone, I'm fuckin' you up!"

As soon as the trio rounded the corner, they had their guns aimed, catching the four dudes off guard.

"Don't *nobody* fuckin' move!" Shameeq hissed, scanning the block for any movement.

The nigguhs playing dice all raised their heads.

"You got it, son. Be easy," one dude said.

Just hearing his voice ticked Lil' B off. He lifted dude with four to the chest. That crumbled him up against the store wall, leaving a trail of blood on the bricks.

"Yo, son! What the fuck?!" the second dude hollered. "Take it, yo. You can have it!" he offered, referring to the pile of money on the ground.

"Who block is this?" Shameeq asked the third cat.

"What you mean, who block?" the dude answered with attitude.

Boom!

Shameeq put the gun to his forehead and blew out the back of his head. "I said who's block is this," he asked the fourth cat before the other cat hit the ground.

"I'm sayin', son, what you talkin' about?!" the fourth cat asked nervously.

"Who get money out here?"

"We do."

"Then it's your block?" Shameeq repeated, lowering his gun.

The cat opened his mouth to say yes, but Shameeq shoved the gun in it and made sure he would have a closed-casket funeral too.

Before he could turn to the second cat, he blurted out, "It's your block, son! It's yours!"

Shameeq smiled.

"Exactly. Now we on the same page. Now you tell whoever the fuck got you out here this Drama's block. You got me?!"

"Yeah, yo, I got you. I got you," the second cat said, nodding his head.

"Now beat it before I change my muhfuckin' mind," Shameeq sneered.

As the cat jogged off, Lil' B kicked him in the ass. "Pussy-ass nigguh! Bring that shit to Bad News again!"

"Let's be out," Shameeq said, tucking his gun.

CHAPTER 9

1989

"Drama? Who the fuck is Drama?!" Gutta barked when the second cat, a nigguh named Divine, gave him the message.

"Yo, son, them nigguhs came outta nowhere! They mercked Lo before they said a word!" Divine explained.

Gutta was furious. He looked at Divine. "And y'all ain't do shit?! Fuck you had this for?!" he questioned, snatching the gun off his waist.

"How?! They had the drop!" Divine replied.

"The drop?!" Gutta smacked the shit out of Divine. "Punk bitch, you shoulda died too!" He punched Divine in the jaw and pinned him against the wall. "And what the fuck is this about Bad News?! I don't even fuck wit' Bad News!"

"But I do."

Gutta turned around to see Sincere standing there.

"I sent a team over there 'cause I know for a fact them Bad News nigguhs fuck wit' that nigguh KG," Sincere explained. "I knew if we hit them and they knew exactly who to hit back, then Black was right, and KG is the one behind this."

"Then who the fuck is Drama?" Gutta questioned.

"Drama?" Sincere echoed.

"Yeah, ain't that what the nigguh said, B?"

"Yeah, son, he said this Drama's block," Divine answered.

"Never heard of 'em," Sincere replied.

"Yeah, well, he gonna hear of Gutta real goddamn soon. KG, Drama, all them Jersey nigguhs can get it!" Gutta vowed.

??????

"Drama, where you goin'?" the chocolate bunny on the bed whined. Her dark, naked skin tone glistened with the afterglow of sex.

"Just chill, yo. I gotta make a call," he replied, putting on his boxers and grabbing his beeper.

"Can't it wait? This pussy still on fire, daddy," she cooed, crawling down to the end of the bed like a panther, then licking Shameeq's ear. He moved his head, irritated. He hated the after-sex cuddling-type shit.

"Well, play in it 'til I get back," he replied nonchalantly.

He got up from the bed and headed to the kitchen. Why the fuck I'm even calling the bitch back, he thought to himself, but the truth was he couldn't get her off his mind. Nya beeped him six times while he was fucking. It made him imagine it was her taking each thrust, her beautiful voice crying out in soft, sensual moans. No matter how much he tried, he couldn't shake it, and he hated the feeling of wanting her, but his curiosity got the best of him, so he picked up the phone and dialed.

"Yo," was all he said when she picked up.

"Jamal?" she said sweetly. The sound of her voice made him imagine how her moan would sound.

"Yeah, this me. What the fuck you want?" he bassed, holding the phone like a grudge.

"Okay, I deserve that," Nya replied, sitting back twirling a pencil and swiveling in her desk chair. She had him on speaker phone while Richard sat across from her.

"I'm really sorry about the way I acted the other day. I was really upset, but I had no right to take it out on you," she explained. Shameeq didn't respond.

"Hello?" she said.

"Yeah, I'm here," he said, fronting like he was swoll, but his insides eased up knowing she had come crawling back to him.

"Can you forgive me?" Nya chimed, winking at Richard. He shook his head.

"Ay, yo, girl, you play me like I'm lint and now you wanna apologize? Fuck you take me for?" Shameeq retorted.

Nya rolled her eyes at the ceiling then answered in her softest voice, "You have every right to be upset, Jamal. Really. But what's done is done, so why waste time on the past when the future could be so bright? Please ... let me make it up to you, okay? I promise I'll be good—or bad, if you want me to be."

Shameeq's dick twitched at her sexual innuendo. He smirked because his pride was restored. "What you got in mind?"

Nya faced the phone and put her mouth near the speaker, "It's a surprise."

"I thought you ain't like surprises?"

Nya giggled. "I don't like to be surprised, but I love to be the surprise," she purred. "I'm taking you out tonight. I'll pick you up around eight. Is that okay?"

Shameeq lit the blunt. "Yeah, that's cool."

"Excellent! So where should I meet you?"

"I'll be on Newton Road in VA Beach, Shameeq replied. "You know the strip?"

"I'll find it. I'll see you then," Nya said. "And, Jamal?"

"Yeah?"

"You *won't* regret it," she purred before hanging up. She looked at Richard.

"You sure this kid can handle it?" he questioned.

"Please. By the time I'm finished with him, he'll be ready to kill the pope for me. Men are so easy," she bragged, brushing her hair out of her face.

"I'm glad you're enjoying your little game, Nya, but this *ain't* a game! I told you that son of a bitch Mark is cooperating! We don't need the feds up our ass. You already know what's at stake," Richard stressed.

"It'll be handled, Richard," Nya assured him.

"I've cut Don off for now. I stopped taking his calls three days ago. I'm beginning our ... exit strategy," Richard said.

Nya thought about it, then agreed. "In light of recent circumstances, I agree. Besides, if this becomes of war of attrition, then we need to cut off all resources."

"Attrition my ass. This thing has to be done yesterday! Now what do we do if this KG kid fails?"

Nya leaned her elbows on the desk and eyed him squarely. "Then *you* will handle it, Richard. Daddy wouldn't have it any other way."

Richard sat back silently.

??????

Don slammed the car phone back into its slot with disgust. He had been trying to get his connect for three days, to no avail. This had never happened before, so he knew something was wrong. He could feel it.

"You alright, God?" Sincere asked, sitting in the passenger's seat. Don gave him a stone look, then answered, "Yeah, I'm peace."

"Still no word on scrams?" Sincere asked, referring to Mark.

"Naw, yo, and that fuck-ass lawyer in Richmond couldn't get his punk ass out so we can get at him!" Don barked, hitting the steering wheel with his open hand.

"You really think he won't hold water?"

"We can't take that chance. I told dude let that shit go, and he disobeyed me! Nigguh gotta face the consequences of his actions," Don told him.

Sincere nodded in agreement.

"Any word on this Drama cat?" Don wanted to know.

"Naw, yo, muhfuckas ain't heard of him. Nobody. Maybe it's them KG muhfuckas tryin' to throw us off," Sincere surmised.

Don nodded.

"Makes sense. Fuck!" Don blurted out in disgust. "We don't need no goddamn fed beef right now! How the fuck we 'posed to go to the mattresses wit' these Jersey nigguhs and the feds on us hard?! Somehow we gotta get to Mark, yo. Somehow."

"Indeed," Sincere nodded. "But if not?"

Don didn't answer.

"Ay, yo, God, I know this ain't the best time to bring this up, but yo, when we gonna discuss that issue I brought to you a few months ago?" Sincere probed.

"What issue?" Don responded, making a left turn.

"When I was sayin' I got a major move brewin' out in Ohio. Shit is official, God, word. And wit' your blessins I could go sew that shit up."

Don grunted.

"You right. This ain't the time."

"No disrespect, but I done brought this up several times. Come on, Don, you know the God been true wit' you, holdin' it down however you needed. Now I just wanna put my own thing together, so when will it be a good time?"

"Whenever the fuck I say it is!" Don blazed him, slamming on the brakes as they reached the light. "*Whenever* I say, a'ight?!"

"A'ight," Sincere mumbled. Looking out the window.

"I said a'ight?!"

Sincere looked back at Don, without fear but not trying to push it either.

"I said a'ight, God."

"Then that's what it is then," Don replied.

??????

"Go 'head wit' that bullshit, Tez," a lanky dude named Tim said, tired of being clowned.

Tez, Trello, Lil' B and Shameeq were standing on Pacific Avenue in Virginia Beach. The strip was brimming with activity as people pumped everything illegal, from drugs to pussy. There was a big crowd, and Tez was the center of attention.

"Go 'head?! Nigguh, that's what I always tell you, wit' your beggin' ass! Ay, remember that time I made you eat shit?" Montez cracked.

"Eat shit?" Shameeq echoed, laughing hard.

"Word, stic, this nigguh here was always beggin'. Chips, candy, soda—he ain't give a fuck. If you had it, he wanted some! So

I said I'ma break this nigguh, right! So one day I see him comin', right, so I get a napkin and some old-ass poodle shit off the ground. You know how when that shit get old it turn white and shit?" Montez chuckled.

"Yeah," Shameeq answered, damn near in tears.

"So I'm actin' like I'm eatin' it. Here come this nigguh," Montez continued, pointing his thumb at Tim, who stood there fuming. "Here he go, 'What's that?' I say, 'It's a snow rocket.' He say, 'Snow rocket? I ain't never heard of that. Lemme get a piece.' So he break off a piece, right, and word, stic, the nigguh chew it for like three seconds and say, 'This ain't no snow rocket, this doo-doo!'" Montez and the whole crowd died laughing.

"Yo, fuck you, Tez, man!" Tim barked, embarrassed.

Montez kept laughing, so Tim added, "Bitch-ass nigguh!"

"What the fuck you say?" Montez asked, still laughing. And before anyone saw it coming, Montez backhanded Tim in his mouth, then proceeded to go to his ass. "

Nya pulled up in a stretch limo just as the fight broke out. She rolled down the window and called out, "Jamal!"

Shameeq didn't answer, not recognizing his alias, until Trello tapped him on the shoulder and said, "Yo, B, who that bad-ass bitch in the limo?"

Shameeq turned out.

"Jamal!" Nya called out again, waving him over.

"Oh, that's me, B," he stated nonchalantly, adjusting his sag as he slow-bopped to the car. He leaned on the limo's roof and spoke to Nya through the open window.

"Is everything okay?" she asked after seeing Montez beat the shit out of Tim.

"What, that? That ain't nothin', just a little misunderstanding, boo. You ready?"

She opened the door.

"No, the question is are you?" she quipped with sexuality dripping from her tone.

??????

Telephone Love, you sound so sweet on this line
Telephone Love, you make my day every time

The sounds of this reggae filled Shananigan's, a hangout spot for Big Willies in Virginia Beach. The way Nya worked her hips, it made Shameeq think she was part Jamaican. His dick was rock hard from Nya grinding against it the last twenty minutes. The outfit she wore made guys and girls do a double take.

She wrapped her arms around Shameeq's neck and placed one leg around his and grinded her body against him Jamaican style. "Do you know what she's singing about?" she asked in his ear.

"Naw," he replied, palming her ass like a basketball.

"Phone sex," she replied. "You ever tried it, Jamal?"

"I never had to," Shameeq answered with a smirk.

Don sat in the VIP with Sincere, Gutta, and a bevy of chicks trying to be down.

"Ay, yo, Don, ain't that your lawyer chick?" Sincere asked.

"Where?" Don asked casually, flirting with the Spanish mami next to him.

"Right there," Sincere pointed.

Don followed his finger to the center of the dance floor, and his blood pressure went through the roof. He was on fire seeing Shameeq's hands all over her ass and Nya all over him. He totally forgot the chick next to him and rose from the booth.

"Who the fuck is dude, yo? Sincere asked, getting up after Don.

"I don't know, but I'm about to find out," Don seethed.

As Nya and Shameeq left the dance floor, Don, Sincere, and Gutta cut them off before they reached a table. Don snatched Nya by the arm, but Nya snatched it right back.

"Excuse *you*!" she hissed.

"Yo, what the fuck you doin' here, and who the fuck is this?!" Don barked, grilling Shameeq.

Shameeq grilled him back, keeping his hand close to the gun on his waist.

"What, you think I don't like to party too? Don't worry, I'm not here to bust up the groove you have going over there," Nya commented, referring to the chicks Don was with.

Knowing he was busted, he redirected his anger to Shameeq.

"Yo, who you, B?" Don bassed.

Shameeq saw how Don's crew was slowly forming voltron, but before he could answer, Nya said, "Donald Baron, do you think you own me?! He has nothing to do with this. Now please excuse *us* because now you're bustin' up *our* groove."

She took Shameeq's hand and led him to a vacant table.

Shameeq's mind was whirling. Donald Baron? He couldn't be the same nigguh who took out the fugazzi robbery charge, could he? It wasn't like the name was all that common, so how many Donald Barons could there be in VA? Still, he could tell the nigguh was heavy just by the way his crew held him down. But why pull a bitch move like a warrant? Shit didn't make any sense.

"Jamal? Jamal? Are you okay?" Nya asked with concern. She made sure to say Don's whole name clear enough so he could hear it, so she had a feeling she knew what he was thinking.

"Yeah, yo, what up?" he replied, finally responding.

"Are you okay? You wanna get out of here?" Nya offered.

Shameeq looked over and saw Don still grilling him.

"Yeah, for real, 'cause it's only so much I can take," he told her.

They made their way to the door. As they were leaving, Black was coming in with his arm draped around a chick. Shameeq brushed past him, which made Black look up.

"Pardon me, dude," Shameeq said, but kept it moving.

Black was so into the chick, he almost brushed it off. A few steps later, he stopped, looked back towards the door, then he told the chick, "Hold up."

He made his way through the thick crowd and went back outside. As he emerged from the club, he saw Nya and Shameeq getting in the limo. His eyes got big as he quickly debated whether he should blaze the limo in the crowded parking lot or go inside to find Don. He opted to find Don. He rushed back inside and straight to VIP. "Ay, yo, I just saw that nigguh KG!"

"Where?!" Gutta barked, rising from his seat.

"Here! He just left wit' that lawyer chick Don fuck wit'!" Black informed them.

Don looked up.

"Who?!"

"The nigguh KG just got in a limo wit' the broad."

"You sure?!" Don probed.

"Hell yeah, I'm sure!" Black assured him.

"What up, son, let's go get 'em!" Gutta growled.

"Naw, naw, chill. Nya in the car," Don answered, rubbing his face.

"So what?!" Gutta spat.

"Fuck you mean, so what?! I said *chill!"* Don ordered, then hurried to beep Nya.

??????

Blue was back in L.E. to pick up the money from the workers. Since Shameeq was arrested, the Squad had basically shut down shop in Lake Edwards. Blue had just come through to collect what they still had out there.

"Yo, Blue! Blue, let me holla at 'cha, stic," Blue heard the boy call out to him.

Blue looked up and saw his little man Peanut peddling over to him on his bike. Peanut was only twelve, but he was always around doing things for all the dope boys, like going to the store, watching out for police and carrying packages. He hook slid his mongoose in front of Blue, kicking up dust.

"A'ight, Nut, you betta watch that shit. You fuck up these new Jordans, I'ma beat yo lil' ass," Blue chuckled.

"Man, later for that. Where y'all nigguhs been? Money been rolling like a muddafucka," Peanut exclaimed.

"Shit got too hot, young," Blue told him, getting in the car.

"Where Drama at? I need to holla at him."

Blue shut the door and started the car. "He a'ight."

"Yeah, but I gotta tell him something, stic. I saw the nigguh that snitched him out to po-po! Ol' punk-ass nigguh named Dion," Peanut told him.

Blue frowned. "Dion? Naw, youngin, his name *Don*. Some cat named—"

"Naw, Blue! I'm telling you, stic, I *saw* the muddafucka in the back of the police car that day, and I know him too. He my cousin's best friend's baby daddy—you know, big butt Tamika!" Peanut exclaimed.

"Naw ... Dion? Peanut, you sure?" Blue questioned. Drama had him looking for a cat named Donald Baron.

"Hell yeah, I'm sure! I saw him wit' my own eyes! I know where he be at too!" Peanut replied, happy to be in the mix.

"Lil' nigguh, you betta not be lyin'," Blue warned. "Come on, get in."

"Hold up. Follow me home so I can drop off my bike," Peanut replied, then peddled off quickly, doing a wheelie off the curb.

??????

Nya was all over Shameeq in the back of the limo, tonguing him down and unbuckling his pants. Shameeq broke the kiss and asked, "Ay, yo, what was all that about?"

"All what?" she responded, still trying to unbuckle his jeans.

"Don't play games wit' me, Nya," Shameeq said, turning his head to avoid her kiss.

"It's complicated. Don is my client, but we also had a relationship," she answered.

"Naw, I ain't talkin' about that shit. I'm talking about his name. That's the same Donald Baron from the warrant?" he asked.

"Yes."

"And you knew this when I came to see you?"

"Honestly, yes."

Shameeq sighed hard.

"So why the fuck you ain't tell me?!" he growled.

"Because it wasn't my place, Jamal. I'm a lawyer, not some gossipy little hoodrat. What difference does it make anyway? Don will use any means to remove anyone he deems a threat to his ... operation, which is why I knew you weren't just some straight-laced college kid like you wanted me to believe," she smirked.

Shameeq looked out the window, letting it all sink in. Nya grabbed his dick again but saw that it wasn't hard anymore. "Jamal, don't be mad at me," she pouted sensually. "It's water under the bridge. If you're a college student, then it's probably all just a big mistake, but if you're not ..." she said, using her finger to turn his face to hers, "then don't get involved with Don. He's a killer." She looked him dead in his eyes, like she was training a pit bull. Her own pit bull.

Shameeq laughed in her face, and the look in his eyes thrilled and chilled her at the same time. "He ain't no goddamn killer! Bitch-ass nigguh use the cops to do his dirty work?! Yeah, you tell your man Don stay the fuck out of my way 'cause that nigguh definitely don't want Drama in his life!"

Nya smirked to herself. She knew the evening had gone according to plan. Now all she had to do was fuck his brains out to put the icing on the cake. She kissed him on the neck. "Now can we get back—"

"Yo, drop me back on the block. I gotta handle somethin'," he said, ignoring her advances.

??????

Blue beeped Shameeq, but when he didn't return his call, he beeped YaYa. He told YaYa the deal and told him to meet him in Bowling Green projects in Norfolk. Blue and Peanut rode over there. When they saw YaYa's Jetta, he signaled for them to follow. They rode around looking for Dion.

"You see him?" Blue asked.

"Naw, not yet," Peanut answered.

"Keep lookin'."

They rode through a second time, then Peanut said "Yo! Go to Raynor Street. He probably at Tamika house."

They pulled to a small concrete-colored home. Tricycles, trash and broken baby dolls littered the front yard.

"Come on," Peanut told Blue, leading the way.

Blue got out, and YaYa followed. When they got to the front door, Peanut said, "Blue, you can't stand yo' big ass where they can see you. Stand to the side."

"Ay, yo, Nut, I'ma fuck yo' lil' ass up," Blue whispered.

YaYa chuckled. "Yo, who is this lil' nigguh?"

Blue and YaYa gave Peanut space while he knocked on the door.

"Hello?" Tamika said from the other side of the door.

"Girl, open the door! It's Nut!" he said.

She sucked her teeth. "Boy, what you want?"

"Just open the door, girl. Where my cousin at?" he asked.

She unlocked the door.

"What yo' lil' mannish ass want?" she grinned with her hands on her ample hips. "Melonie ain't here."

"Dion over here?" he asked.

Tamika sucked her teeth again. "Yeah, he here wit' his sorry—"

That's all Blue and YaYa needed to hear. They pushed Tamika back and ran up in the crib. She hadn't even noticed them standing in the shadows. She started to holler, but Blue put his massive hand over her mouth.

"It ain't nothin', shorty, so don't make it somethin'. We just need to speak to your man. Where he at?" Blue probed.

"In the room," she whispered nervously. Blue may've said it was nothing, but the guns in the two men's hands told Tamika something totally different.

"Show me," Blue told her, taking her by the arm and leading her down the short hallway. He heard her take a deep breath, so he jerked her arm and stopped. "Yo," he whispered, breathing through his mouth, "don't even *think* about yellin' for the nigguh. We ain't gonna hurt him; we just wanna talk to him."

Tamika jerked her arm back but failed to loosen the grip of Blue's ham-like hand. "Whateva, just don't hurt me."

"Play fair, and I won't. He got a gun?" Blue probed.

"No," she said, then added quickly, "not that I know of."

"A'ight, come on."

As they approached the last bedroom down the dimly lit hallway, they could hear the sounds of Eddie Murphy's "Raw" on TV.

"Ed-deee! I want to talk to youuuuuu!"

They entered the room to find Dion lying in bed, shirt off, smoking a blunt, his son asleep on his chest. When he looked up to say something to Tamika, he saw Blue, YaYa and Peanut. He started to sit up, but Blue raised the gun. "Hold up, playboy, you good right where you at," Blue hissed.

"No, you hold up and let me get my baby," Tamika huffed, going around Blue and taking the sleeping infant off Dion's chest. She gave him a "what'd you do this time" look.

"Yo, man, what the hell you doin'?!" Dion exclaimed nervously.

"Be easy, yo, and we won't go hard," YaYa told him, standing over him with the gun on his side.

"Muhfuckas sayin' you dropped a dime on my rap-dog, yo," Blue accused him.

"Dropped dime?! Nigga I ain't no goddamn snitch!" Dion bellowed. He started to sit up, but YaYa put his hand on his chest.

"You's a lyin' muddafucka, nigguh! I saw yo' bitch ass in the police car!" Peanut barked like a young pitbull.

"Oh, hell no! Dion, I know you ain't no snitch!?" Tamika squealed. She was hood through and through. She hated rats of all kind, the rodent and the human variety.

"B, if lil' man said he saw you, fuck he gonna lie for?" YaYa asked calmly.

"Man, it wasn't me!" Dion claimed.

YaYa cracked the side of his face with the pistol, then cocked it back and put it to his forehead. "Now, I'ma ask you one more time ... did you snitch on my man Drama?"

Dion was dazed by the pistol blow, which also let him know these nigguhs were serious.

"Man, it wasn't me! I mean, I ain't do it *for* me. I was in the country jail on a robbery charge, and she told me she'd get me out if I did it. I ain't want to. I don't even know the cat. I—" Dion spoke so fast that YaYa had to cut him off.

"Hold up, hold up. She? Who she?" YaYa asked.

"The lawyer chick, yo. Braswell! She like Johnny Cochran, man, and I ain't wanna go to prison, man! I ain't want to do it, man. Please don't kill me," Dion sobbed.

Tamika shook her head.

"And you said they dropped the charges!"

YaYa looked at Blue like "what the fuck?"

"Braswell?" Blue repeated, just to make sure he heard him right.

"Yeah man, Braswell. Nina or Nia or something. That bad-ass lawyer chick all the big dope boys fuck wit'. Man, don't kill me. I just had a son!"

"You good, stic. That's all we wanted to know," Blue said, tucking his gun. They were about to walk out, but Tamika said, "Oh, hell no! Take that piece of shit wit' you. Get him the fuck out my house! My daddy doin' life 'cause of a muhfucka like you. Probably yo' goddamn daddy! Get out!"

Blue chuckled. Since he did run up in her crib, he felt it only right to do her a solid.

"You heard the lady, stic. Raise up outta here."

Blue yanked Dion off the bed and marched him to the door. He stopped in front of Peanut and told Dion, "And, yo, this my lil' rap. He tell me you so much as looked at him wrong, I'ma leave you stinkin' somewhere, you got me?"

Dion nodded.

"Man, I ain't worried about this nigguh doin' nothin' to me!" Peanut boasted, then spit in Dion's face. "Pussy muddafucka!"

YaYa laughed.

"Yo, I *like* this lil' nigguh!"

??????

Nya wrapped her arms around Shameeq's neck and one leg around his and gave him a long kiss goodnight. A kiss Shameeq was totally detached from. Nya felt it, but she knew he was preoccupied with the thoughts she had planted in his head.

"You okay?" she asked, caressing his cheek.

"I'll call you," he said.

Nya smiled.

"When?"

"Soon," he one-worded her, then untangled himself from her embrace. Jamal, I hope tonight didn't damage anything. I told you Don is the past. He just ... won't let go," Nya explained.

Shameeq nodded.

"I'ma call you tomorrow."

"For sure, Jamal?" she whined, fronting like she was pressed.

"Yeah, ma, for sure."

Nya watched him walk away and said to herself, "Yes, KG, there's definitely more to you than meets the eye."

??????

Shameeq rounded the corner in the Jetta. He checked his beeper because he had it on vibrate all night. He didn't want Nya all in his business. He noticed Blue had been beeping him. He pulled over at a pay phone and called him back. Blue told him to meet him at his crib, so Shameeq drove straight there.

When he entered, he saw Peanut sitting on the couch, smoking a blunt.

"Yo, who the lil' nigguh smokin' up all the weed?" Shameeq chuckled.

"The young God solved the mystery, B," YaYa said cryptically once Shameeq reached the kitchen.

"Mystery?" Shameeq frowned.

"Of the warrant," Blue answered.

"Yeah, yo, I met that bitch-ass nigguh Donald Baron tonight. He one of the New York nigguhs we been goin' at," Shameeq informed them.

"Yeah, that's peace, but he ain't the one that took out the warrant," YaYa told him.

"Huh?" Shameeq grunted, taking the blunt from YaYa.

"The nigguh that really took it out is some bamma name Dion," Blue said. "We just went and saw the nigguh, and he admitted to the whole shit! That's why I was paging you like that."

Shameeq inhaled the ism, then said, "Naw, B, Nya read the fuckin' paperwork. The shit said Don, not *Dion*."

YaYa smirked.

"B, that's who put Dion up to it!"

"Who?"

"Who you think?! Fuckin' Nya!" YaYa stressed.

While Blue ran it down to Shameeq, he puffed the blunt and paced the floor. At first he was confused, then the picture got less and less cloudy.

"So that's why the nigguh ain't know who the fuck I was! He had his whole team there! If I supposedly robbed 'em, fuck a warrant, any nigguh in that position gonna serve justice!" Shameeq snarled.

"Yo, B, the bitch set you up," YaYa chuckled.

Even Shameeq had to admit she got that off. Now it all made sense. How she played the hot and cold game to reel him in. He knew the game worked because he had it mastered. He just hadn't had it run on him before.

"True, indeed, B, true, indeed. I can't front, she got her shit off. She set the God up nice," Shameeq admitted.

"Yeah, but the question is for what?" Blue added.

"Oh, don't worry," Shameeq smiled, now having the element of surprise back on his side, "I intend to find out."

??????

Nya walked into her spacious bedroom and kicked off her shoes. Her mansion was out in Charlottesville, an expensive community three hours from Virginia Beach. She wore no panties or bra, so once she peeled herself out of her cat suit, she was completely naked. Her nipples were hard, and her pussy was dripping. She wanted to be fucked so badly, she started to make a booty call but decided not to. She wanted to fuck Shameeq. He turned her on in so many ways she knew no other man would quench her thirst that night. She intended to use him because the situation was urgent. But she also intended to possess him. Keep him like a pet in her dirty cage. She just didn't know he couldn't be tamed.

Her fingers worked their way down her stomach, and she pretended they were Shameeq's hands. She started to pull the hood of her clit back, but the ringing phone jolted her back to reality. She sighed hard, then picked up the phone full of attitude for being disturbed.

"Yes."

"I heard about your conversation with Richard," the male voice hissed, momentarily stopping her heart. "And if anybody kills Dion, it'll be *you*, bitch! You brought him in, so you better take him out."

Click.

She hung up and found that her pussy had completely dried up.

??????

"Nigguh, wake yo' punk ass up!"

Shameeq heard the voice, but he thought he was dreaming. He turned over on his other side.

"Nigguh, you heard me," she said again, then pinched his nose because she knew he hated that shit.

He snorted and sat up, ready to hook off.

"Yo, what the fuck?!" he exclaimed angrily. He looked up to see Egypt standing over him.

She smiled and said, "What up, *little* brother," she teased, referring to the fact she was the older twin by three minutes.

Shameeq snickered and yawned.

"Yeah, whatever girl. How you? It's good to see you," he yawned, then stretched.

"I know. It's good to see you too," she replied, sitting down next to him and putting her arm around his shoulder. She made a face, then held her nose. "Damn, Sha, what, you ate some shitty boots last night? Go handle that, for real."

"Shut the hell up, dummy," he retorted, heading to the bathroom to wash his face and brush his teeth.

Egypt came and stood in the bathroom door. He had his back turned, taking a piss.

"So what up? VA a goldmine like YaYa thought it was?" she asked.

"Damn, Egypt, can't you see I'm pissin'?!"

She sucked her teeth. "Boy, please. Ain't nobody thinkin' 'bout that shit. Oh! Guess who made a record!"

Shameeq grunted, unconcerned, as he washed his hands then his face.

"Remember that chick Dana? I think her last name Owens. She used to fuck wit' the twins in EO, Keith and Kevin."

"Yeah," Shameeq answered, brushing his teeth.

"Used to play ball for Clifford Scott. Her. Yeah, she call herself Queen Latifah. She got all afrocentric and shit. But that come from the God Lakim and Shakim. Ain't no money in the rap shit unless you old-ass Run DMC," she giggled.

"Wha aba soool" he said in toothbrush talk.

"Huh?" she said even though she knew that he had asked what about school.

Shameeq gave her that look because he knew she knew what he said.

"Skoo," he said, mouth full of toothpaste.

"What, YaYa?!" she yelled, then turned back to Shameeq. "Hold up, YaYa callin' me."

She jetted out the room. Shameeq knew YaYa didn't call her. She was avoiding the question. He spat out the toothpaste, rinsed his mouth, then headed into the living room. YaYa and Blue were on the couch playing Nintendo, while Trello and Casper smoked a blunt in the kitchen. Egypt was at the stove frying turkey bacon.

"Look, Sha, I made your favorite: pancakes and turkey bacon!" she smiled.

Shameeq knew if she was volunteering to cook, something was up.

"Egypt, I know you heard me!" he sneered. "What up wit' school?!"

She shrugged, keeping her attention to the stove.

"I stopped goin'."

Shameeq stepped up to her, "You did what?"

"Look, Sha, it ain't that serious, okay? Shit just got hectic, that's all, and I had to handle somethin'. I can always go back," she told him.

"Handle somethin' like what?" he asked.

Egypt smirked.

"Like that 111 code on KG beeper," she answered.

"What you mean you handled it?" he probed.

Casper knew shit was about to hit the fan, so he spoke up.

"Ay, yo, B, I tried to tell—"

Egypt cut him off.

"Chill, Casp, I got this." Then she turned to Shameeq and said, "The nigguh called, lookin' to get paid, so I went down to Grafton and gave him and his mans what we owed em'. End of story," she explained, defiantly returning to the stone gaze Shameeq was giving her.

Smack!

Shameeq smacked her in the mouth. Egypt took the blow and swung a straight left that Shameeq easily weaved. He had taught her well, but she was fighting out of emotion. She grabbed at his face with her nails, but Shameeq mushed her back by her face. Casper jumped between them and grabbed Egypt.

"You lost your mind?!" Shameeq barked.

YaYa and Blue ran in the kitchen.

"Get yo' fuckin' hands off me!" she yelled at Casper, slipping out of his grasp and grabbing a knife out the sink.

"She got a knife!" Trello warned, pushing his chair out harm's way.

Egypt swung the knife, just missing Shameeq's face and cutting him on the shoulder. Shameeq lunged at her, but YaYa held him back while Casper finally got hold of Egypt's wrist.

"Casper, get yo' goddamn hands off of me! Just 'cause you eatin' my pussy don't make you my fuckin' man!" Egypt huffed, breaking loose again.

"You what?" Shameeq's temper shot up another hundred feet.

"Nigguh, you fuckin' wit' my sister?!" he growled, but YaYa again held him back.

"Yo, B, it ain't like that," Casper replied.

"Fuck you mean, ain't—" Shameeq started to say, but Egypt cut him off.

"Nigguh, don't talk to him, talk to me! I pushed up on *him.* What he gonna say? No? Look at me!" she bragged, gesturing to her beauty. "If you wasn't my brother, I'd have you eatin' it too!"

Blue stifled a chuckle. "Yo, lil' mama crazy."

"You takin' yo' ass *back* to Newark, *back* to college!" Shameeq bassed.

"How? I blazed three muhfuckas in broad daylight! You think I'm goin' back up there now? You crazy as fuck. What's done is done, and I did what I did! Why? 'Cause that's what I do! College ain't for me, Sha, so stop tryin' to make me somebody I'm not!" she stressed, fighting back the tears.

Shameeq just looked at her and shook his head. He hated that he raised her so well. At the time, it was needed because they had to be hardened to survive. But now it was like he had created a monster that he could no longer control.

She put the knife down and walked towards him.

"The food's ready. I hope you choke on that shit," she hissed playfully as she walked around him. She stopped at the door and added, "And instead of worrying about me, you need to be worryin' about that country-ass bitch that played you. What? You want big sis to beat her up?" she winked, then walked out.

Shameeq looked at YaYa. Ya shrugged with a smile, then him and Blue went back to the Nintendo.

"Fuck both of y'all," Shameeq barked, making his way over to the stove. He looked at Casper, who was watchin' him, and chuckled. "I can't even be mad at you, B. How the fuck you let a broad beat you for the head and not even get no pussy?!" He ate a piece of turkey bacon and mumbled, "Stupid muhfucka."

Casper gave him the finger.

CHAPTER 10

Present Day 1994

YaYa lay in his cell, smoking a cigarette. The word was already all over the jail that somebody in the notorious Drama Squad had turned rat. After all the years of money, murder and sex, one of the so-called gangsters had switched sides. YaYa could hear the whispers because all eyes were on him, Blue, and Rivera.

Every time they were called from the pod to go out, people speculated about which one was the snitch. Nigguhs who used to fear them now laughed behind their backs, though never to their faces because they were still cowards at heart.

YaYa sat up and flicked his cigarette in the toilet. The hiss of the cigarette being extinguished by the water momentarily held his attention until, out the corner of his eye, he saw Rivera on the phone. It was the third time in thirty minutes Rivera had used it. It wasn't strange for dudes locked up to sweat the phone, whether it be for money, their lawyer or a girl. But Rivera wasn't his usual laid-back self. He looked nervous. YaYa didn't know if he had ever been locked up or if he had a guilty conscience, but YaYa knew he'd better keep an eye on him.

"Yo," Rivera spoke into the phone after the call was accepted. "Tell me something good."

"Nothin' changed since the last time you called fifteen minutes ago," the man on the other end replied like he was bored.

"Bullshit, man," Rivera whispered harshly, eyes scanning his immediate vicinity to make sure he wasn't being overheard. "You guys have gotta get me outta here! If these guys find out who I am, I'm a dead man!"

The man said, "Look, Rivera, it's not my call, okay? This isn't our case, it's the D.E.A.'s. If we pull strings to get you out, it could totally jeopardize the case. Just sit tight. No formal charges have been filed."

"Yet," Rivera emphasized. "Look, I've done a lot of work for you guys, haven't I? Remember Chino in Philly? Mark in Richmond? I even got you up close and personal with Drama *himself*! But I'm not about to lose my life over this shit.

"Everything's taken care of. Have we ever let you down? Just sit tight. If things get outta hand, then we'll spring you," the man lied. He was using Rivera as shark bait. The first shark that took a bite would be hooked and gutted. Never mind that it would probably cost Rivera his life.

"Yeah, you bet—" Rivera started to say, but looked up to see YaYa standing in his face.

"What up, papi? Everything good?" YaYa smiled.

"Yeah, yeah, man. Just bitches, man," he told him, then said into the phone, "Bitch, just make sure you send me my fuckin' money, a'ight?!" He slammed the phone on the hook. "Bitches think 'cause a muhfucka locked up, shit is sweet," Rivera huffed.

"Yeah, yo, I feel you. But ain't shit sweet 'bout you, huh, papi?" YaYa quipped. He could damn near smell the fear coming from the short Puerto Rican.

"Naw, YaYa, not at all," he answered.

Rivera retreated to his cell as YaYa watched with murder in his heart.

??????

1989

The night was going as planned for Nya as well as Shameeq. Both thought they had the other rocked to sleep. Their individual arrogance made them underestimate one another.

Throughout dinner, Nya was all over Shameeq, feeding him and grabbing his dick under the table. Shameeq played the game like he was truly open, when in reality he wanted to choke the shit out of her.

"I want to be honest with you, Nya," Shameeq said while caressing her cheek.

"About?" she chimed.

"You were right when you said that I wasn't the college type. I'm, like you said, goin' O.T." Shameeq admitted.

"Jamal, I already figured that much out," she smiled, glad that he was opening up, because it symbolized his trust.

"I just ain't want you to look at me, you know, like some street cat," he explained in his best lame style. "But after seeing how it is you deal with Don Baron, I figured maybe I stood half a chance."

Nya kissed him gently on the lips.

"You have *more* than half a chance," she replied, feeling as if she were the spider and Shameeq the fly.

"Now you be honest with me. What up with you and Don," Shameeq asked.

Nya took her hand away from Shameeq and looked down. Damn this bitch is good, Shameeq thought to himself.

"I ... I really want it to end, Jamal, but he doesn't want to let me go," she began.

"Neither would I," Shameeq smiled.

Nya mustered a small fake smile.

"But I know you wouldn't do the things to me he does. He's ... he's very abusive, Jamal. He ... he hurts me," Nya told him with water in her eyes.

Shameeq saw her angle. She wanted him to feel like if Don wasn't around, she could be all his. But out of the way for what? And out of the way how? How far did she think he would go?

Shameeq turned her face to his. "Nya, for real ... I would never hurt you," he lied, imagining her gasping for life.

She kissed his palm.

"I know, Jamal, and I thank you for that, but Don...he's a very powerful man. I don't want you to get involved," she lied.

"Nya, listen to me. I really like you, and I'ma be there for you. I couldn't just turn away from you knowing you were in pain.

Let me be the one, Nya, the one you come running to, and I'll protect you with my life," Shameeq gamed.

A part of Nya cried, check mate! He had fallen hook, line and sinker. But there was a small part of her that liked the idea of having a knight in shining armor.

She kissed him passionately.

"Let's just enjoy the time we have, even if it's only for one night," Nya told him.

??????

By the time they got inside the door of the suite, they were all over each other. Shameeq pulled the spaghetti-strap dress and allowed it to tumble to the floor. Being Nya, she was totally naked underneath. Shameeq couldn't front; Nya's body was flawless. Her full C-cup breasts sat up perky, and her skin was blemish free. Her pussy was shaven bald, and her low-slung hips curved out into a phat little ass.

Nya unbuttoned Shameeq's pants and grabbed his thick dick with her tiny hands, barely able to get one hand around it. The girth alone made her pussy drip with anticipation.

"Jamal, fuck me now! Don't make me wait," she breathed heavily in his ear, but Shameeq had other plans.

He started to put subtle pressure on her shoulders, willing her to drop to her knees. He then put one hand on top of her head and pushed her down.

As she sunk lower, she looked up and smirked, "I love a man to take charge."

Shameeq responded with an evil smirk as she pulled his dick from his boxers.

"Hmmmmm, is all this for me?" she purred, sticking her tongue in the hole on the head of his dick.

"*All* of it," Shameeq replied, ignoring the pleasant sensation and pulling her head onto his dick.

As she opened wide to take him all in, she felt a hot burst of salty liquid.

Piss!

Nya gagged, but Shameeq wouldn't let her go. She struggled against him, gargling his piss. "What's the matter! I thought you wanted it all," he taunted.

He released her, letting her fall to the carpet on her back. He continued to piss in her face, but to his surprise, she didn't turn her face away. In fact, by the way she was squirming and moaning, she was actually enjoying it!

The bitch is a freak! Shameeq thought. He had done it to degrade and humiliate her before he beat her ass, but she changed his mind, thinking she was probably a pain freak too!

"Jamal, why ... why ... are you doing this?" she gasped.

Shameeq looked around trying to figure out what to do next. His gaze landed on the balcony. A devilish smile crossed his face. He snatched Nya up by the hair, then half dragged her—she half crawled—to the sliding glass door.

"Jamal, stop! Please!! Why are you—"

"Shut the fuck up, bitch," he growled, snatching open the door and throwing her, face down, on the balcony. She looked up, hair wet from his piss and matted to her face.

"Look at me! Are you crazy!" she yelled, her tiny voice all but drowned out by the crash of the ocean waves seventeen stories below.

Shameeq snatched her to her feet, pushed her against the iron railing and pulled his gun from the small of his back.

"Climb over," he hissed.

"Climb?! Helllp!" she screamed as loud as she could, only to be rewarded with a vicious slap and a pistol to her forehead.

"Do that again and you won't be alive long enough to hear the sound," Shameeq warned her coldly.

From the look in his eyes, Nya knew he was dead serious.

"What is this about, Jamal?" she questioned.

"Climb."

"You won't get away with this! Do you know who I am?!" she answered, trying to sound defiant, but her fear made her voice tremble.

"You gonna be the dead bitch on the front page of tomorrow's paper if you don't do what the fuck I tell you!" Shameeq sneered.

Nya opened her mouth to reply, but Shameeq was beyond negotiations. He jammed the gun in her mouth so hard it bruised the roof of her mouth and damn near chipped a tooth. She knew then there was no turning back.

Nya hurriedly climbed over the railing, placing her feet on the bottom border and gripping the top.

"Okay...okay, Jamal. Are you happy now? I climbed!" she cried out in anguish.

Shameeq smirked and tucked the pistol in his waist. He placed his hands on the rail, outside of hers.

"Now talk. Why the fuck did you set me up with a fake robbery charge and try to make me think it was Don?" Shameeq questioned.

Nya's mind went into a frenzy, trying to figure out how he knew. Who told? The question also gave her a slight degree of relief because she felt like his intention wasn't to kill her. She kept her composure and replied without hesitation. "I have no idea what—"

Bam!

Shameeq brought his fist down on her left hand hard, making her let go, dangling seventeen stories from a hard ocean landing. She quickly grabbed the rail with her throbbing left hand.

"You're gonna kill me!" she gasped.

"Let's try this again," Shameeq said calmly. "Why did you set me up?"

Nya hesitated then said, "Jamal, I don't know who you've been talking to, but I swear I didn't—"

Bam!

He banged her right hand, and she squealed in pain, but this time she didn't let go.

"Wrong goddamn answer! Next time I'ma hit 'em both at the same time!" he threatened.

"Jamal, I don't know why you're so upset, but if I die, you're going to prison. There are cameras all over this place. The desk clerk saw you come in with me. Jamal, think...please. It's cold out here," Nya tried to reason with him, but Shameeq just smiled, then banged both her hands. The force was so painful, she let go with both hands. Shameeq grabbing her by the throat was the only balance she had. She tried to grab the rail, but he banged her hand again while continuing to apply pressure to her throat.

"Do I look like I give a fuck about prison?! Huh, bitch, do I?!" Shameeq gritted and she gasped for air.

"Jamal ... I can't ... breathe."

"Now I'ma ask you again. Why did you—" He began letting her go in midair and allowing her to grab the rail with her elbows.

She was woozy as she blurted, "It was Don's idea! He knows you're really KG and that you set up the beef with his guys and the other NY guys! He wanted you out of the way!"

Shameeq laughed in her face.

"What New York beef?! Now I don't know what you're talkin' about. Extend your arms," Shameeq told her. He knew she was lying because he knew Don wouldn't go such a roundabout way to remove a crew that wasn't getting half the money he was.

"What?" she asked

"Grab the rail with both hands and lean back, fully extend your arms."

Nya did as she was told. Shameeq reached back inside and pulled a chair out on the balcony. He sat down and kicked his Timbs up on the rail. "Just relax, 'cause you seem like you want to be here a while."

"Jamal, I don't know what this is about, but I didn't set you up, I swear," Nya pleaded.

Shameeq ignored her.

"Please, Jamal, I'm freezing. What do you want? I have money. A ... a safe in my home. I'll give you everything in it if you let me go," Nya begged.

"Who's Dion?" he asked.

"Who?" She feigned ignorance.

"Never mind."

Shameeq sat back and made himself comfortable while the swift ocean breeze whistled and swirled around Nya's urine-dampened body. Five minutes of silence later she finally said, "Dion … is Don's cousin. He's nobody. Don just used him to set you up."

Shameeq shook his head.

"You good, ma, I'll give you that. Just not good enough to lie your way off that rail," Shameeq quipped.

"What do you want from me, Jamal?! Why in the world would I set you up?! I don't even know you!" she tried to reason.

"That's what you're going to tell me."

Forty-five minutes later, Nya's teeth were chattering uncontrollably and her knuckles were red from holding on to the rail for dear life. Shameeq just sat back, content to watch her plunge to a watery death if she refused to tell him the truth. Her eyes had been closed, until she slowly opened them and said, "I … I wanted you to … to kill Don."

Shameeq stood up and came over to her.

"For what?"

She looked him in the eyes and replied, "Because I was tired of the abuse, tired of him hurting me. I didn't know what else to do."

Shameeq eyed her closely, then asked, "Why me? How did you know about me?"

Her eyes came alive.

"Because of the beef. Don has so many people afraid of him that when I heard what you had done, I knew you already had a reason. I … I … I was going to offer you money, but once I saw you" she said, gazing intently into his eyes, "I … I wanted you for myself. I'm so sorry, Jamal, but I needed you, and that need became a want, so—"

Shameeq turned around and began walking away.

"Ma, it's getting cold out here. Call me when you ready to tell the truth," he chuckled.

He went back in the suite and closed the glass door.

An hour later, he could hear her humming to herself, trying to calm her frazzled mind. Her whole body was numb. She couldn't feel her hands or feet. Her forearms ached with a burn and her bronze skin had an ashy hue. Shameeq opened the door and stood there.

"I wanted you to kill Don," she whispered weakly.

"Why?"

"I … I can't tell you," she sobbed.

Shameeq could see that she was broken. At least now he knew there had been a plan in which he was supposed to be the pawn. But just like in chess, a pawn that makes it to the opponent's side could choose to be any piece he wanted to. In the game of life, Shameeq chose to be king. He lifted Nya's limp body over the rail like lifting a child out of their playpen. He then scooped her up and carried her inside.

"See what you made me do, Nya," he whispered softly. "Why we had to go through all that? Just tell me why you want Don dead?"

"I … I can't, Jamal. They'll kill me if I do," she admitted, which was the most truthful thing she said all night.

"Who is they?" Shameeq probed, but she didn't answer.

He laid her down on the bed and started to pull the covers over her, but she pulled him down with her and wrapped her body around him. It wasn't sexual; it was simply human comfort, his body heat a welcome relief.

"Don't," she told him, holding him tightly.

Feeling him so close, Nya's pussy was the first thing that heated up. Soft whimpers escaped her lips as she pulled him even tighter and grinded against the bulge in his jeans. Her body was so soft to Shameeq's touch, he had to explore it. He ran his hands down her back, over her ass and started finger fucking her from the back. She came instantly all over his finger.

"Jamal, don't tease me … fuck me," she moaned, fumbling with his pants. She used her feet to work his pants to his knees as Shameeq rolled on top of her.

Nya grabbed his dick and slid it inside of her wet, creamy pussy, wrapping her legs around his back and urging him deeper inside.

"Ohhh, fuck, Jamal! Th--that's my spot," she moaned, arching her back to meet his thrust.

Shameeq grasped her around the waist and pulled her into a sitting position while he positioned himself on his knees. He bounced her on his dick as he pressed her against the wall. He stood up on the bed, still bracing Nya against the wall as he pounded away at her pussy.

"Owwwww, yesss, Jamal, right there! Harder! Give it all to me!" she begged, pouncing on his dick and clawing his back.

"Like this?! Tell me to beat this pussy! Tell me!" he grunted.

"Oh, Jamal! Fuck my ass, daddy! I cum so hard when you fuck my ass!"

Shameeq wasted no time, putting her down, then turning Nya to face the wall. She grabbed her ass cheeks and tooted her ass as he slid his thick dick in her tiny asshole. He penetrated her with the full length of his shaft, long-dicking her furiously while he squeezed and pulled her clit.

"Ohhhhh, make it squirt!" she squealed as her pussy did just that. Even her ass came, coating Shameeq's dick and causing him to cum deep in her ass. They both collapsed onto the bed, spent.

??????

The next morning, Shameeq felt Nya stir and instantly woke up, although he kept his eyes closed. He was a light sleeper, but he wanted to watch her to see if she would try and go for his gun.

Instead, she went in the bathroom. He heard the shower come on. He thought about joining her but decided against it, instead lying back and thinking about his next move. Whatever Nya was involved in, Shameeq smelled a payoff. He knew Don was getting major paper, so if Nya went through all the trouble to get him killed, it had to be big.

Nya came out the bathroom a few minutes later with a towel wrapped around her. She saw Shameeq lying back on the bed, smoking a blunt, and smiled.

"Good morning."

"Come 'ere, girl," Shameeq replied.

Nya came over and straddled his naked body.

"So when you gonna answer my question?" Shameeq asked, then inhaled the blunt.

Nya looked at him mischievously but didn't answer. Instead, she traced her fingers over the large tattoo on his chest.

"So your name isn't Jamal either, I see," she quipped.

"Neither is KG," he smirked.

"The God Shameeq," she said, reading the tattoo. "Wow, talk about arrogant. God?"

He chuckled.

"Naw, love, that ain't arrogance. Every black man is God, maker, owner, cream of the planet Earth, father of civilization, God of the universe," Shameeq explained.

"Is that your *real* name?" she probed.

"Yeah, yo. Shameeq, shy and meek. That's me"

She looked at him and they both laughed.

"Then that name *definitely* doesn't fit you," she giggled.

Nya traced lower to the tattoo on his stomach. "Now *this* is more like it. What is Drama Squad?" she wanted to know.

"That's family," he replied.

"You mean your crew," she smirked, feeling his left tricep and reading the tattoo on it. "Psalms 37:11? You don't strike me as very religious."

Shameeq laughed.

"I'm not, but I respect truth. Psalms 37:11 is the meek shall inherit the Earth."

Nya caught on to his play on words. She knew he meant *Meeq* and not meek. "The Earth, huh? You must want it all."

"The world, chica," he replied, imitating Scarface, "and everything in it."

Nya smiled.

"Not everybody has what it takes to handle it all. Do you?"

Shameeq traced his finger around her nipple. "Now I've answered your question, so you gonna answer mine?"

Nya eyed him closely, enjoying his touch, then said, "Don is...was one of my clients. He also used to ... deal with another one of my clients. A very powerful one."

"I'm listenin'," Shameeq told her, blowing out a stream of weed smoke.

"Don ran into a problem, one that compromises my other client"

"What kind of problem?"

"A legal one."

"Don snitchin'?"

Nya smirked.

"You can say that. Anyway, my very important client doesn't want to...deal with Don *ever* again," she explained.

Shameeq inhaled the blunt, assessing the situation. It was easy to see if this client was worried about Don snitching, then this client had to be his connect.

"How much is this client willing to pay?" he asked.

"A hundred thousand," Nya told him.

Shameeq nodded.

"So you was gonna gas me up to do it, and keep the hunnid large for self, huh?"

Nya didn't respond. Shameeq shrugged.

"I ain't mad at 'cha, ma. It's a sucker born every minute," he said as he put the blunt out. "On the real, I'd kill that clown for free, but I'll take the hunnid too. But I wanna meet the client."

"For what?"

Shameeq smiled.

"To pick up where Don left off."

Nya smirked. She could see Shameeq caught on quick.

"I can make that happen, but Don—it won't be as easy as you think," she warned.

"It will be, once you do what I tell you."

Nya frowned.

"No. I can't be involved," she protested.

"You won't be, but, ma, that ain't no suggestion, that's a demand," he said, caressing her ass and spreading her cheeks.

She instinctively grabbed his dick and slid it inside her, riding him slow like an ocean wave.

"And, Nya," he added, stopping his thrust and looking her dead in the eye, "if you ever try to play me again ... I'll kill you."

CHAPTER 11

"Ay, yo, Nya, where the fuck you been?! Why you ain't been returnin' my beeps?!" Don barked through the phone.

"I was on a business trip, if you must know," Nya replied calmly, sitting in her office. She had been avoiding Don's beeps, but returned them once Shameeq told her the plan.

"Not at or around my office," Nya had emphasized to him.

"A trip to where?!" Don probed.

"What do you want, Donald?" Nya sighed.

"Who was that dude you were wit' the other night at the club?" Don asked, driving through Norfolk.

"Why?" she toyed with him.

"Just answer the question," he gritted impatiently.

"A client."

"What's his name?"

"Jamal. Why? What about him?"

"Where you at?" Don grilled her.

"At my office. Why are you questioning me about Jamal?"

"I'll be there in 15 minutes."

Click.

Nya smiled to herself, then beeped Shameeq all 7's, like he told her.

??????

Shameeq sat on the passenger's side of a stolen van while Trello sat behind the wheel of a stolen Buick. Shameeq checked his beeper.

"That's our cue, B," he told Trello, picking up the walkie-talkie. "He on the his way."

"Bet," Casper squawked on the other end.

"Yo, B, how you know we can trust that bitch? She might be settin' us up!" Trello asked.

"Naw, B, the shit's official. Bitch want this nigguh out the way bad! Don't sweat it," Shameeq assured him.

While the Drama Squad was on Don, Gutta and Black had found out where Shameeq rested his head.

"Yo, son, are you sure?" Sincere stressed over the phone in his hotel room.

"Positive!" Gutta exclaimed excitedly. He could damn near taste Drama's blood. "This bitch he fuckin' named Sherrie, her cousin fuck wit' Black's man. She told Black that she dropped Sherrie off over there, and she said Sherrie said she was fuckin' wit' this Jersey nigguh name Drama!"

Sincere smiled to himself. "How she know it's his rest?"

Gutta replied, "She said it was mad clothes and shit all around, son. I'm tellin' you, it's his rest!"

"A'ight, that's what it is then. Go serve justice, God," Sincere said.

"'Nuff said," Gutta shot back and hung up.

He walked back in the living room where she was sitting on the couch.

"I'm tellin' you, Black, them nigguhs be on point. Nicole, the chocolate bunny Black's man was fuckin', told them! "How many be up in there?" Gutta asked, sitting on the arm of the loveseat.

"Like five or six, sometimes more, but never less than three," she replied.

"They keep dough up in there?" Black greedily asked.

"I don't know all that," she answered.

"Fuck dough! I got dough. All I want is they blood," Gutta barked.

"The only way you gonna get up in there is if somebody they know go to the door," she told them.

"Somebody like you?" Gutta quipped.

Her eyes got big as plates, "Oh, hell no! I ain't signed up to be no accessory. Y'all said y'all would pay me for the address! I ain't wit' all that!"

Gutta jumped up and put the gun to her forehead. “Bitch, you wit’ whatever I say you wit’. Now get yo’ ass up and let’s go!”

??????

“Yo, peace, where you?” Sincere asked, talking on the phone.

“VA Beach. What up?” Don replied, static from the bad car phone connection crackling in his ear.

“Son just called. They found out where scrams rest at,” Sincere informed him.

“Word?! Scrams from the club?”

“Naw, that lil’ VA Beach situation.”

“Bet! I’m ’bout to get the math on the dude from this club right now from shorty. We gonna handle all this shit and let nigguhs know how BK get down!” Don bassed.

“Gutta say they be deep in the spot,” Sincere said.

“Say no more. Tell G I’m sending a team now! Peace!”

“Peace!”

??????

“Yo, where the fuck he at?” Casper asked into the walkie-talkie.

“Be easy, he comin’,” Shameeq replied over the air.

Casper was down the street from Nya’s office, in a stolen Honda Accord. “Yo, Egypt, you good?”

“Always,” she squawked back from her post. “You just be on point wit’ that whip.”

“Always,” he smirked.

Casper saw the burgundy Benz coming down the one-way street in his rearview. He sunk in his seat as it passed.

“Yo, he here,” he said into the walkie-talkie. Just then a blue BMW with four black dudes came right behind Don. When Don parked, the BMW parked right behind him. “Yo, the nigguh got company,” he said into the walkie-talkie.

“Company?!” Egypt squawked.

"It's cool," Shameeq squawked.

"Cool? It's only me, and I count four more heads!"

Just then Don got out and walked over to the BMW. He bent down in the driver's window for a moment.

Instinctively looking up and down the street. Don spoke,

"Yo, Sincere said Gutta got the math on scrams that did that VA Beach caper," Don told him.

The driver just nodded because he was a man of few words.

"So look, I want y'all to go handle that shit then. Young nigguhs too wild, too emotional about the shit. Fuck around and hit a little kid or some shit. Go make sure that shit is clean and effective."

The driver nodded again, then asked, "What about you? You a'ight?"

"Yeah, son, them lil' nigguhs ain't tryin' to bring that level. Go 'head, handle your biz," Don told him.

Casper breathed a sigh of relief.

"They about to leave," he told Egypt.

"I know," she replied, and she could hear his smile through the walkie-talkie.

The driver started the BMW and pulled off as Don walked into Nya's office.

"What up, gorgeous? Nya back there?" Don asked, flirting with the Kim.

She blushed, then replied, "Yes, she is, and she's expecting you."

Don swagged down the hall like he owned the place. He didn't even bother to knock, he just walked into Nya's office.

Nya was sitting behind her desk. She looked up and smiled her most captivating smile and said, "Hello, Don. I missed you."

She rose from her chair and came around the desk to greet him.

"Hmph, you missed me so much you didn't return my beeps for three days?" he quipped with manly attitude, although he wasn't as mad as he wanted her to think. He could never stay mad at Nya for long because she had him open.

Nya threw her arms around him and tongued him deeply.

"Baby, don't act like that," she pouted, caressing his cheek with her thumb. "You know how I get at these lawyer conventions. I just don't know how to stop running my mouth."

"Next time stop runnin' long enough to respect my call," he replied, melting into the moment.

Nya licked her lips sensually. "I can think of an even better idea to do with my mouth."

"Oh, yeah?"

She nodded slowly as she dropped slowly to her knees. "Oh, yeah," she said.

Nya undid Don's silk slacks and removed his thick savage-like dick from his boxers and slid it in her mouth.

Just like Shameeq told her to.

??????

The BMW pulled up outside Gutta's spot in Norfolk. Gutta came out and leaned in the passenger's side, smiling his gold-grilled smile. "What up, Tink? Shit is goin' down today. Word to mother, son, it's not a game," he said giving the passenger strong dap.

"Where the bitches at?" the driver asked.

Gutta jerked his head toward the house. "I got the bitch on ice. She gonna get us in the door, unlock the back and—" Gutta made a gun with his finger and aimed it at Tink's head. "Boom!"

Tink crossed himself. "Yo, don't mark me, son!" he told him seriously.

"My bad, son, pardon the God," Gutta replied, then looked at the driver. "You ready?"

The driver just nodded.

??????

Don had to brace himself against the desk after the brain game Nya had just put on him. It was like she was trying to suck the life out of him, just like Shameeq had told her to. She even swallowed his load, something she'd never done to him before. She came out of her office bathroom after freshening up. She stopped and looked at Don. "Why are you looking at me like that, Don?" she asked with a nervous giggle.

"Remember what we talked about?" he said.

"What?" she replied, coming over to him.

"You know, about making this thing official. I mean you and me. The game ain't the same, and I done had a nice seven-year run. I think it's time I get out of the game and settle down," he told her.

Hopefully real soon, she thought, wrapping her arms around his neck. "Don, are you asking me to marry you?"

"Hell no, I don't ask for shit. I'm tellin' you we gettin' married," he shot back, bravado masking his nervousness. When she didn't answer right away, he quickly added, "I ain't talkin' about tomorrow or nothin', but soon, and for the rest of our lives."

Nya got on her tiptoes and kissed him on the nose.

"Let me think about it."

"Yeah, you do that," Don replied as Nya went back around her desk.

"Now, what was so urgent about Jamal Jenkins?" she asked.

"Nothin' for you to worry about. I just need an address on him."

"Don," she said, like she was scolding him, "that would violate his attorney-client privilege. I could lose my license."

"Come on, Nya, I promise you, just this once," he swore.

She looked at him like she was thinking about it, then handed him a piece of paper. "You owe me," she smirked.

Don took the paper, read it and smiled. "Then I'll pay you back tonight. *All* night," he winked.

"Sounds good," she responded, hoping to herself he wouldn't live that long.

As Don headed for the door, she called out, "Don."

He turned around.

"I'll definitely think about what you said," she winked. "We'll talk about it tonight," she told him.

He smiled and walked out.

??????

Gutta and Black sat down the block in the lead car, while the dudes from the BMW sat nearby in a black Ford Taurus. They were watching the two-story house down the street. A cab pulled up and Nicole got out, just like they had told her to.

"Yeah," Gutta nodded, "the bitch better had hold it down. Murder that bitch whole family."

"Man, that bitch heard you say two G's and got dollar signs in her eyes," Black chuckled.

"Stupid bitch, she ain't gonna see a dime. Leave that trifling' bitch layin' in them nigguhs' blood," Gutta smirked evily.

"Naw, stic, we can't kill that bitch! Think, stic. Her cousin know she turned us on to this nigguh. What you think she gonna do if she dead in that muhfucka," Black reasoned.

Gutta rubbed his chin and nodded, "True indeed, son, true indeed. Fuck it, kill her and her cousin tomorrow," he snickered.

Nicole rung the bell. YaYa came to the door and hugged and kissed her, then she went in. YaYa looked up and down the street, then closed the door.

"Here we go," Gutta chuckled, locking the Mac-II.

??????

"Here we go," Casper said into the walkie-talkie as he started the car.

"I'm ready," Egypt squawked.

"Bet," Shameeq squawked back.

Don had just walked out of Nya's office, smiling to himself. To possess a woman like that made a man feel good about himself, so Don was definitely feeling himself. He jumped in the Benz and pulled off a few seconds later, but neither Casper nor Don saw the blue sedan halfway down the block pull out behind both of them.

??????

Black's beeper went off. "It's on, stic," he exclaimed.

Gutta, followed by Black and the four other dudes, wasted no time getting out. They cut through a backyard four houses down and crept up on the Drama Squad's spot. They all had their guns locked and loaded as they pulled the ski masks over their faces. Gutta lead the way in a low squat. He reached the back door and peeped through the door's window. He could see the kitchen and straight into the living room. He scanned the rooms for any movement.

They were empty.

He nodded to his crew, then slowly and quietly turned the knob It was unlocked. He smiled at Black, who winked back, and Gutta opened the door slowly. He paused with it halfway open, listening for any sounds. He heard nothing, so he ducked and walked inside, gun aimed and ready to rip. His crew followed him inside. They could hear voices coming from upstairs, but they carefully checked each room on the first floor before starting up the stairs. The sound of voices and a money machine got louder.

"Didn't I tell you VA was a fuckin' goldmine, Drama!"

"Word to mother!"

"Ay, yo, Sherrie, hand me that bag. Let me scale it up."

"Damn, Drama, you ain't scared being up in here with all that money?" they heard Sherrie say. The whole crew got dollar signs in their eyes as they reached the top of the stairs. Underneath their feet, the carpet felt soggy, but no one paid attention to it.

??????

Don neared the corner of the block with his mind a thousand miles away. With the feds a potential step away, the outcome of the Jersey beef and the penchant for the number seven, the number of years of his run, he felt like marrying Nya would be the move to make. She was smart, sexy and classy. Plus, she had money. It would be a marriage of equals. He knew with the dough he had put away, he could launch any kind of business he wanted. In his heart, he was convinced it was time to retire from the drug game.

The light turned green. He caught a quick movement out of the corner of his eye. He quickly turned his head and saw a young dude coming off the sidewalk on a bike. He blew his horn and slammed on the brakes, but it was too late. He hit the bike, knocking the boy and the bike onto his hood. The boy rolled off the hood, then disappeared from Don's view.

"Shit!" he cursed, getting out of the car as Egypt came off the curb.

"Oh, my God!" she cried, wearing a long wig to cover her dreads.

"You hit my baby!"

"Yo, miss, I'm sorry! He came out of nowhere," Don claimed. He rounded the front of his car to see Peanut on the ground with his eyes closed.

When Don looked up to ask what he could do, ready to pay her off, he saw the barrel of a .45 automatic pointed directly at him.

"Drama Squad, nigguh!" Egypt laughed, then put two in his face at damn near point-blank range.

Boom, boom!!

Don's body jerked as blood and brain matter flew out the back of his head from the force of the dum-dum bullet. He hit the ground just as Peanut scrambled up. Egypt stood over him and hit him three more times in the head for good measure.

Right on time, Casper sped up and swerved around the Benz on the narrow one-way. As Peanut jumped in the back, Egypt looked up and saw the blue sedan, which was like half a block away, pick up speed. She quickly got in and screamed, "Drive nigguh! It's the fuckin' police!"

Casper skidded off, and the chase was on.

??????

"Fuck that shit, B, we gotta push them New York nigguhs the fuck outta VA! I want *all* the money!" Gutta heard another voice exclaim, and he was on fire. His crew hurriedly opened the two other room's doors and the bathroom door to make sure they were empty. Gutta waved them on impatiently and pointed to the door the voices were coming from. The crew got ready as Gutta grabbed the knob. They all pointed their guns at the door so that as soon as it opened, they could blast whomever moved.

Gutta nodded, then threw the door open as the crew opened fire with semis and automatics, but all they did was bust the windows and put holes in the walls. The room was empty except for the boom box in the middle of the floor, which was playing the tape of the voices they heard. "Fuck New York!" YaYa yelled on the tape. Then they heard a barrage of gunfire behind them.

??????

Casper wasn't as good a driver as Trello, but he could definitely handle a car. He whipped in and out of traffic, even using the oncoming traffic to elude the police, then made a sharp left. Egypt squawked into the walkie-talkie, "Shit! They still on us!"

"I see 'em," Shameeq squawked as Trello struggled to keep up with the chase in the slow-ass van.

Shameeq's heart was in his stomach. He had only allowed Egypt to be involved in the Don hit because he felt it was an in-and-out job. Afterwards, he could relocate her to a safer spot until the war with the Brooklyn nigguhs was over. But somehow the police were on the scene in an unmarked, and now they were on Egypt's ass.

"Push it!" Shameeq urged Trello.

"I am!" he barked back, damn near running over a person crossing the street.

Shameeq gripped his gun tightly. He was prepared to murder the police before he let them take Egypt to jail. He didn't know what he'd do if his twin went to prison because of him.

??????

Montez and YaYa had been hiding the closet in the room on the opposite end of the hall. They had heard the dudes open the door, but they didn't bother to come in. The dudes had left the door open, so once Montez and YaYa crept out of the closet, they had a clear shot at the whole crew at the other end of the hallway.

They lay on the floor, staying low in the open doorway, and as soon as Gutta opened the door and saw the setup, they opened fire, killing the driver and two other members of the crew before Tink could orient himself and return. He aimed too high, not seeing them on the ground. YaYa and Montez rolled to opposite sides of the door to take cover as Tink, Black and Gutta checked out inside the setup room and slammed the door.

"Aarghh!" Gutta howled in disgust, shooting through the door and into the hallway.

"Stupid muhfuckas, joke's on you!" YaYa laughed, then squeezed off at the door.

Tink sniffed, "Yo ... what the fuck is that smell?"

Black and Gutta smelled it too, but before they could comment, they got their answer. Smoke began to seep under the door, and they heard the roar of a fire on the other side of the door.

"They set the fuckin' house on fire!" Black exclaimed, heading for the window. Tink opened the door and saw that the whole hallway was on fire and spreading fast—the carpet had been soaked with lighter fluid.

YaYa and Montez opened fire again, pinning them in the room.

Black yanked open the window and slung his leg out. "I'm out, stic!" he shouted.

"No, son, them nigguhs gotta leave too! Then we bounce! Them nigguhs waiting for us to do that!" Gutta hollered, thinking fast.

The fire started to lick the walls and ceiling like a blanket of liquid heat, cutting of any possibility of leaving through the door.

Black grabbed the ledge with his hands, then lowered his body in order to hang jump.

Boom, boom, boom!

Three shots from below went through his back and pierced his heart. He fell to the ground.

Gutta saw the dude in the yard behind the backyard and squeezed off, picking the gunman off.

He quickly scrambled out the window, followed by Tink. Just as Tink hit the ground after Gutta, YaYa and Montez rounded the corner dumping shots from AK-47s. Gutta just made it around the neighbor's house, but Montez caught Tink in the back of the head, the impact pushing him over and causing him to skid forward on his face. Gutta started to go back for him, but the vacant look in his open eyes let him know Tink was gone.

Gutta crossed himself while back pedaling away. "Damn, son, I hope I ain't mark you."

Then Gutta jumped the fence and got away.

??????

Casper pushed the Accord hard, hoping to shake the police. He knew if the chase lasted much longer, the police backup would join the chase. He had to lose them. His opportunity came several seconds later when he spotted the city bus lumbering down the street towards him. He slowed up, slightly allowing the police to gain ground.

"What the fuck you doin'?! Punch this shit!" Egypt urged, reloading her gun while nervously looking in the rearview.

"I got this," Casper assured her intensely.

Trello saw the bus too.

"Tell him use the bus! Use the bus!" Trello barked.

"Use the bus!" Shameeq squawked.

"Use the bus!" Egypt echoed after Shameeq squawked.

"Everybody shut the fuck up!" Casper bassed, leaning into the steering wheel and grasping the emergency brake.

As the bus neared the side street that separated it from Casper, he punched the gas hard, then locked the car into fishtail right in front of the bus. The car slid right into the path of the bus. The tires smoked, then regained traction and darted onto the side street. The bus driver blew his horn, then applied the air brakes, making the bus skid to a stop, blocking the side street. The police skidded to a stop, and the driver jumped out, waving the bus out of the way. By the time it was clear, Casper was long gone.

"Yeah, nigguh!" Shameeq hollered into the walkie-talkie as they drove past the blue sedan in the middle of the street. "Make a left, then a right. We'll be right there!" Shameeq told Egypt.

By the time Shameeq reached them, they had already gotten out of the Accord. Trello scooped Casper, Egypt and Peanut and sped away from the scene.

CHAPTER 12

Present Day 1994

"Richard Rivera! Lawyer here to see you!" the U.S. marshal called over the intercom.

"About time," Rivera huffed, getting up from the metal table in the pod.

YaYa watched him walk out. "Ay, yo, Blue, let me holla at you," YaYa said, breaking into a fit of coughs.

??????

"You ready to continue?" Mullins asked him.

"Whenever you are," he said, pulling a cigarette from his Newport pack.

"You know, you really do smoke too much. Keep that up and you'll die from cancer before your crew gets to carve you up," McGrady quipped.

"Hopefully," he mumbled as he stuck the match to light the cigarette.

Mullins ignored the sarcastic banter.

"Now, who killed Donald Baron?"

"I just told you, we did," he answered.

"No, you told us *how* he was killed and where. I want to know who pulled the trigger."

He looked at Mullins without responding.

"I want a *name*," Mullins said calmly, but firmly.

"Egypt. Egypt pulled the trigger," he said, looking away, then down at the table.

"We don't have Egypt Stevens on this indictment!" Jacobs told Mullins.

"We do now," Mullins smiled at him. "Get a warrant for her arrest! I want her in custody yesterday." When Jacobs left the room, he dropped his head.

"Okay, you say Drama Squad stuck twice at the same time, Don and his crew, right?" McGrady asked.

"Yeah," he mumbled, blowing out smoke, then coughing.

"Well, how was it that there was no major organization in Virginia? They just let you guys waltz in and take over without a fight?"

"With Don gone, they lost their pipeline. Most of his peoples were just block huggers and gun hustlers. Without Don to supply them, they had nothing to fight with!" he explained, taking a pull of the cigarette. "Besides, Sincere was Don's right-hand man. So once he got wit' us ... he himself made sure the transition went smoothly."

"Sincere," McGrady echoed confusedly.

He looked at all the 9x12s of the whole crew until he found Sincere's picture. "Him."

Mullins looked at the picture and read the bio. "Joseph 'Sincere' Glover. He was killed two years ago in Brooklyn," Mullins said.

He chuckled.

"Yeah, them Brooklyn nigguhs found out he had been down wit' us all these years since Don's murder and nodded him in the front of Junior's," he explained

"Brooklyn? You sure it wasn't your crew?" McGrady probed.

"Why would we do it? He played his position and made us a lot of money," he replied, blowing out smoke.

"So did Taylor, Evans, Mitchell ..." Mullins quipped, reading off a few names of the countless murders being credited to the Drama Squad.

"One more question," McGrady cut in. "At the time of Don's murder, did you know that the officers involved in the pursuit were, in fact, federal agents tailing Baron at the time?"

He chuckled. "Naw, we just thought we had buzzard luck. We didn't find out until later, when we found out who the federal informant in our crew was."

Mullins was all ears.

??????

1989

The young girl sashayed from the gold Benz 190 she just got out of. "I'll call you," the driver told her, watching the sway in her hips as she walked away.

"Okay, boo, good night," she chimed, now fifteen hundred dollars richer.

She was only sixteen, but her body made her look twenty-four. She had been juicing ballers since she was fourteen, doing whatever it took to get that paper. She knew all the major and minor ballers in the seven cities because she had been run through them countless times.

She was approaching her apartment in the projects when a shadow came out of the cut.

"Yo," Gutta said.

"Do I know you?" she replied, giving him attitude.

Gutta didn't bother to respond. He aimed the gun and blasted her in the chest twice, deading the scream in her throat.

"That's for setting us up," he spat, then splattered her brains for good measure. Gutta tucked the gun and disappeared into the night.

??????

Sincere couldn't believe his ears. He was leaned up against the hood of his Saab as Gutta explained what happened when they went to kill Drama.

"Son," Gutta said, shaking his head, "I can't front, them nigguhs caught us slippin' bad"

Sincere looked at him. Gutta wasn't his usually amped self who rocked from foot to foot. No elaborate use of his hands when he talked. He could see that the young dude was totally psyched out.

"We underestimated these nigguhs," Sincere commented almost to himself, thinking back to the Brooklyn-Harlem beef Drama had orchestrated. Being a thinker, Sincere could appreciate a well-executed plan. He just seethed from the fact that it was his people who had been executed.

"And that bitch, yo, she played that shit to a tee. Triflin' bitch. I ain't get her yet, but that bitch's good as a memory, son," Gutta spat.

"Yo, why ain't this nigguh callin' me back?" Sincere said, preoccupied with his own thoughts.

He opened the passenger door and sat down as he picked up the car phone to beep Don. Then he called Don but got no answer.

"Don probably laid up wit' a bitch, son," Gutta surmised, irritated by the thought that Don was somewhere chilling while the cream of his team lay in their own blood.

"Yeah, the God did say he was goin' to see his lawyer for that other nigguh KG address," Sincere remembered. Gutta looked at him coldly.

"Word to mother, I don't trust that high-post bitch, God! She was there when I told Don about KG, and then, next thing we know, she in the club with 'em?!" Gutta huffed venomously. "Don got the bitch too close, talkin' around her and protectin' her. If he woulda let us get at her, this shit never would've happened! 'Cause I know that bitch fuck wit' this nigguh Drama!"

The more Gutta talked the more amped he got, and the more amped he got, the more he convinced himself of his own logic. Sincere nodded. He knew Nya dealt with a lot of street nigguhs. Hell, she was a criminal defense attorney, but at that point, that was all they had.

"Yo, I'm wit' you, son. We gotta get at Don. After tonight, I know he'll take the gloves off with the bitch," Sincere replied, rounding the car to the driver's side.

Gutta got in the opened passenger's door and closed it. "No disrespect, but I don't give a fuck what Don say. He worried about gettin' money, but this shit personal wit' me! That bitch gonna talk, or I'ma have the paramedics breathin' soft on her," Gutta vowed as they pulled off.

Shameeq, Egypt, Trello, Casper and Peanut pulled in the apartment complex driveway. They were in Elizabeth City, North Carolina, a stone's throw from the Virginia border.

They entered the apartment to find Montez and YaYa on the couch smoking a blunt.

"Yo, look, B, that shit on the news!" YaYa told them between puffs.

"A mysterious house fire still blazes as we speak. Afterward, neighbors say a shootout occurred. One man was found shot dead outside the home, while two bodies were found inside," the reporter explained.

"Yo, y'all missed one," Montez snickered. "If the bastard ain't ashes by now."

YaYa turned the TV on blast so they could talk.

"Yo, B, they talked about that other shit before y'all came in," YaYa said. "Everything looked good."

"Fuck no, shit wasn't good, B! It was fuckin' plain clothes in the area, B! Muhfucka chased Casp!" Shameeq barked

"Word?! Muhfucka ain't say police gave a chase or nothing," YaYa replied.

Shameeq thought to himself that it was strange that the news didn't mention it. They never miss an opportunity to big-up the police to assure everyone how close they were to the case. Before Shameeq could reply, Sherrie came out the back and wrapped her arms around Shameeq's neck.

"I did good today, daddy?" she cooed, kissing him and biting his bottom lip.

"Yeah, boo, you did your thing," Shameeq answered, still preoccupied. "Do me a favor: Go back in the room. Let me speak wit' my peoples."

He slapped her on the ass as she walked away, then he looked at Montez.

"Where Blue and Lil' B?"

"They had some problems out Norfolk wit' some of those wannabes from New York. Virginia nigguhs—they got wind of that shit and tried to holla back," Montez explained. "But the shit wasn't 'bout nothin', B, and Blue a'ight. They in DC."

Shameeq nodded. Virginia was on fire, so it was good that the whole Squad relocated for the moment.

"Shit gonna be hot for a minute 'cause nigguhs ready for war," Montez commented.

"Shit, we already set it," YaYa chuckled, giving Montez a pound.

"Naw, ain't gonna be no war," Shameeq said, sitting down.

"The hell it ain't. You think them nigguhs gonna just lay down?" YaYa questioned. "Fuck no!" he added, answering his own question.

"YaYa right, Meeq," Egypt chipped in.

"Go to war wit' what?" Shameeq asked, looking from face to face. "Without Don, they well dried up. You can't fight a war without paper. Yeah, the few Brooklyn nigguhs left probably in they feelings, but them Virginia nigguhs, they loyal to who feed 'em. If it ain't New York, then they'll be Jersey nigguhs," Shameeq chuckled, looking at Montez.

"You got a point there, playboy. Them bammas just foot soldiers," Montez agreed.

"Naw, the only thing I'm worried about is Nya," Shameeq said, deep in thought.

"Yeah, 'cause them nigguhs gonna go at her 'cause they know she know you," YaYa reasoned.

"No question," Shameeq replied, rising from his seat as the thoughts came to him. "And if she don't tell 'em where I'm at, then they gonna kill her."

"And we did all this for nothing 'cause then we don't meet the connect," Egypt said, verbalizing Shameeq's thoughts.

"Egypt, gimme your keys," Shameeq told her.

She threw them to him. "What you gonna do?" she asked.

"Call Nya. Get her mind right and let her know when they come, tell 'em we holdin' Don for ransom," Shameeq smirked.

"And what's that gonna do?" Montez wanted to know, but Egypt knew how Shameeq thought and answered for him.

"Give 'em back the connect. You said Nya told you Don eatin' in three other states. That's a lot of mouths to feed," she explained.

"But what if they already seen the news?" YaYa interjected.

"All the more reason to get at me. Nya just gotta get me on the phone with the nigguh. If not, we blowin' Virginia and we migratin' down here," Shameeq answered, then turned to Egypt,. "Either way, you, Trello and Casper stayin' here to set up shop 'cause, regardless, we expandin'."

Egypt didn't argue. Besides the fact the police got on the hit, she'd have her own spot without Shameeq on her back.

"What about her?" Montez asked, jerking his head toward the back where Sherrie was.

Shameeq thought about it. Sherrie was a trooper, no question, plus she was well connected through the sack chasers. She could be useful; the question was, could she be trusted?

"She good ... for now," Shameeq concluded.

"You sure?" Egypt checked.

"No question," he answered.

CHAPTER 13

Nya kept a close eye on the headlights in her rearview. She had no doubt that she was being followed, because she had made a series of turns and the car stayed right behind her.

Shameeq had already prepared her for this. She remembered the conversation they had a half hour earlier.

"Let them abduct me?! Are you mad?! They'll kill me!" she yelled.

"Then they wouldn't bother to abduct you," Shameeq shrugged. "They think you know where they can find me, so they won't kill you if you tell 'em."

"Where are you?" she asked quickly.

Shameeq laughed.

"You're gonna use me as bait, aren't you?" Nya probed in a shocked tone.

"Naw, ma, you already the bait. But don't worry, I got you," he told her.

"So why can't you set them up too?"

"Nya, I think you misunderstand your position, boo. This ain't for me, this is so *you* can live. If you don't do it my way, they'll kill you for sure because you don't know where I'm at," Shameeq explained calmly.

"What do you want to do, Shameeq?" she questioned, fully realizing that her fate now rested in his hands.

"Tell them I'm holding Don for ransom, and I want a million dollars," Shameeq told her.

"What if they already know he's …" she let her voice trail off.

"Then you tell 'em you know how to get me. Bottom line, get dude on the phone with me."

She took a deep breath.

"And what's that supposed to do?"

"Save my connect, number one, and save your ass, number two!" Shameeq shot back.

"But what if it doesn't work?" Nya stressed.

"You ask a lotta goddamn questions for a sittin' duck! 'Cause that's what you are. Your client has you on front street. His problem is solved. Now the mess is in your lap to clean up. If it doesn't work, I'm out, they win, and you lose your life," Shameeq broke it down.

Nya didn't respond.

"You in deep, love. My way is the only way out," Shameeq added.

Deeper than you think. I just didn't want to get my hands dirty, she thought, then said, "Okay, Shameeq, I understand."

"Get him on the phone, Nya. Your life depends on it."

Click.

Nya took a deep breath as she turned into the apartment complex Don had his spot in, just like Shameeq told her to. He didn't want Don's people to have any reason to blast first. If she was going to Don's spot, they'd feel more comfortable and know it wasn't a setup.

Nya was scared to death. She had thought briefly about going to the police but quickly dismissed it. With all that she had going on, she definitely didn't need the police around. Besides, she knew her father would never approve. It was dangerous, but she knew Shameeq's way was the only way. She knew she couldn't hide from Don's people forever. If they really wanted her dead, then they'd get her. She had dealt with Don long enough to know that.

"Yo, son, the fuck she comin' here for?" Gutta questioned as they pulled into the apartment complex behind Nya. Sincere didn't respond. He just watched his surroundings closely. He had underestimated these Jersey nigguhs once, and he was determined not to be caught slipping. He parked two rows back and watched Nya get out, then climb the steps to Don's apartment. He was waiting for Don to come to the door, but he never did. Nya waited a few minutes, then put a note on the door.

"Let's go," Sincere told Gutta, gripping his pistol in his right hand.

He and Gutta got out and walked towards Nya's car. Nya saw them but kept her composure. Inside she was shaking like a leaf, but she knew fear would make her look guilty.

"Peace, Nya. How you? Lookin' for Don?" Sincere asked with a smile, concealing his gun behind his leg.

"Yes, I am. Have you seen him," she asked innocently, with just a hint of sexuality.

"I was about to ask you the same thing," Sincere replied.

She looked at Gutta, who watched her with a stone face.

"What's the note for?" Gutta asked.

"Ummm, just something for Don," Nya replied.

Gutta went to retrieve it.

While Gutta was gone, she quickly went to work on Sincere's emotions. Of the two, she knew Sincere was the one to appeal.

"Please Sincere, I swear I didn't want to! He made me!" she whispered feverishly, making sure she made body contact and Gutta didn't hear.

Sincere instinctively grabbed her and raised his gun, looking around for any movement. If anybody would've had the bad luck of going to his car, he would've squeezed off. That's how tense he was.

"Made you do what?"

"Yo, son, I told you this bitch was greasy!" Gutta growled, coming back with the note. "They kidnapped Don, son!"

Gutta backhanded Nya to the ground. She started to scream, but Sincere put the gun to her head. "Shhh, be easy. Let's go!"

He grabbed her by the hair and pulled her up. Gutta snatched the keys from her and got in her Jag while Sincere drug her to his Saab. He popped the trunk and stuffed her inside.

"Please don't kill me," Nya sobbed.

"That'll be up to you," Sincere replied coldly, then locked her in total darkness.

Now there was no turning back.

??????

"Yesssss, dadddy, punish this pussy. Awwww!" Sherrie squealed as she rode Shameeq reverse-cowboy style.

Shameeq loved fucking Sherrie in this position because her ass was so fat., Every time he drilled her, it would wobble like jelly from the impact. He spread her ass cheeks and slid his thumb in her asshole, something that drove Sherrie crazy.

"Oh, my God!" she gushed. "Yo, that makes me—" her words stopped in her throat as her whole body shook with her third orgasm. "Sha, please, cum ... cum all in this pussy, baby," Sherrie urged him.

Sherrie's pussy farted as the thickness of Shameeq's dick pushed the air out again and again. He pulled her down hard on his dick and grinded her until her eyes rolled up and she began shivering like she was cold. Shameeq's body spasmed, then he released deep inside her with a grunt.

Sherrie curled up next to him, throwing her leg over him and putting her head on his chest.

"You hungry, daddy?" Sherrie asked, caressing his chest.

Even though he hated to cuddle, he was too tired to object.

"Naw, I'm good, baby girl," he replied.

Shameeq couldn't front—Sherrie had the best sex game he had ever had. Her head game wasn't great, but that said to him that she hadn't done it a lot. But her pussy stayed wet, her sex song was magnetic and she was so flexible she could put both legs behind her head. Fucking her like that brought out something junglastic in Shameeq.

On top of that, he dug her style. She was laid back, southern with a drawl, slow as molasses and had a little-girl quality that tempered her black goddess–like sexuality. Plus, she wasn't all about money. She didn't hound him for paper to shop and get her hair done. Sherrie just wanted a good man to love her, which made Shameeq feel a little guilty because he knew he would never be a good man.

The vibration of his beeper on the nightstand brought his mind back to the business at hand. He picked it up and smiled.

"I gotta make a call," he mumbled, getting up to get dressed.

Sherrie sighed.

"I know, business , right? Be safe, daddy."

"Always, baby girl. Preservation is the first law of nature," he smirked, putting on his clothes, then headin' out the door.

Shameeq used the convenience store pay phone across the street from the complex. It was three in the morning, so the streets of the small town were deserted.

"Yo, somebody beep the God?" he asked once Sincere picked up on the other end.

"This KG or is it Drama? Or is the two one in the same," Sincere replied, having figured out the façade.

Shameeq smiled. "The God has many names. Call on them all."

"Where's Don?" Sincere probed, ignoring Shameeq's sarcastic remark.

"Who's this I'm speakin' to," Shameeq said.

"Sincere."

Shameeq chuckled to himself. He thought he'd be talking to a lackey, but he had Don's Capo_direct. It would only make his plan that much easier. It also told him if the crew's Capo had been forced to get his hands dirty, then the crew must've been real thin. Shameeq looked at it as another advantage.

"Peace, Lord. I heard a lot about you."

"Nigguh, ain't pressed for convo. Is we gonna do business or what?!" Sincere bassed. "You think shit is sweet? A'ight, I'ma play your game. Put my man on the phone, then you get your mil. But you better run far and fast or you won't live long enough to spend it!" Sincere spat, having no intention on paying; he just wanted to get at Shameeq.

"You'll speak to him in a minute, B. Right now, I'm talking to you," Shameeq spat back.

"Nigguh, if Don bleed, the bitch bleeds," Sincere warned.

Shameeq laughed.

"The bitch? Who, Nya? That's your bitch. I just borrowed her long enough to get my point across. Kill her and you'll be doin' me a favor. Bitch know too much as it is," Shameeq told him, glad to hear that Nya was still breathing.

"Put Don on the phone."

"I can't."

"Fuck you mean you can't?!" Sincere barked, Gutta looking at him like, what up?

"'Cause Don dead," Shameeq told him plainly.

"Nigguh—"

Shameeq cut him off and talked fast knowing that success or failure depended on what he said in the next few seconds. "Do the knowledge, God. You could react off emotions and fight a war you can't win, or you could recognize the situation as the opportunity that it is."

Sincere didn't respond, so Shameeq continued.

"I don't want a war wit' you no more than you want one wit' me, even though I got the advantage, not because I'm smarter, but because I moved *first*. Now you gotta rebuild, but without Don! How? We both know who had the connect. He was the man, but wit' him out the way, *you* the man, and all them spots Don was eatin' in is yours. I'ma supply you and *we* get money. But if you wanna go the emotional route, may the best man win," Shameeq concluded. Now the ball was in Sincere's court.

Sincere assessed the situation. War was no option. He'd have to go back to Brooklyn and bring another team. One he couldn't fund because his pockets weren't long enough. Sincere loved the lavish lifestyle, so the money he had put up couldn't supply three states that comprised 15 cities and fund a war at the same time. Besides, he'd have to find a new connect—and quickly, because once the other spots went dry, he'd have to reestablish himself in those areas and probably have to go to war again to reclaim his spots.

But what Shameeq had said about opportunity was true. Being the heir to the throne, with Don gone, the throne was now his. Sincere was a thinker, so there was no way he wasn't going to give it thought.

"A'ight, tomorrow morning at nine. You have Don there, and I'll have the mil ticket," Sincere said.

Shameeq smiled because he read between the lines. He wanted to think it was over.

"Peace, God. Next day," Shameeq said.

Sincere hung up without responding.

"What he say, son? You speak to Don?" Gutta wanted to know . Sincere looked at Nya, and she could tell he knew the truth.

"Naw, I ain't speak to him, but he safe," Sincere lied. "He begged me not to kill the bitch, so I know he'll play fair."

Gutta looked at Nya and got down eye level to the chair she was tied to. "You see this face, bitch?! I *promise* you once we got my man back, it'll be the last one you see!" he growled, then walked away.

Nya looked at Sincere and smiled to herself. He had lied to Gutta, so that could only mean one thing.

??????

While Gutta slept, Sincere contemplated things, damn near until dawn. Sincere claimed to be a God, but his God was money. He worshiped it and was willing to sacrifice for it. Because he didn't believe in anything he couldn't see, his outlook was materialistic in nature. Everything had to be concrete, real, and money represented the value of reality to him. What Shameeq was proposing was the opportunity of a lifetime. The only question was, how could he trust him?

"How I know Don dead?" Sincere asked Nya.

"He is dead, Sincere," Nya replied.

"I wanna know for sure," Sincere emphasized.

"I can call homicide. I have a friend in—" Nya explained, but Sincere cut her off.

"Call the police? Yeah right."

"Then turn on the news. The early edition is on," Nya remarked.

Sincere turned on the TV, keeping it low so as not to wake Gutta. Five minutes into the broadcast, the reporter said, "Police still have no leads as to the murder in downtown Virginia Beach yesterday. The man was killed at this intersection," the reporter said, as the news cut to the burgundy Benz, its door wide open. The police were all around it and had it roped off with yellow tape.

Sincere cut off the TV.

"I wouldn't lie to you, Sincere. Don's gone now. It's your turn. All the businesses Don had, the paperwork went through me. It won't be hard to backtrack and redirect. It's all to you," Nya offered, appealing to his greed. "The laundromats in Virginia, the real estate in Maryland and Pennsylvania. Even the shoe store and strip club he just opened in Ohio."

"Ohio?" Sincere echoed in disbelief.

"Yes, Don had me set that up a few weeks ago. The ink's still not dry yet, so transferring that would be even easier."

Sincere chuckled to himself. He knew how Don operated whenever he set up shop in a spot: He always started a legit business first. Don was getting ready to cross him out of the spot Sincere had set up. It was a dirty game.

Sincere snorted a chuckle. "Ohio, huh?" he said, more to himself than to Nya.

She picked up on the tone of his voice and realized there must be some significance to the place, so she echoed, "Yes, Ohio."

Sincere again asked himself if he could trust Shameeq's offer. Putting himself in Shameeq's shoes, he could see Shameeq had all the cards in his favor. Sincere realized that trust wasn't the issue, because there was nothing Shameeq could do to be trusted. The real question was what could Shameeq gain by tricking Sincere into the open only to kill him? The answer he gave himself was nothing could be gained. Dead or alive, Sincere was in no position to threaten him; he was an convenience at most. His offer was an appeasement and a way for Shameeq to expand all in one. Sincere's heart was for it, but there was one thing standing in his way.

Gutta.

Sincere knew Gutta would never agree to a deal. If Sincere worked the deal, Gutta would definitely take that back to Brooklyn, and Sincere would have a price on his head. No, there was no way he could take that deal as long as Gutta was still alive. Therefore, there was only one thing left for Sincere to do.

He got up from the couch and went into the bedroom. He stood in the door for a moment. Gutta was asleep on this stomach. Sincere had his gun in his hand. He paused. He couldn't shoot him in the back. He deserved better than. Sincere went over and sat on the bed. Since Gutta was a light sleeper, he woke up.

"What up, son? It's time?" Gutta asked.

"Naw, son, not yet. I just needed to speak to you. Turn over, son. I ain't talkin' to yo' ass," Sincere chuckled.

Gutta turned over and sat against the headboard.

"So what up? How we gonna do this?"

"Yo, Gutta, you a soldier, son. A real muhfuckin' soldier," Sincere complimented him.

"No question, I'm from the ville!" Gutta replied, gold grill gleaming.

"Indeed, son, indeed. But sometimes soldiers fight wars they don't understand, because soldiers don't *need* understanding. They fight from the heart. I used to be a soldier, but now I'm a general. You know what the difference between a soldier and a general is, Gutta?" Sincere asked.

"Yo, God, what is you talkin' about ?" Gutta chuckled confusedly.

"The difference is a soldier lives to fight, but a general...a general lives to win," Sincere concluded.

"It's too early for plus degrees, son," Gutta said, about to lay back down.

"Naw, this ain't no plus degree, Gutta, it's the first law of self-preservation," Sincere replied and raised the gun, holding it sideways.

Before Gutta realized what was happening, he was gone. His brains splattered on the wall behind him. His dead body slowly fell to the bed.

"It's a dirty game, son," Sincere told Gutta's dead body, then stood up and left the room.

Nya sat listening to the silence. The single gunshot made her jump. Sincere walked out and entered the room. He walked up to Nya with the gun at his side. He eyed her silently.

"Please, Sincere," Nya begged, not knowing his state of mind.

Sincere walked behind her and began to untie her. "Go beep your man."

CHAPTER 14

The sun rose as Sincere followed a black Cherokee into a clearing on the outskirts of Elizabeth City. Behind him was a gray Cadillac Coup Deville. They drove out onto an old airstrip. Sincere looked at the display before him. At least four Blazers and several other vehicles sat on both sides of the runway. At the end sat Egypt's white Volvo and Shameeq's Mercedes-Benz 190. At least three people stood around each vehicle. Sincere estimated at least fifty, soldiers, armed and trained to go. As he neared the Benz and Volvo, the Cherokee pulled to the side and Blue got out, followed by three of his workers. Behind him, Lil' B stopped the Cadillac. Shameeq emerged from the Benz, and it was then that Nya realized he was a real boss. Gone was the look of the street thug, replaced with a red and green Gucci suit, a pair of Gucci sneakers and Gucci shades. The Gucci link around his neck was at least four fingers wide, with gold and diamond stars and the number seven, the symbol of the nation of the Gods and earth.

YaYa and Montez got out of Egypt's Volvo and leaned on the hood.

Sincere smiled to himself because he knew what this was. It was a show of strength. Shameeq was letting him know he offered peace, but he was fully prepared for war. He walked up to Shameeq with Nya by his side. As soon as they met, Nya took Shameeq's shades off his face, put them on, then wrapped her arms around his neck.

"I missed you," Nya said, pecking his lips with a quick, sensual kiss.

"Go wait in the car," Shameeq replied, unmoved by her presence. He then approached Sincere. "Peace, lord. I'm glad you decided to bless me wit' your presence."

"You made your point," Sincere replied, stone faced, referring to his surroundings.

Shameeq shrugged and clasped his hands behind his back.

"I ain't know if you was comin' for peace or for war."

Both men assessed each other. They were about the same height, so they saw eye to eye in more ways than one.

"So where we go from here?" Sincere asked.

"I want it all, but I ain't greedy, nigguh," Shameeq began. "Don had spots in at least three states. You get one for yourself. That's all you. I'ma give it to you. For what I get it for. The other two, it's 70/30. That peace?"

"Do I have a choice?" Sincere smirked, liking the way Shameeq was handling the situation.

"I'm not a hard man to get along wit' to those I get along wit', you know? So what up, can we get along?" Shameeq said, offering his hand.

Sincere paused, then shook it firmly.

"Which state you want?" Shameeq asked.

"Maryland," Sincere replied, securing Ohio and Maryland for himself, because Shameeq didn't know about that spot.

"That's what it is then. Lastly, me and you peace, but I know some of your peoples won't like this agreement. Do us both a favor and relocate the ones you give a fuck about," Shameeq told him.

Sincere nodded.

"You lost people, but we did too," Shameeq reminded him, "so any bad blood that's allowed to mix would be bad for business, you know?"

"I'll handle it," Sincere assured him.

"Then I guess that's it."

"KG."

Shameeq smiled.

"Naw, God, call me Shameeq."

Sincere smirked.

"Shameeq, when we get started?"

"Hit me in three days. And Sincere?" Shameeq said, pausing to make sure he had his attention. "My word is bond, and my bond is life. If you ever try to cross me, I will find you."

Sincere returned his gaze.

"Never bite the hand that feed you. But if that hand should stop..." Sincere let his voice trail off.

"Fair enough. I'll see you in three days. Peace," Shameeq said as he walked away.

"Peace."

??????

Nya watched Shameeq as he drove. His confidence and arrogant swagger worked like an aphrodisiac on her senses, making her want to fuck him on the spot. But Shameeq kept an emotional disconnection between them, so she settled for massaging the back of his neck with her left hand. "You're amazing, you know that? I knew there was more to you than meets the eye," Nya said.

Shameeq chuckled.

"Yeah, 'cause you thought you just had a boy with the heart to do what you wanted and not a man with the mind to figure it out," he remarked.

"Maybe you do have what it takes to have it all," Nya quipped.

"So when do I meet your client?" Shameeq questioned.

"Soon," she said coyly.

"Tomorrow," Shameeq retorted, looking at her sternly.

He pulled over to the side of the road, and YaYa pulled over behind him. Shameeq left the car running and started to get out.

"Shameeq, where are you going?" Nya asked.

"Home," he replied simply.

"Why can't I go with you?" she asked sensually.

"Because trust is something we don't have, love. I'll see you tomorrow."

He got out and switched cars with YaYa and Montez. YaYa got on the driver's side, and Montez got behind Nya.

"Where to?" YaYa asked Nya.

Nya watched Shameeq pull off. She realized Shameeq was playing the same game she did, but she was determined to show him she played it better.

??????

Shameeq walked along the dock between various sized yachts and sailboats, looking for the one named "The Admiral". Caucasians curiously watched him pass as he spotted Nya a few boats ahead, smiling and waiting for his arrival. She was standing where the 30-foot Admiral was docked.

"Good morning, Shameeq. How are you?" she beamed.

Shameeq smiled back. He had to admit, Nya was one of the baddest women he'd ever seen. Her multicolored sundress flapped softly in the breeze and accentuated her figure. He could tell she wasn't wearing a bra by the way here nipples pressed against the fabric.

"What's up, Nya? This you?" he asked, referring to the boat.

"I'm not The Admiral," she winked. "He's inside. Shall we?"

Shameeq held her hand as she descended the three steps into the boat. He followed her inside the spacious cabin area. Shameeq chuckled upon seeing the familiar face. Richard turned around with a drink in his hand and saw the smirk on Shameeq's face.

"What, you were expecting a Colombian or something? Que pasa, amigo?" Richard quipped.

Richard was a little hesitant dealing with Shameeq because that hadn't been a part of the plan, but Nya had convinced him that Shameeq definitely had potential.

"I shoulda known," Shameeq replied, remembering Richard from the sheriff's office when he paid his bond. Shameeq now truly saw how far they went to set him up. Now that he knew how important it had been, he intended to juice it for all it was worth.

"I didn't think it would come to this," Richard remarked, "but seeing the way you handled the situation—well, the rest is now history. Drink?"

"Naw, I'm good," Shameeq said, sitting down on the small leather couch.

"So ... Shameeq Stevens. Funny, you look much older than twenty," Richard quipped, letting him know he had checked him out. "There a very short rap sheet on you back in Newark, so I figured you're either smart or a novice. But I think it's safe to say we both know you're not a novice," Richard said, raising his drink to Shameeq then downing it. He turned to Nya. "Nya, will you excuse us while we discuss things I'd rather not—" Nya nodded.

"I understand, Richard. I'd rather not either," she winked, then left the cabin.

"I appreciate what you did for me. I have the hundred—"

Shameeq leaned forward, resting his forearms on his knees and said, "Keep it. I was doin that number at seventeen. I want what you gave Don."

Richard nodded and smiled, pouring himself another drink.

"Nya told me as much, but what I was giving Don?" Richard shook his head. "Those are some pretty big shoes to fill."

"Yeah, and I filled 'em with dirt," Shameeq retorted.

Richard smirked.

"Fifteen a key."

"I can move twice as much as Don, twice as fast. He kept everything for himself and fed his crew crumbs. But me? I represent a...a coalition of sorts, so all boats rise together. Make it ten," Shameeq replied.

"Ten?" Richard echoed. "That's out of the question. Thirteen-five."

"Ain't how much money you make, it's how fast you make it. You givin' us five a brick to make ten three times faster. Why let five stop you from making thirty," Shameeq shot right back.

Richard chuckled.

"I like you, Shameeq. You're a thinker," Richard remarked, then sat his drink on the table, rested his forearms on his knees and looked Shameeq in the eyes. "I'll make a deal with you. You move 500 keys in the next thirty days for twelve-five, and I'll do ten from then out. But anything I give you on consignment stays fifteen. Deal?"

"No question," Shameeq smiled.

"Five hundred, Shameeq, not four ninety nine. If you can't do what you say, then in my eyes, you'll be a fraud, and I have no time for frauds. One last thing: I'm an old navy man, so I believe in protocol. I only deal with you. This coalition has nothing to do with me. Understand?"

"I wouldn't have it any other way," Shameeq agreed. He planned on allowing his people to get the same number he was, but he definitely would keep the connect to himself, which would allow him to keep the edge. The two men stood up and shook hands.

"Yeah ... I think we'll get along just fine," Richard said.

"And Richard? Being that I'm the only one that will know you, you don't have to worry about another Don situation. I'll never flip. But if I do catch a case, don't bother sending nobody at me, because unlike Don, I already know how you rock!" Shameeq smiled, but his tone was unmistakable.

Richard nodded.

"I'll beep you in two hours with a time and a place."

"I'll be waiting," Shameeq told him.

Shameeq left the cabin to find Nya, who was wearing his shades, lying back in a patio recliner on deck. She stood up as he came out.

"Should I kiss your ring?" she quipped.

Shameeq stepped closer to her, then removed his sunglasses form her face. Putting them on, he said, "I was wondering where these had gone."

He started to walk away, but Nya put her hand on his arm. "Shameeq, I know we got off to a bad start, but I really do want to get to know you. That is, if you'll give me a second chance," Nya said, maintaining eye contact.

"Second chance? I don't do the—"

"Hello, my name is Nya Braswell," she said, extending her hand. "And you are?"

Shameeq let a slight smirk creep over his face.

"You should know. Didn't you have it ran?"

"I know, but it doesn't work if you don't play along. And you are?" she asked again, hand still extended. She then deepened her voice, like Billy Dee Williams on "Lady Sings the Blues" and said, "You want my hand to fall off?"

Shameeq couldn't help but laugh, and her beauty softened him up. He shook her hand. "Shameeq."

"Shameeq, shy and meek. Yeah, that's you," she quipped and they both laughed. "So what are you doing tonight?"

"Me and my peoples throwin' a party at Shananigan's," he replied.

"Sounds fun. What time should I be there?"

"Naw, love, I never bring sand to the beach," Shameeq chuckled.

"Did I say I was coming with you? I said what time should I be there. Don't worry, you'll know when I'm there. And Sha? How can you build your castle without sand?" she winked, then walked back in the cabin, leaving Shameeq watching the sway in her hips.

CHAPTER 15

Present Day 1994

The marshal led Rivera into the small square room where his visitor sat at the small metal desk. Rivera took a seat.

"You got a cigarette?" Rivera asked desperately.

This is a federal building—no smoking," the agent retorted.

"Fuck a buildin', I need a smoke," Rivera replied, rubbing his handcuffed hands through his thinning hair.

The agent saw he was frazzled, so he extended his pack to him. Rivera took one and looked at it. "Marlboro?" he asked, then shrugged. "Gimme a light."

The agent lit the cigarette with his lighter, then Rivera sat back and blew the smoke in the air.

"You told 'em you're my lawyer, huh?" Rivera said.

"Yes. No one must know what's going on, not even the D.E.A.," the agent replied, then added, "You're gonna have to sit for a few more days."

"A few days?!" Rivera echoed nervously. "I can't stay in here a few more days! Look," Rivera began, taking a long drag of his cigarette, "I know for a fact that it's coming outta the naval boatyard."

"How can you be so sure?" the agent asked, his interest piqued.

Rivera leaned forward and spoke near a whisper.

"Because we were supposed to meet them *tonight*," he smiled. "Drama himself told me so."

The agent nodded knowingly. Everything had already been confirmed. The FBI had been tracking the Virginia pipeline for years. It began with a simple traffic stop in Hartford, Connecticut, that uncovered sixty kilos of cocaine. That led to the arrest of Rivera in the Bronx. He wasted no time cooperating and becoming a C.I. In his mind, it was a win-win. He'd be able to continue business as usual, as long as he fed the FBI enough to justify his position.

Rivera got several dudes in New York busted, which led to a Philly connect. Philly led to Maryland, where he first started dealing with Don's people. He was Don's top man in Virginia, but once bodies started dropping and the trail turned cold, the investigation ended there. That is, until he met Drama Squad. That, along with the official federal investigation, made all arrows point to Virginia. The feds were able to link the pipeline all the way back to the initial bust in Connecticut. Now they were so close they could taste it. They would fry the Drama Squad, but after they found out who they really were, they would make popping a million-dollar-a-week drug organization look like peanuts. The agent knew what was at stake, and he was prepared to go the distance, even if it cost Rivera his life.

"And guess what," Rivera continued. "Word around the jail is that somebody from the Drama Squad is talking to the D.E.A. as we speak."

"Here?!" the agent stressed, pointing to the table. "Fuck! Okay, look, let me make some calls, pull a few strings. Gimme a few hours and I'll have you out. You've *got* to make that meeting," the agent said.

He knew with all the hoopla, the big fish may be scared away if he hadn't been already. The meeting could be the last chance before the big fish swam into the deepest abyss. Then the trail could go cold permanently. "But in the meantime, you may want to ask for protective custody," the agent suggested.

"P.C.?! Es tu loco?! I can't go to PC. Muhfuckas look at me funny. Naw ... but," Rivera smiled, "I do have an idea. Gimme a cigarette."

The agent saw where he was going with it, so he handed him two.

"Ay, policia!" Rivera called out, "I'm ready to go!" he yelled, then winked at the agent.

??????

Present Day

The club in Norfolk was packed. Word spread quickly that there was a new team in town, so everybody wanted to know who the Drama Squad was.

They didn't disappoint.

YaYa, Casper and Trello had a crew of chicks from Newark drive their cars down. YaYa pulled up in a black Porsche 944, with Trello right behind him in his money-green drop-top BMW 325i. The hammer rims on both vehicles made it look like the wheels were going backwards as they entered the parking lot. Blue had just copped a brand-new midnight-blue Chevy Blazer. He fucked the game up being the first in VA with a Batman kit on his Blazer. Montez and Lil' B kept it Virginia pimpin' in Cadillacs, Montez in the Seville and Lil' B in the El Dorado. Egypt pushed a Volvo while Casper pushed his burgundy kitted Nissan Maxima. Shameeq brought up the rear in the 190, with Peanut riding shotgun.

The Squad brought extended members of the crew along to make sure the place was packed. Anybody wanting to bring it had to have an army because they'd damn sure be facing one. The party was invitation only, but Drama made sure to extend the invites far and wide to make people feel like they were among the elite.

Inside, the party was bananas. It was filled with young black gangsters who had been raised on the bitter milk of poverty and were just beginning to taste the good life. The DJ kept the music spinning while couples who looked more like they were fucking than dancing grinded and gyrated to the rhythm. Others flicked it up or toasted the Drama Squad. Peanut, the youngest by far, got dap from the dudes and cheek pinches and kisses from the ladies, but all he wanted was a drink.

"Come on, man! I got money! I want a muhfuckin' forty!" he yelled at the bartender.

"First of all, I don't sell no goddam forties, country-ass lil' nigguh" the bartender said in a thick southern drawl. "Second, I wouldn't sell you one no how! How the fuck you get in here?!"

" 'Cause I'm Drama Squad, motherfucka. You just the goddamn bartender! Fuck you!" Peanut hollered, then bopped away. He found Shameeq in VIP sitting with YaYa and a gang of chicks.

"Yo, Drama! Drama! Man, that punk-ass bartender won't sell me no forty! Holla at 'em for me, stic," Peanut said as he bopped up to the table.

Everybody at the table laughed.

"Yo, Nut, chill, B. Ain't nobody sellin' your young ass no alcohol," Shameeq chuckled.

"Man, y'all let me pump on the block, but you won't buy me a drink? That shit crazy," Peanut remarked.

"Who this, Drama? Your lil' cousin? He so cute, wit' his mannish ass," a thick redbone remarked.

"Yo, Drama, who she is?" Peanut asked, eyes glued to her exposed cleavage.

"You digging her, Nut? What up, you wanna hit that?" Shameeq snickered.

The girl shot Drama a look.

"What?" Shameeq said incredulously. Peanut looked her up and down.

"Hell yeah," Peanut exclaimed.

"That's what it is then. Val, take care of my lil' man," he told her with a flip of his hand.

"Hell no, Drama. I ain't doing no shit like that! Why you tryin' to play me?" Val protested, trying to sound firm, but coming off weak.

"Come on, baby, let me holla at 'cha," Peanut cooed, taking her hand.

Val snatched her hand away. The girls at the table giggled nervously. They were all watching Val's reaction, glad it wasn't them, although they were all willing to do what Drama said just to be in his circle.

"Word? You tellin' me no? It's like that?" Shameeq questioned her, staring her down, until she dropped her eyes.

After several moments, Shameeq added, "Go 'head, Val. Get outta here. Handle that or hit the door."

Val sucked her teeth and sighed hard. "Come on, boy!" she huffed, grabbing Peanut's hand, the leading a smiling Peanut away.

"You dead wrong, yo," YaYa chuckled.

"Fuck that. Ain't no bitch gonna defy the God and remain in my orbit. The moons revolve around the sun. You know the drill," Shameeq spat, then downed his drink.

Then Nya walked in.

Her entrance made the song "The Men All Paused" come to life. Her attitude was in every step, and she strutted like she meant it. Nya wore open-toed stilettos with the straps that wrapped around her calf. Her v-cut dress exposed both legs up to her waist and hugged her fat ass. She had on a halter-like top that stopped above her belly button and tied around her neck. She wore her hair in a bun, one lock of hair hanging loose, grazing her face. Every man in her line of fire froze like deer in headlights, letting Nya know her presence was felt.

"Yo, baby, could I holla at you?"

"Damn, you killin' that dress!"

"Baby, I wish today was yesterday, 'cause you somethin' to look forward to!"

Her compliments were punctuated jealous glares and evil eyes from all the females. Nya's light was eclipsing, but when a woman knows she's the one, her radiance is so strong the haters are forced to bow down. Shameeq saw her approaching. She looked so good, he couldn't help but be glad she had come. The two of them had an undeniable magnetic attraction, but the secret of magnetism is that it repulses and attracts simultaneously. They repulsed each other because they were so much alike, and they were attracted to each other because they were so much alike. The combination of love and hate is a powerful aphrodisiac.

"We're gonna be late," Nya said, disregarding the ill looks she was getting from the women at the table.

Shameeq bit his bottom lip slightly and a sexy smirk crossed his face. "Yeah? Late for what?"

"Our flight to Macau, Hong Kong's island of decadence," she replied.

Shameeq chuckled. "Word? That's how you comin'? And I ain't even packed no clothes."

"Don't worry," Nya winked, "for what we'll be doing , you won't need any." Then she began to strut away.

Shameeq downed his drink, gave YaYa a pound and got up. "Yo, I'm out, B. Bitch got boss game."

As he caught up with Nya, Lil' B approached. "Yo, Egypt said she out."

"Where she go?"

Lil' B shrugged.

"She left wit' some nigguh."

"What?!" Shameeq growled, then shook his head. Lil' B wanted to see what he wanted to do. Shameeq sighed, then chuckled. "Man, fuck it. Let her do her thing. Just beep her in an hour, make sure she good," he told Lil' B, then he and Nya walked away.

??????

When they got to the airport, Shameeq expected to be flying first class; he wasn't prepared for private class. Nya pulled the Jag up to a single airplane hangar, where a sleek white G-4 sat outside with a boarding steps leading to the open door.

As they both got out, Shameeq asked, "How we gonna miss the flight if the plane is yours?"

"It's rented, actually, and they charge extra if you're late. I love to spend money but hate to give it away," Nya replied, taking his hand.

One of the plane's crew approached.

"Hello, Ms. Braswell. Shall I get your bags?" he asked politely.

"We didn't bring any," she answered.

"Very good, ma'am. The captain's aboard. We're ready to leave when you are."

Shameeq and Nya boarded the plane. Shameeq looked around the plush interior with supreme satisfaction. The floor was covered with a brownish carpet that his Timberlands sunk into with every step. On either side of the aisle were two brown leather seats that reclined fully. Behind them was a bar and a leather love seat. Behind that was a closed door that led to the plane's bedroom.

Shameeq nodded.

"Yeah, love, I could get used to this."

"And you will," Nya replied, strapping in for takeoff.

After the plane leveled off, a tall blonde stewardess came into the cabin and fixed drinks. She handed one to Nya; Shameeq didn't want one.

"That'll be all," Nya told her. The stewardess nodded and left the cabin. Nya unbuckled her seatbelt and turned to Shameeq. "Relax, Shameeq. I didn't put anything in your drink," she giggled. "All the games are behind us now. I want to show you what the future looks like.

"Don't take it personal, ma. I just wasn't thirsty," Shameeq commented.

Nya put down her own drink. "But I am."

Nya got up and crossed the aisle. She lowered herself to her knees and undid Shameeq's jeans. She freed his dick from his boxers and squeezed it as it quickly grew longer in her hand.

"Mmmm," she moaned, licking the swollen head. "I missed you too."

Nya ran her tongue along the shaft, tracing the veins, then put his balls in her mouth. Shameeq sat back and grunted from the gut. Her tongue was as soft as wet feathers. Nya ran her tongue back up the shaft, then said, "Damn, your dick is beautiful. I want to make a mold of it so I can have you anytime I want." Then she stuck her tongue in the head of his dick, causing Shameeq to squirm.

"You act right and you can get that anyway," Shameeq answered, putting his hand on the back of her head.

Nya slid his dick into her relaxed throat and began to bob slowly. She used her throat muscles to contract and expand, massaging his dick as he fucked her mouth. It felt so good Shameeq gripped her hair, but Nya removed his hands and pinned them both to the arm rests. She bobbed quicker and quicker, long-dicking her throat until she felt his body begin to jerk. He pushed his dick as far down her throat as it would go and let off with a long grunt of relief. Nya pulled up her dress to her waist and straddled Shameeq, not giving his dick time to lose its girth. She slowly rode it back to full mast and initiated him into the mile-high club all the way to Macau.

Since Hong Kong is half a day ahead of America, they arrived in the earliest part of the day. Shameeq took one look at the large city and said, “This shit look like New York.” He wasn’t expecting that.

“I know, and twice as corrupt,” Nya replied as they made their way through the throngs of people. He found out how corrupt the place was when they reached the entrance point. He also found out that Nya spoke the Chinese dialect of Mandarin when she began talking to the Chinese guard. She flashed her passport, then he spoke to Shameeq.

“Yo, B, I don’t speak that shit,” Shameeq snickered.

Nya flashed her passport again, but this time there were five one hundred dollar bills on top. The guard looked around, then quickly pocketed the money. “Madame-san,” the guard replied, bowing slightly.

“You speak that shit like you a native,” Shameeq complimented her, impressed with her knowledge of another language.

“Thank you,” Nya giggled. “It’s one of the languages I learned in college.”

“One? How many do you speak?”

“Five.”

They chartered a helicopter to a small, run-down airport on the island of Macau, then they were driven by cab to Hotel Liscoa, which sat in the heart of the Sun Ma Lo district. They checked in but didn’t even go to the suite. Nya was eager to show him the city, and

Shameeq was just as eager to see it. This was his first time outside of America, let alone the tri-state area. The farthest he had been was Miami. Despite his swag, the fact was his style was strictly street. Nya was showing him a whole 'nother world.

As they walked, Shameeq saw Macau as more of a Chinese city like he imagined. Along the Ban Cheung Tong, the main boulevard, drab brick buildings housed small shops that lined the streets. People hawked their wares to tourists and natives alike. The streets were congested with loud, red double-decker buses and small matchbook-sized vehicles like Fiats and Le Cars. The only traffic making progress was the endless stream of bikes, mopeds and rickshaws. It made traffic in New York at rush hour look like a drive in the open country. The air smelled of salt water and seafood as they traveled from the old district of Si Ka Hou to Macau Square. Here shops with more familiar names—Hermes, Yves Saint Laurent and Chanel—and fine jewelry stores filled the square.

They walked into a mid-sized store, whose awning was written in Chinese. Shameeq looked around at all the expensive wares. Along one wall ran an extensive display of shoes, ranging from ostrich to gators to Ferragamo. Human mannequins stood on pillars among racks and racks of designer brands.

"You see anything you like?" Nya queried. As they browsed, a small Chinese woman walked up and began speaking what sounded like Spanish to Shameeq. Nya replied in her language. Shameeq asked, "They speak Spanish in China?"

"No, Portuguese. It just sounds similar. Ooh, Sha, look," Nya cooed, tracing her finger along a white silk outfit. "You'd look delicious in this. Will you try it on?"

Shameeq looked at the outfit skeptically, but replied, "Yeah, I'll try it on."

Shameeq backed out of the dressing room looking like he was ready for a *GQ* cover shoot. His outfit consisted of white-on-white ostrich shoes with subtle black trim, pleated silk pants and the matching shirt. Nya walked up to him and topped the outfit off by putting a white fedora with a black band on his head and cocked it ace-deuce.

"Now, that's hot," she commented, stepping back and taking him all in.

"Yeah, you think?" he replied, stepping in front of the mirror to check himself out.

He looked at himself and chuckled.

"What?" Nya asked.

"I look like my uncle Wayne Perry. Unk used to be on the fly shit every day," Shameeq reminisced. "I used to look at that nigguh and wanna be just like him, 'cause Unk was the man."

Nya walked up behind him and wrapped her arms around his waist and looked at their image in the mirror.

"Now you're the man, Shameeq," she remarked.

Shameeq admired himself in the mirror. A strange look crossed his face for a moment.

"You okay?" Nya asked.

"Yeah, yeah. I'm a'ight."

"You wanna try on something else? Whatever you want—you can get a whole new wardrobe."

Shameeq turned to face her.

"What you tryin' to say? You don't like the way I dress or something? Ya' tryin' to make me Don?" he questioned.

"Of course not! I just ... wanted to see you in a different look. Besides, Timberlands and Macau don't mix," she smirked.

Shameeq chuckled.

"Yeah, okay, I'm peace wit' that. I do the gators from time to time, but, Nya, don't ever think I'm Don, okay?" he warned her with a smile.

"Believe me, I already know that," she replied.

Before they left, Nya spent more than twenty grand on several outfits for Shameeq. She wasn't interested in shopping for herself, so they slid by a small café for a quick bite to eat. Many of the dishes were a mix of Portuguese and Cantonese styles, including ginger milk, stir-fry curry crab and egg tarts. They even had a dish called galinha-a-africana, which Shameeq ordered because of the reference to Africa. When it turned out to be African chicken, he snickered and said, "Halfway around the world, and they still put chicken on the menu for black people!"

After their conversation lulled, Nya asked, "Shameeq, how old do you think I am?"

Shameeq looked at her. He wanted to say twenty-one, but he answered, "Twenty-seven, twenty-eight."

She smiled and replied, "Thank you, but no, I'm thirty-four."

"You definitely wear it well," he complimented her.

"I didn't tell you that to fish a compliment; I just want you to understand I've been where you are before—young, hungry, ambitious, willing to do whatever it takes—but I don't want to see you make a lot of mistakes I've seen others before you make," Nya explained.

"Believe me, love, I'm on point. I now this game won't last forever, if that's what you mean by mistakes. Muhfuckas get caught up in the hype. That ain't me. The game is just a stepping stone," Shameeq replied.

"To what?"

"Bigger things."

"Such as?"

Shameeq shrugged. "Like going legit, getting into some businesses—you know, a couple of hair salons, strip clubs, real estate. Shit like that."

Nya smiled and reached across the table to touch his hand. "It's bigger than that, Shameeq. I like you. I do, which is why I brought you here. I've never done that before, but I feel like if you're given the right opportunity, you could be much more than just a street legend."

Shameeq nodded.

"I'm listenin'."

Nya looked around to make sure no one was within earshot and leaned into the table.

"I'm going to introduce you to a few people later, very important people,. I know you're going to like Macau, because it's run by gangsters," she giggled.

"I like it already," Shameeq chuckled.

"China is a communist country, which views capitalism as a poison, but every gangster is a true capitalist, which is why when Mau Se Tung cracked down inland China, the triads fled to Macau to continue their operations."

"The Chinese mafia," Shameeq replied, letting her know he knew what the triad was. They practically ran Chinatown in New York.

"Exactly. Anyway, they made Macau their base of operations, running the golden triangle from right here," she told him, pointing at the table. "Not too long after I got out of law school, I met a few Chinese girls—call girls. A simple case, but because I spoke Chinese, they felt comfortable talking to me. To make a long story short, I helped a group of them get into the country. That's when I met Stanley Ho."

"Stanley Ho?" Shameeq echoed. "He triad or something?"

Nya shook her head. "He's in the casino business ... among other things. In 1962, the Chinese government issued a monopoly license to handle Macau's gaming. He had it ever since."

Shameeq could only imagine how much money Ho had if he had it on lock for almost thirty years.

"But Britain, which has China as a colony, runs out in 1999. That's where we come in," Nya told him, biting into her egg tart. "But we'll discuss that later. I brought you here for two reasons: business and the business of pleasure," she winked.

She could see she had Shameeq's full attention, and she intended on keeping it that way because she loved to keep 'em dangling.

That night, after going back to the hotel for fucking and freshening up, Nya took Shameeq to the Hung Cheung Mun, Macau's red-light district. Chinese, Portuguese and a few black prostitutes worked the corners as luxury cars crowded the streets. Shameeq watched the hustle and bustle of the Macau's nightlife as they rode around in a Benz limo. They arrived in front of a red brick building on an unusually desolate block in the busy area.

"This is it," Nya informed him as the driver got out to open the door for them.

"This is what?" Shameeq asked.

"You'll see."

Nya and Shameeq got out, then Nya spoke to the driver in Chinese. The driver nodded, then got back in the limo and pulled off.

Shameeq looked at the building. It looked like an old warehouse. There were no windows and only one door. Nya walked up to the door and pulled a gold key out of her clutch. "A lot of people would kill for this key," she told him with a mischievous smile and handed him the key.

Shameeq could tell from her gleam that it was solid gold. With a key like that, he could only imagine what it opened the door to. Nya had already put him on to a connect of a lifetime, and with what she told him about the triad, his mind thought of heroin and heavy weaponry. All kinds of things went through his mind, so he was prepared for anything—except what he saw.

They entered a narrow hallway that was lit with purplish-blue light. Two slim Chinese dudes stood there. As they approached, Shameeq could tell by the way the stood they were nice with the martial arts, but the bulges under their coats let him know if the kicks didn't stop you, the bullets would.

Nya exchanged a few words with them and showed them the key. Then the two men escorted them to one of the many doors that lined the left side of the hallway.

They entered a small, sparsely furnished room. The only furniture in it was a small couch and a tiny wet bar, and there was a closet.

Nya opened the closet door, then kicked off her shoes. She looked over her shoulder at Shameeq with a lustful smile.

"Well? What are you waiting for? Take off your clothes."

"Take off my clothes?" Shameeq smirked. "We coulda stayed at the hotel and fucked."

Nya slipped out of her strapless dress and allowed it to fall into a pile of silk at her feet. Her beautiful bronze hour-glass figure was always a sight to behold. She walked over to Shameeq, kissed him gently, then began unbuttoning his silk shirt.

"This is the business of pleasure, and I promise," she purred, flicking her tongue from his nipple to his neck, "you won't be disappointed."

"Oh, yeah?" Shameeq replied, squeezing her soft, voluptuous ass. "What, you got an Asian ménage à trois in mind?"

Nya giggled and moved away from him. "Remember you said trust is something we don't have?"

"Yeah."

"Well, now is the time to establish it. Trust me, tonight I open up a whole new world to you—access to the shadows that control the light. And I'm trusting you not to speak of this to anyone," Nya said, her voice becoming firmer as she spoke.

"Yo, Nya, what is this?" Shameeq asked with concern.

"Will you trust me?" she asked seriously.

Shameeq eyed her for a long pause, then replied, "Yeah, yo, but don't ever break that."

"I expect you to do the same, Shameeq. Now, take off your clothes."

Shameeq hesitated, then began to undress.

"Ay, yo, Nya, don't let this be no crazy shit."

Nya giggled.

"Oh, *trust* me, it is. But after this, your life will never be the same again."

Nya pushed a button concealed in the corner, and the wall panel opened. They could hear a Chinese woman singing—though she sounded more like she was fucking. The Chinese -style music was accompanied by the smell of opium being smoked and raw sex. When Shameeq looked, he couldn't believe his eyes. The first thing that came to his mind was that if there's a such thing as hell, everyone in that room was definitely going. The large, cavernous room reminded him of fire because of the red halogen bulbs that lit it.

"This is the VIP section of the world," Nya cooed, taking his hand and giving him a mask that covered his eyes as she put on hers.

Every sex act imaginable was going on in the room, from wall to wall. In one corner, there were several dominatrices clad in shiny black leather and boots to their thighs, whipping and pissing on a group of writhing men. Eight females formed a daisy chain that snaked halfway across the room, with the last girl sucking some dude's dick as the first girl got fucked from behind. Two guys on a girl or two girls on a guy was as common as air. But many women paired off because it was obvious the women outnumbered the men. Various groups sat around large bongs and smoked opium from long hoses. The one thing that turned Shameeq's stomach was the men-on-men action. He stopped short when he saw it and told Nya, "Ma, I ain't wit' that gay shit."

"Don't worry, if you don't give off that energy, they won't bring it to you," she assured him.

Shameeq looked around at all the masked faces and noticed that he was one of only three black men in the room. Voluptuous bodies of various lighter shades made him lick his lips like a fat kid in a candy store. Nya saw his dick stand at attention, so she dropped to her knees and gave it hers. The color of his skin made him stand out, as four women approached him, surrounding the God with their heavenly bodies. One petite woman joined Nya on her knees, and they tongue kissed over the head of Shameeq's dick, licking and sucking it in turn while another woman got behind Nya and sucked her pussy from the back.

Before long, Shameeq had five women around him. He fucked a woman as Nya lay on top of her sucking her titties. Shameeq was in heaven. Two dudes came over to join him in the feast of flesh, but the look he gave them made them walk off in search of pussy unspoken for.

He played in Nya's pussy with three fingers while he fucked the shit out of the girl under her, until Nya creamed his fingers and begged, "Sha, please fuck me. Fuck me now!"

He slid his long dick straight into her just the way she liked it: rough. One of the other girls slid underneath Shameeq and began licking his balls while he pounded Nya. The sexual energy was so intense that even when he came his dick didn't go soft. The smell of sex and the opium contact had him in a zone. He grabbed a handful of Nya's hair and pounded her pussy relentlessly. She tried to wiggle away, but he had her by the hips, pulling back into every thrust. She shook her head furiously until Shameeq lost his grip on her hair.

"Don't ... don't pull my hair," Nya moaned.

"Shut the fuck up and take this dick!" Shameeq spat through clenched teeth, grabbing her hair.

"No!"

She shook loose, but he grabbed it again. This time, she lost it.

"Don't pull my fucking hair!" she bellowed, bucking back hard against him and pulling away.

She fought and scratched at a shocked Shameeq. He grabbed her waist to stop her. "Yo, what the fuck is wrong with you?!"

"Get off of me!" she screamed in his face, then broke away and headed back towards the room. Shameeq went after her. The incident barely registered in the room. People just continued with their scandalous behavior.

Shameeq reached the room right before the wall panel slammed shut. Nya was in the closet trying to put back on her dress.

"What the fuck is wrong with you?!" Shameeq asked, but she ignored him.

He grabbed her by the arm and turned her to face him.

"Nya! I'm talkin' to you!" he barked.

"I don't want to talk about it! I just want to go!" Nya spat back.

Shameeq looked into her eyes and saw a scared, blank look on her face. It was a look so uncharacteristic of her he knew something was wrong.

"Love, talk to me, a'ight? What's the matter? Why you flip like that when I pulled your hair?"

The mere mention of the act and the look of sincere concern in Shameeq's face made the terrible memories overwhelm her, and the tears turned from a trickle to a torrent.

Shameeq pulled her tightly and hugged her to his chest. “Shhhh ... Nya, it’s okay, love. I got you. Just talk to me,” Shameeq urged her.

She shook her head, but Shameeq put his hand under her chin and gently lifted her head, looking into her eyes. “Now I’m asking you to trust me.”

Nya studied his face for a moment, then walked over and sat on the couch. Shameeq sat down next to her.

“Shameeq, let’s just go, alright? I just ... I don’t like to talk about this. I *never* talk about this,” she mumbled.

Shameeq took her hand and squeezed it.

“Nya, whatever it is, you can’t run from it, because you can never escape, you know? I’m here for you, love. I wouldn’t do anything to hurt you.”

Nya took a deep breath and said, “My ... my father, he used to grab me by my hair.”

“What? He used to beat you?” Shameeq frowned.

My mother was a very beautiful woman. Creole, from Louisiana. Men just wanted her, wanted to possess her, but she was a free spirit—you know, she wouldn’t be tamed,” she began. The memories became so vivid it was like she was a child again. “She met my father. He was in the Navy. He made good money, and he was hardly there, which fit my mother’s lifestyle perfectly. Anyway, my father, he worshiped her. They got married, and he bought a home in Chesapeake. One day he came home and found my mother with another man. He was heartbroken, but she had him wrapped around her finger. She was wild, Shameeq, ghetto fabulous, but it all caught up with her, and she died of AIDS when I was nine,” she told him as he wiped her tears from her eyes.

“I’m sorry to hear that.”

“After she died, my father became distant, then sullen, then angry. I reminded him so much of someone he loved— and hated— so passionately. That’s when he began to ... he began to...” her voice trailed off, and she began sobbing.

Shameeq just dropped his head because he knew where she was going.

"Yo, that's sick, man," he uttered.

"He ... he molested me until I was thirteen. I ... I had my first orgasm with my own father! It made me feel so ... so dirty, so ... *nothing*. And every time he would pull my hair, calling me his dirty little slut, like my mother! He hurt me, Shameeq. He hurt me real bad. I can't have children," she told him, then fell into his arms, crying.

Shameeq was sick. He shook his head. "Yo, a fuckin' child molester is fuckin' scum! A nigga like that—"

She cut him off.

"He isn't black."

"Huh?"

"My father, he's white," she told him.

"Where is he?" Shameeq asked with murder in his heart.

"He ... he's dead," Nya lied.

It was like the window of Nya's vulnerability was slammed shut once she lied. Shameeq detected the change in her quickly. The blank look was gone, and her wall of defense returned. A part of Shameeq just wanted to protect her, but another part, the hustling womanizer, wanted to exploit the weakness he had found. Nya was definitely well connected, so to break her down and control her could take Shameeq a long way. He knew it wouldn't be easy. Besides, he didn't know which side of him would win the struggle.

CHAPTER 16

"Wake up, sleepy head. I want to show you something," Nya told Shameeq, waking him with a kiss.

They got dressed, then left the hotel in the same Benz limo from the night before. They drove past Senado Square, then entered the Si Ka' Hou district. They came to a row of stores and pulled over. Nya got out, and Shameeq followed.

"Remember I told you the British are leaving in 1999?" Nya reminded him.

"Yeah."

That's when Stanley Ho's monopoly runs out, and this," she said, referring to the group of buildings, "is where we get a piece of the pie."

Shameeq looked at the small shops, puzzled, so Nya explained. "I own this section of Si Ka'Hou. Once the British leave, then all this will be torn down, and in its place, a hotel and casino. Mine," she smiled.

Shameeq nodded with a smirk.

"Like I told you, it's bigger than the game, hair salons and barber shops. A casino will be worth hundreds of *millions*," Nya remarked, "and the rest of the block is still up for grabs. You want real estate, then this is where you plant your flag. You've been introduced to people you don't know, but who know you. People that make things happen internationally. When your money is right, we'll come back. Until then, I'll help you set up the account necessary to purchase land in Macau."

Shameeq's third eye was opened to the possibilities. He pulled her close and kissed her on the neck. "I'm very fortunate to have someone like you in my life, and my bond, I'll never take that for granted."

He leaned in and tongued her down.

"You said you want it all. Here's your chance," Nya smirked. "Oh, before we go, we have one more stop to make. For my mold."

Shameeq shook his head, chuckling.

"You serious, huh?"

"As a heart attack," she replied as they got in and pulled off.

??????

Present Day 1994

YaYa entered Blue's cell and found him sleeping. An old memory flashed through his mind. It was something a cop had once said during an interrogation: "You lock two guys up for murder, come back the next morning and the one that's sleep is the guilty one. Why? Because he know he's caught!"

He tried to shake the thought, but it snowballed. Blue had been called out a lot since their arrest. Since word spread someone from the Squad was snitching, Rivera had only left once, and YaYa couldn't see it in Blue. But pressure bursts pipes, and they're made of steel, so what could pressure do to an emotional human being?

"Yo, Blue, wake up," YaYa said loudly.

Blue's eyes popped open lazily.

"Fuck you doin sleep in here wit' your door open?" YaYa asked.

Blue sat his Buddha-like frame up and sucked his teeth. "I ain't worried about none of these coward-ass nigguhs, stic. I *know* I'm good."

In a situation like this, how could you be so sure, YaYa thought, but he let the comment pass. "Yo, that cat been actin' real shady."

"Who?"

"Who you think? Rivera," YaYa replied.

"What makes you say that?" Blue probed.

"Damn, B, where you been? You ain't been peepin' the shit? He been back and forth, blowin' the phone up. Fuck is all that about?" YaYa remarked.

The statement made Blue think about his own actions—he had been blowing up the phone as well. In the back of his mind, he wondered if YaYa was looking at him in the same light.

"Naw, stic, that ain't 'bout shit."

"Man, I walked up on the nigguh while he was all hush-hush on the jack. Then when he see me, he act like he was askin' a broad about some gwop," YaYa said, shaking his head. "I'm tellin' you, B, the muhfucka suspect."

"Yeah, yo, now that you mention it, he has been on some distant shit. Not really playin' us close," Blue remarked. "Shit, we in this together."

The statement made YaYa think about his actions. He hadn't been playing either one of them close. It made him wonder if Blue saw him in the same light and was just throwing that out subliminally.

"You talk to anybody?" YaYa asked.

"Lil' B still in Mexico. Ain't nobody seen him. I talked to Montez, though. He good. He said them people ain't even come to none of his spots, but he bounced to be safe," Blue informed him.

"He talked to you on a federal jack?!" YaYa questioned. "I know Tez ain't slippin' like that. Muhfuckas only do that if they feel safe."

"Naw, Ya, you paranoid, stic. Tez ain't carry it like that," Blue said.

"Yeah? How you know? Show and prove," YaYa challenged.

"Come on, Ya, Montez? Playboy got mo' bodies than me *and* you. Nigguh family," Blue reminded him.

"Yeah, and only family close enough to hurt us. Tez my nigguh, B, but yo," YaYa shook his head. Fire reduces all matter to its basic elements, revealing what you truly made of.

Both men got quiet for a moment.

"What about Drama?" Blue asked. "You talked to him?"

"Naw, but the God wouldn't answer anyway knowin' the situation." YaYa shook his head, then punched his fist.

"I told the God not to trust that bitch!"

"Yeah, stic, a nigguh in love'll do anything," Blue remarked.

YaYa looked at him and wanted to respond, but he remembered his own statement. He felt like he knew Shameeq, but in a situation like this, how can you be sure?

A dude walked up to the cell and knocked on the opened door. "Yo! Your boy just flipped out at his lawyer visit!" the dude exclaimed. "He tried to sneak some cigarettes back, but when they peeped it, he swung on the police!" the dude told them and walked away.

"Damn," Blue chuckled, "he musta wanted to smoke bad as hell."

YaYa stood up, irritated. "Fuck outta here wit' dat! Nigguhs sell cigarettes in here! The God sees shit for what it is and not what it appears to be! Dude did that shit so he wouldn't have to come back up here, 'cause he knew I peeped him!" YaYa exclaimed, pacing the floor. "Think about it, B. Who else knew we was 'posed to meet dude? Tez ain't know and Lil' B in Mexico! Who else knew?!"

"Yeah, that's true," Blue nodded, "Except ..."

"Except what?"

Blue looked at YaYa, knowing he wasn't trying to hear what he was about to say.

"Drama knew."

YaYa stopped pacing and looked at Blue. He thought for a minute, then replied, "I'ma call him again."

Then he walked out of the cell.

??????

"After that, the Squad never looked back," he said, then coughed.

"Nya put us in a position to be bigger than the game, so we ran with it, we expanded."

"So is this when the Drama Squad found out who was supplying Nya?" Jacobs asked.

"Naw," he replied, "that came in time."

"So who was it?" McGrady chimed in.

He smirked, and Mullins watched him intently. He returned the stare.

"Look, you want me to snitch? You want me to turn rat? Agreed, but I'ma tell it my way. PERIOD. Now, as I was saying ..."

"You mentioned several names," Mullins said, cutting him off. "I'm going to repeat them, and I want you tell me if any of them are or have ever been federally indicted or are in any position to become federal informants."

"What's that got to do with anything?" he wanted to know.

"*Everything,*" Mullins gritted, then began. "Montez Phillips."

"I don't know."

"Bernard Gross aka Lil' B."

"Not that I know of."

"Larry Jackson, Mo Green, Charles Covington," he probed.

"Ummmmm, the three stooges," he quipped.

"Don't be a smart-ass."

"Bill, why don't we just call the bureau and find out if they have a C.I. within the Drama Squad," Jacobs suggested.

"Because those smucks in the bureau want all the glory. They wanna bust the case before us," Mullins objected.

"No way. The Drama Squad's all mine!" he chuckled.

"Let me find out you alphabet boys don't work together."

"Just interoffice rivalries, but we're totally united against *your* kind," McGrady seethed.

"My kind?" he echoed. "You mean black? Are you a racist, officer?"

"Of course not! I--I meant criminals, lowlifes like yourself! Fuckin' rats running from the responsibilities of your actions!" McGrady huffed.

"Without *my* kind, you wouldn't solve any cases," he shot back. "Yeah, you're racist, but only against black men. You know why? 'Cause we got bigger dicks!" he laughed.

"That's a fuckin' myth," McGrady spat.

"Wanna see?" he smiled. "But what you don't wanna see is one big, fat, long dick in your women's pussies. You don't wanna see how she takes this big black—"

"Get back to the fuckin' story!" Mullins yelled, banging the table, making McGrady jump.

He held up his hands in mock surrender. "Easy, big guy. Didn't know you were so touchy," he snickered. "My point is, pussy is a motherfucka. Wars been fought over it, and in the end, whole kingdoms have fell over it. Just like ours."

??????

1990

"Yo, baby, what you got in them titties, skim milk?"

Shameeq laughed at the comment as he and Nya sat in the theatre watching *New Jack City*. Shameeq hated the movie, so he was glad when it was over. As they were walking out, Nya said, "That was good."

"Good?" Shameeq snickered. "That shit was fake as fuck! How dude making a million dollars a day, but when he go on the run, he hidin' out in a Harlem apartment?! Get the fuck outta here. A real nigguh woulda got ghost."

"True," she giggled, "but Wesley is a good actor."

"Yeah, I bet he wasn't actin' when he was talkin' 'bout that red devil dust. He even said the real spot and everything. Yeah, he done been dusted before."

"See? That's what I mean. He was good. Even you said it was real," she countered.

"Yeah, but what wasn't real is him taking the fuckin' stand," he gritted. "I hate a fuckin' snitch, especially when a so-called kingpin rat out his family. That's some fucked up shit."

"Everybody has a breaking point, Shameeq."

"Fuck that, my word is my bond, and my bond is my life. I'll give my life before my word shall fall! The God'll never snitch."

As they strolled through the lobby, people treated him like a real life Nino Brown. Cats who only knew his name and face greeted him, making sure everybody in the room knew they knew him, even if only superficially. Haters hated from the sidelines, but that's where they stayed because they weren't cut to fuck with a real don.

The females were even worse. They called out his name. Two even gave him hugs, to the chagrin of Nya. He took it in stride, blessing them with, "Peace, love. How you?" And he kept it moving.

Looking around, he could see his influence shining in the eight months after returning from China, he had stepped his game up. He still rocked the Timberlands, jeans and jogging suits, but gator shoes, Polo boots and Gucci loafers became the norm, not the exception. Everything he wore was tailored. Gone were the big, obnoxious ropes and herringbones and chunky nugget watches; in their place were Movado, Tag Huer and a single-diamond pinkie ring on both hands. Nya even had convinced him to get manicures. Shameeq was getting his grown-man shit on, and Nya loved it.

She also loved the way he handled business. If she ever had a doubt whether or not he could handle it, those doubts were quickly dispelled. The Drama Squad was moving in two weeks what Don was moving a month. Besides, the spots they still controlled through Sincere, Egypt and Trello had expanded into Elizabeth City and Raleigh. YaYa had spots in South Carolina, and Blue had set up a distant cousin in Charleston, West Virginia. They didn't expand through intimidation; they expanded simply by giving better prices. Since Shameeq gave his team the same number he was getting, they, in turn, gave their customers discount, thereby moving the product much faster.

Nya was impressed with his business acumen and the way Shameeq had begun to carry himself like a shadow. The one thing she wanted the most, though, continued to elude her: his heart. She liked a challenge, but the pursuit was frustrating.

Shameeq, for the most part, was feeling Nya as well. She was everything he wanted and needed in a woman, except she had deceived him from the jump. She had beat him at his own game, and that was something his pride wouldn't let him get past. He kept her at arm's length—or dick's length, depending on the situation—but in his heart, he willed her closer. He had to somehow even the score, and if he could, then maybe his pride would consent to truly embracing her. As it stood, they were more opponents than opiates to each other's emotions.

"Shameeq, I know what you do, but you don't have to be so disrespectful," Nya commented as they exited the theatre.

"Disrespectful? They know me, yo, I don't know them," Shameeq replied arrogantly. "Why you ain't say somethin' to them?'

"Because it wasn't my *place*," Nya spat back, vexed, her high heels clicking across the parking lot pavement.

Shameeq sighed.

"I can't help if they like what they see. I ain't buggin' 'cause the nigguhs be in your face. Fuck you want me to do? Live in a bubble like Michael Jackson? Don't let nobody in but my monkey, Bubbles? You gonna be my Bubbles?" he smirked.

Nya stopped. "Oh, so I'm a monkey now, Sha—" She wanted to spaz on him, but the monkey face he made with this tongue making his upper lip protrude made her burst out laughing. "You make me sick," she said, shaking her head. "And whoever is in my face, I don't disrespect you with it."

"Yeah, whatever," Shameeq replied, chirping the alarm on his brand-new black Mercedes 500SL. He hated to know Nya had nigguhs in her face when he wasn't around, but he kept his cool as he opened his door. "We just beautiful people, love, and beauty is a magnet."

"Yeah, for jealousy," she mumbled, as she got in.

"Huh?"

"Nothing," she replied.

He started the car and backed out of the parking space.

"I'm hungry," Nya remarked.

Shameeq glanced at his Movado.

"Ma, it's damn near midnight. Only thing open is McDonald's or Burger King. Have it your way," he said sarcastically.

"Please," she said, brushing the comment off. "No, I know this little bistro down by the beach. It stays open 'til two."

"I can't, love. I gotta handle somethin'," Shameeq replied, stopping at the light.

"Oh," she said, paused, then added, "are you coming back to the house tonight?"

"Naw."

"Well, what is it? I like Nikki too," she smirked and made Shameeq chuckle.

It was a running joke between them because of the ménage à trois they had been having. Nikki was a reference to Prince's song "Darling Nikki." Nya wasn't really that into girls; she just didn't like the idea of Shameeq fucking another woman and she not being a part of it.

"Naw, it ain't Nikki," he chuckled. "I gotta meet somebody."

"Then I'm going with you."

The light turned green and Shameeq pulled off. "Why?"

"Why not?"

Shameeq couldn't help but smile at her comeback. He saw she was adamant about going, so to avoid an argument, he relented.

"Okay, cool. Let's go."

"Where?"

"To a dog fight."

??????

They drove out to the country, where Lil' B had a pit-bull farm. And on that farm, he bred and sponsored pit-bull fights. The farm was set back in the woods, far from the vigilant eye of animal control and the ASPCA. Shameeq pulled the Benz into the busy gravel parking lot. From the looks of the parking lot, you would've thought it was a club. Cars and trucks bumping the latest hits filled it. The gold diggers were deep as well, knowing some of the biggest ballers came to fight their dogs or bet on the dogs being fought.

Nya looked around at the spectacle as she and Shameeq got out.

"All this over a dog fight?" she remarked in surprise.

"A lotta money changes hands over these dogs, yo," Shameeq replied, checking his clothes for any signs of the dust that covered the entrance to the barn. The barn was huge. All Nya could hear was the roar of the crowd, loud barking and growls and the pungent smell of heat and animals.

"This place stinks," she remarked. "I hope we won't be here long."

"You said you wanted to come, right?" Shameeq reminded her.

Before she could reply, Lil' B came through the crowd, counting a large stack of money.

"What up, Drama? How you?" Lil' B greeted him with a gangsta's hug.

"Not as good as you," Shameeq smirked, referring to the money.

"This? Shit, I'm 'bout to double this, stic! Muhfucka put twenty grand on a red nose against my grand champion! He goin' home broke tonight!" Lil' B said. He and Shameeq laughed.

"Which dog?"

"My bitch Lady."

"Lady? Shit put ten on her fo' me," Shameeq told him.

"You're covered, slick," Lil' B assured him.

"What's a grand champion?" Nya wanted to know.

"A dog that's won five fights. Shit, I got four grand champions already outta my bloodline," Lil' B boasted, then turned to Shameeq. "You see Lo out there?"

"Naw, where he at?"

"He waitin' for you in the parking lot. Blue Blazer—you can't miss 'em. He the only muhfucka out there pumpin' that go-go," Lil' B replied.

Shameeq nodded, then said to Nya, "Wait here wit' B. I'll be right back."

"Shameeq," she protested.

He pecked her lips. "Right back. Then we out."

"Don't worry, lil' mama, you in good hands," Lil' B assured her. "Come on, let's go check the pits."

"The pits?" she echoed.

"Yeah, where the dogs fight. You don't know what a pit is?"

She shook her head.

"How you gonna live in VA and ain't never seen a dog fight?" Lil' B chuckled.

Shameeq saw the blue Blazer, and just like Lil' B said, go-go music was blasting. The sounds of "Ruff it Off" by Junkyard Band seemed to make the gravel vibrate. He walked up to the driver's side just as Montez's cousin Lo got out the truck.

"What's up, young," Lo greeted in his laid-back, gravelly voice, his eyes sleepy. The toothpick in his mouth bobbed with every word.

Shameeq snickered as he shook his hand. "Lo, you the coolest muhfucka I ever met, being that I ain't never had the pleasure of meeting myself."

Lo smiled slow and easy. "Yeah, young, you the second-coolest muhfucka I know too."

After the lighthearted banter, Lo got down to business.

"I wanted to holla at 'cha 'cause shit wide open in DC right now, and I might have the muhfucka that could plug the hole."

"Speak on it."

"Youngin' named Tony. He from New York somewhere. Spanish nigguh. Now e'ry since that bitch-ass Alpo pulled that bullshit on Silk and them, I ain't been too big on New York nigguhs, but this Rivera jive alright," Lo explained.

Shameeq nodded to let Lo know he was listening.

"E'ry since Rayful Edmond got popped, DC ain't really had no steady supply. What me and my people been coppin' from you, we been hittin' Tony wit, 'cause he be spendin' that paper. He fuck wit' some nigguhs out Barry Farms that'll leave you at the go-go. They real live."

Shameeq looked a little confused, but Lo knew why.

"Leave you at the go-go, meaning leave you layin' at the go-go," Lo chuckled.

"He solid?" Shameeq wanted to know.

"I can't speak on that, young, but he got that paper. Problem is, what he need, I can't supply. He got a few spots that suck that shit up like water."

"How many he move a week?"

"Wit' us, three or four, but young be doin' 'bout eight a week. He jive fuck wit' a few other nigguhs, but yo, shit so raw, he move our shit twice as fast. That's why he asked me to speak to my peoples," Lo replied.

"What you tell 'em?"

"No more than he knew before he walked in the door. But I'm tellin' you, 'cause the nigguh a opportunity."

Shameeq pinched his bottom lip as he contemplated, then said, "A'ight, I'ma come through in the next few weeks. I'll beep you when I get there."

Shameeq really planned on coming in the next two days, but he never telegraphed his true intentions.

"I'll let em know."

"Naw, don't hit 'em 'til I come. Then we'll go meet 'em," Shameeq told him.

They shook hands.

"A'ight, young, I'm gone," Lo said.

"Peace."

Shameeq went back in the barn and heard, "Hey, daddy."

He turned his head and saw Sherrie approaching him, looking like a chocolate goddess in her black en vogue dress and clog heels. She wrapped her arms around his neck and tongued him down, letting all the females know exactly where she stood.

"Peace, queen, how you?" he said, greeting her wit' a sexy smile.

"Peace, king. I'm better now," she cooed, basking in the light of his attention.

Sherrie was Shameeq's good girl, the one every bad boy wants but doesn't deserve. He had moved her in with him after the devastation of losing her cousin. He felt partially responsible for that, so he took her under his wing. He was paying her way through school at Norfolk State, where she was pursuing a career in child care. Sherrie was loyal, responsive to his needs and easily satisfied, and she kept the house. Everything he didn't deserve. "I hope you don't mind, but I just got bored at home. My girlfriend called—"

Shameeq cut her off gently.

"Ma, you good. My door open just as easy as it close. I ain't tryin' to keep you under lock and key."

"You comin' home with me? I got something to show you," she flirted.

"Oh, word? Well—"

"Shameeq!"

He knew exactly who had called his name: Nya. None of the other broads he dealt dare call him out like that.

She had been in the throes, watching the two pits tear away at each other while the crowd around the top of the six-foot-deep pit and cheered them on. She had never been to a dog fight, so the savagery amazed her. When she looked up, she saw Shameeq come back into the barn. She also saw Sherrie approach him. She knew exactly who Sherrie was, because it wasn't like Shameeq tried to keep it a secret. The other females meant nothing to Nya; she knew they were just food for Shameeq's sexual appetite.

But she saw Sherrie differently. To Nya, Sherrie wasn't just another woman, she was the other woman. One who seemed to have the upper hand for reasons Nya couldn't understand. Nya hated to lose, because she had never lost, especially to someone she saw as less than. In Nya's eyes, she was international, Sherrie was country. She was wealthy and independent, Sherrie was broke and dependent. She was smart, Sherrie was simple. And when it came to appeal, she was the color of Egyptian gold, Sherrie was the color of warm shit. There was no way, in Nya's mind, that Sherrie could compete, but there she was with her arms around him and her tongue down his throat. And Nya intended on checking him on the spot.

"Shameeq!"

By calling his name, causing him to turn around, Nya unknowingly saved his life.

When he looked around as Nya approached, he saw three dudes pulling out weapons. Their eye contact was instantaneous, but Shameeq didn't hesitate to react. He grabbed Sherrie, shielding her with his body, then grabbed Nya by the forearm and yanked her to the ground with them. The gunshots whizzed over their heads, hitting two girls and a dude. The whole barn broke out in pandemonium as gunfire and feminine screams filled the air. Lil' B's people quickly returned fire, pushing the gunmen back and killing one.

The stampede of people provided Shameeq the opportunity to take cover and pull his weapon. He was poised to fire back. By the time he did, the remaining two gunmen had disappeared in the crowd.

Just as quickly as it had begun, it was over. The only thing that remained was the frenzied roar of the crowd and mental alertness.

Lil' B and Lo ran up to Shameeq as he helped Nya and Sherrie off the floor.

"Yo, stic, you a'ight?!" Lil' B asked, looking Shameeq over to make sure he wasn't hit.

"I'm good," Shameeq replied, looking around and gripping his pistol tightly.

"Yo, young, I was 'bout to bounce when I heard the shots, so I came to see what up. Whoever they was, I caught one of them bammas slippin'," Lo said, referring to the dead gunman he had murdered.

"Them muhfuckas came outta nowhere!" Lil' B gritted, pissed that the shit went down at his spot.

Shameeq walked over and looked at the body.

"You recognize 'em?" Lo questioned.

Shameeq shook his head. His composure was calm, but his insides screamed for blood. He turned to Lil' B.

"B, get Sherrie home. Follow her tight," he told him firmly.

Lil' B nodded, then he and Sherrie walked away.

"You need me to stick around?" Lo wanted to know.

"Naw, Lo, I'm good. Them nigguhs had they chance. Now it's my turn," Shameeq replied.

Shameeq turned to take Nya's arm, but she snatched away and stormed off. He didn't know what her problem was, but he would soon find out.

??????

"Yo, what the fuck your problem?!" Shameeq exclaimed as Nya tried to slam the front door in his face when they got to her house.

She had given him the silent treatment the whole ride.

"Just get out," she bellowed, kicking off her shoes haphazardly.

She looked at her dirt-stained dress and snatched it off in disgust, then flung it at Shameeq. "And you get this cleaned!" She stood in the large front room of her seaside mansion, totally nude, and pissed. She was pissed.

Shameeq let the dress hit him, then hit the floor. "Yo, I saved your fuckin' life and this how—"

"You grabbed *her* first?!" she said.

Shameeq realized what she meant. He flashed back to the hit, seeing his reaction as the guns went off. He did it out of instinct, a reaction that he only had milliseconds to compute."Ma, I grabbed you *both.* I wasn't thinkin' about—"

"That just makes it worse," Nya shot back.

If he grabbed Sherrie unconsciously first, then his reaction spoke volumes to her.

Shameeq sighed hard and shook his head. "Nya, look, in a situation like that, you just react."

"Do you love her?" she probed, arms folded over her bare breasts.

"What? How you go from—"

"Answer me, Shameeq! Do ... you—"

"No, a'ight? It ain't that serious, yo," he answered.

"She lives with you, Shameeq. How is it *not* serious?" Nya wanted to know.

Shameeq snickered lightly.

"Come on, ma, who else gonna cook?"

He tried to make light of the situation, but Nya remained stone-faced. Shameeq approached her. "Sherrie, she cool, a'ight? She a good girl, and I just wanna make sure she good. It ain't goin' nowhere."

Nya looked him in the eyes trying to abate the scorn she felt building within. "Where is *this* going? Us?"

"What you mean where it's goin? It's here, it's us, it's now, it's real."

He tried to convince her. Shameeq reached out to pull her close, but she stiff-armed him and eluded the embrace.

"Nya, why the fuck is you makin' this a big deal?!" Shameeq didn't understand how his decision affected Nya.

"I refuse to be second to anyone, Shameeq, so let's deal with *firsts,"* she smirked. "We started out doing business, so that's what it'll be: *business*."

"So what you sayin'? Just call you when I need a lawyer?" Shameeq replied, meeting coldness with coldness.

"No, you misunderstand. Since you work for my client, indirectly, you work for *me*," she smiled.

"Naw, Nya, *you* misunderstand. I don't work for no-fuckin-body!"

"Then get a better connect," she shot back.

Shameeq glared at her. He knew he'd be hard pressed getting a connect with the prices and quality that Richard was giving him. He was vexed, but he wasn't about to let his emotions overrun his intellect.

"Okay ... boss," he smirked.

She turned to walk up the stairs, her apple-bottom ass swaying with every step. "And I want to know about any and all expansion. Anybody new you may want to bring in. I no longer trust your judgment. What are you going to do about tonight?"

"Nothing."

"Nothing?"

He shrugged, "Let 'em think the move shook us, and they'll get bolder and expose their hand," he surmised.

"Keep me informed."

"No problem," he replied, boiling on the inside. He grabbed the door to leave.

"Oh, and, Shameeq," she called after him, "don't forget the dress. Have it dry-cleaned."

Shameeq eyed her coldly but smiled evenly. He scooped up the dress and walked out.

??????

Two days later, Shameeq made the trip to DC. He took Nya along because he didn't want to jeopardize the connect. He knew a woman's emotions were volatile, and if Nya found out he had made a major move in DC, there was no telling how she'd react. Besides, it was a good excuse to see her again.

He beeped Lo when he got there. Lo told Shameeq to meet him at a restaurant called Houston's in Georgetown. Fifteen minutes later, Lo walked into Houston's with Tony, and they made their way to Shameeq's table.

"Drama, what up? This Tony. Tony, this Drama," Lo introduce, as the two shook hands and sat down.

"Hey, it's good to meet you, man," Tony said, shaking Drama's hand firmly.

"Same here. Lo says you're doing big things," Shameeq remarked.

"Tony waved him off. "Peanuts," he said, then looked at Nya. "Mi dios! Que hermosa!"

Nya lowered her eyes demurely.

"Gracias."

"Drama, I like you already. You have excellent taste," Tony said, toasting him with his water.

"Yeah, this my girl," he said, glancing at Nya. She rolled her eyes, but in her heart she liked the way it sounded. "So talk to me. Lo tell me you from New York."

"Si," Tony replied, "the Bronx, born and raised. And a Yankee fan before that. You?"

"I'm from Newark."

"You like baseball?"

Shameeq looked at Nya and smirked, "Naw, never watched a game in my life."

"Figures. Beisbol is to the Hispanic, like basketball is to the black people—the only way out of the fuckin' slums, unless, that is, you have some good friends like yourself, eh?" Tony said.

"Indeed."

The waitress brought over the drinks. Tony sipped his, then said, "Newark, eh? I used to be in Newark back in the late 70's early 80's. The Zanzibar used to be the spot."

Shameeq chuckled. "It still is."

"It used to be called something else. I can't remember. Anyway, I was there the night Grace Jones came to the Zanz. And this was when Grace was the shit. So she's performing uh ... uh ... uh ..."Pull Up to the Bumper Baby," right? Big hit, everybody's lovin' it. International star at the Zanz! The place is bananas."

Shameeq laughed because he knew how the Zanzibar could get.

"I don't know," Tony continued, "in Europe, they have this thing where the performer spits on the crowd."

"Spits?" Shameeq echoed.

Tony nodded and mimicked spitting on the floor.

"Yeah, actually spitting on the crowd. In Europe, they love it, fuckin' wierdos. But Newark? Man, this puta started spittin' in the crowd," Tony began, laughing. "It musta been like half the club up on stage beatin' Grace Jones' ass!"

They all broke out laughing.

They talked for the next twenty minutes. Tony kept them laughing with story after story. Shameeq liked his style, and he could tell that he'd been around the game for a minute. What he didn't like, though, was the way Nya kept openly flirting with Tony. Tony tried to overlook it, but it was clear. Shameeq knew she was doing it out of spite, and he was heated. He kept his composure, but he planned on getting at her as soon as they were alone.

"But listen," Tony said, finishing his third Henny, "enough of the small talk. I'm sure you're a busy man, Drama, and I would like to get busy, no?"

"Indeed," Shameeq agreed. "So what kind of numbers you lookin' to do?"

"First, let me ask you this: Are you the policia?" Tony asked, looking Shameeq in the eye.

Shameeq wasn't offended, so he simply replied, "Naw, B, are you?"

"No, I'm not. No offense, but it's not like we're about to discuss a nickel bag in the park. Big numbers bring *bigger* numbers, dinosaur time, so it's always good to get that out of the way, you know?" Tony said, leaning on the table.

"I couldn't agree with you more," Shameeq concurred.

"So," Tony began, interlacing his fingers, "you give me a good price, and I give you good business."

"Nineteen-five," Shameeq told him, sipping his drink.

Tony bobbed his head. "That's a very good number. I like it, but that's the same number I'm already getting from Lo here, and I thought if I spoke to el jefe, you know, the boss, and we could see eye to eye, I figure—" Tony shrugged. "Maybe eighteen?"

Shameeq snickered.

"I have no problem wit' eighteen, but I'm not the man you need to speak to," Shameeq replied, gesturing to Lo, "he is. That's my people in DC, and I ain't the type to cut my own people's throat."

Shameeq could tell Tony wasn't feeling what he said, but Tony hid it well.

"Well, I definitely wasn't tryin' to cut anybody's throat. I just thought—that's cool."

"You sure?"

"Si, si," Tony affirmed quickly as he turned to Lo. "Well, mi amigo, what do you think?"

Lo was surprised by the way Shameeq handled it, but he was too cool to show it. He thought Shameeq would want to cut out the middle man as well.

Lo shrugged. "If it's twenty or better a pop every cop, then that's cool, slim."

Tony shook Lo's hand.

"*Always* twenty or better," he said. He turned to Shameeq and extended his hand. Shameeq shook it. "Tu me gusta. A man who knows how to spread his wealth and not be greedy, he can last a long time in this business. Until we meet again. Maybe I'll take you to your first Yankee game!"

Shameeq chuckled.

"Maybe."

Tony stood up, then to Lo he said, "I'll call you in about an hour or so."

Lo nodded, then Tony looked at Nya and bowed slightly.

"It was nice to be in your presence."

"Maybe I'll see you again. Soon," Nya smiled.

Tony didn't want to reply to that, so he left on that note. Shameeq was vexed. He grabbed her by the arm.

"Let's go," he gritted.

"I haven't finished my drink," she replied slyly.

Shameeq took the drink from her hand and poured it on the floor. "Now you are."

After he paid the tab, he, Lo and Nya walked across the street to the underground parking lot. Shameeq handed Nya the keys.

"Wait in the car."

She wanted to say something, but she knew he was upset. Besides, she was already satisfied with the fact she had gotten under his skin. She took the keys and walked away.

"What up wit' yo' shorty, young?" Lo questioned.

"Bitch like to play games," Shameeq replied.

"Ay, yo, I appreciate the position you put me in," Lo smirked. "You ain't even had to carry it like that and put a nigguh on so strong. That's love, young," Lo told him, giving him dap.

"If I fuck wit' you, I fucks wit' you, straight up. The God only deal in equality, whether in reward or in punishment, you know what I'm sayin'?"

"Yeah, young, but speakin' of punishment, what up wit' that shit from the other night? You find out anything?"

Shameeq grinned. "All you got to do is feed the streets dollars 'til they start makin' sense, you know? Them nigguhs 'bout to feel the wrath of God!" Shameeq laughed and gave Lo dap. "But yo, B, go handle your business. I got you across the board."

"Same here, young."

"That's what it is then. Peace."

They parted ways, and Shameeq got in the Benz. Nya had Sade's "Love is Stronger than Pride" playing. Shameeq turned the music off and grilled her.

"Yo, the fuck is wrong wit' you?! I tell this nigguh you my girl, and you play me like that?! I should break your fuckin' neck!" Shameeq huffed.

"I didn't tell you to tell him I was your *girl*. *You* said it. I told you it's strictly business between us! Period!!" Nya shot back.

"Oh, word?! Well, until we do business again, get the fuck out my car!" Shameeq barked. He hated to show any emotions, but Nya had a way of getting under his skin that he hated.

"What?!"

"You heard me. Get the fuck out," he hissed, starting the engine and leaning back in his seat.

Nya studied the side of his face for a moment, heated. "You know what, Shameeq, you're an asshole! Fuck you!"

"Bitch, breeze," he spat back smoothly.

"Gladly," she replied, fumbling with the door, then throwing it open. "I'll have a ride in seconds! Fuck you!"

Nya slammed the door and stormed away. Shameeq put the car in reverse and threw his arm over the passenger's seat. As he backed out of the parking space, he saw Nya approach a black dude coming out of the restaurant. Shameeq watched her as she subtly flirted her way into the passenger's side of the Lincoln the dude was driving. As the dude opened the door for her, their eyes met over the roof of the Lincoln. She rolled her eyes and got in.

Shameeq was boiling, but he didn't know what he was more angry about: the fact she was getting in another man's car or the fact that he even gave a fuck. He quickly drove up behind the Lincoln. The dude had to put on the brakes to keep from hitting the Benz.

Shameeq jumped out and went around to the passenger's side and knocked on the window.

"Yo, get out the fuckin' car!" he growled.

"No! Move your car so I can go!" Nya shouted through the closed window.

Shameeq tried the door, but it was locked. He bent down and looked at the driver. "Ay, yo, my man, unlock the door for me."

The driver looked at Nya wide-eyed.

"Don't look at her, look at me. Open the fuckin' *door*," Shameeq said calmly, but punctuated his statement by hitting the window.

"Hey, man, I don't want any problems," the driver said.

"Then open the fuckin' door!" Shameeq barked. "Nya, open the fuckin' door!"

"Go to hell!" Nya screamed.

"You want me to call the police?" the driver asked, picking up his car phone.

"No!" Nya and Shameeq yelled at the same time.

"Open the goddamn door!"

"Okay!" Nya huffed and got out.

"Are you going to be okay?" the driver leaned over and asked.

Shameeq leaned down. "Fuck you mean? Of course she okay! Fuck outta here!" he said, then slammed the door.

He turned to Nya and snatched her to face him. "You tryin' to make me crazy?!"

"I should ask you the same thing!" Nya yelled in his face.

"Why you keep playin' these games?!" he yelled right back in hers.

"No, Shameeq, it's you that's playing games now. I told you there were no more games with me!" She took a breath. "Look, Shameeq, I understand that you feel I got the best of you in the beginning, okay?! It's a dirty game, and you're the big boy. Get over it! I did it when I thought you were someone else, just like you thought I was someone else. Why can't you get past that? Because I'm trying to show you who I really am now!" Nya explained.

Shameeq shook his head.

"First impressions."

"First impressions? If I went by first impressions, I'd still think you were lame, green and naïve," she smirked.

"Lame?!" Shameeq growled, then he thought back to his school-boy façade. First he smiled, then looked at her and chuckled. Then he laughed, "Okay, you got that."

Nya laughed.

"Straight sucka," she said, trying to sound street.

The dude blew his horn, and Shameeq looked back with a scowl.

"Let's just go," Nya said, touching his arm.

They got in the Benz and pulled off.

??????

I won't pretend that I intend to stop living. I won't pretend that I'm good at forgiving, but I can't hate you, though I have tried I still really want you Love is stronger than pride.

Sade's CD played on the surround-sound system in Nya's spacious bedroom as Shameeq awoke the next morning. Nya was asleep with her head on his chest and her legs thrown over him.

He glanced down at her sleeping face and thought about what she had said the night before. She had assessed the situation perfectly. His pride remained unmoved. She had tricked him once, and he wasn't about to give her another chance. No matter how much he was feeling her, his emotions were still at odds, because every thug needs a lady, not just a bevy of bitches or a clique of chicks. Sherrie was good to him but not good for him. Her passivity was no challenge. Nya, on the other hand, was the steel that sharpens steel. The only problem was she cut both ways.

His beeper broke his train of thought. He picked it up off the nightstand and saw YaYa's code. He grabbed the cordless and dialed the number.

"Peace," Shameeq greeted when YaYa picked up on the first ring.

"Knowledge, knowledge. Where you?" YaYa asked, smoking a Newport.

"In VA Beach. What's the science?" Shameeq answered and asked.

"Red rum, God," YaYa informed him, using the code red rum because it was "murder" spelled backwards.

"For past transgressions?" Shameeq probed, referring to the attempted hit at the dog fight.

"Indeed," YaYa confirmed, "so meet me at the spot in an hour."

"Say no more."

Shameeq hung up.

"You gotta go, huh? " Nya said, still lying on his chest.

"Every closed eye ain't sleep, huh?" Shameeq cracked.

"That's what they say," Nya replied, pecking him on his lips, then sitting up. "Good morning."

"More like good afternoon, love. It's damn near one o'clock," Shameeq said, putting on his boxers.

"Great sex'll do that to you," Nya snickered and stretched.

She watched for a moment as he got dressed, then said, "You know what our problem is?"

"What?"

"We're too much alike. We're both used to being in control," Nya surmised, wrapping her arms around her quilt-covered knees. Shameeq sat on the side of the bed, putting on his Timberlands.

"Oh, yeah? So how do we solve it?"

"By going with the flow, accepting each other for who we are. I know you're young and not ready for anything ... serious. Maybe I'm not either. But I know I like being with you," Nya said.

"I like being with you too," Shameeq replied.

So let's not jeopardize it. All I ask is don't make me second to anyone, and I won't make you second. And—" Nya suggested, but Shameeq cut her off.

"What you mean I won't be second? I'm the *only*," he responded firmly.

"Come on, Shameeq, let's be mature about this. If you're not going to be monogamous, how can you expect me to be? I'm trying to compromise here. Everything can't be your way all the time," Nya quipped.

Shameeq pulled his Polo rugby over his head.

"Whatever, yo," he mumbled.

"Look, we're both going to do what we want to anyway. I just wanted to be up front about it and lay some type of boundary."

"Just don't let me catch you doin' it," he warned her.

She ignored his last comment and drew closer to him.

"And because you didn't let me finish, hear me out. I've told you things I've never told *anyone*. Things ... I didn't even freely admit to myself," she began, then took a deep breath. "You know I can't have children, Shameeq, and why. It's something I really wish I could do, so if you did ... it would really ... hurt me. No matter what you do, all I ask is that you don't have any children on me. Please," she stressed, and Shameeq could see the potential pain in her eyes.

He caressed her cheek to assuage her fears and replied, "Love, this ain't the type of life I would bring a seed into, you know. So that's something you definitely don't have to worry about," he assured her.

Nya searched his eyes until satisfied, then lowered hers and said, "Okay, I'll trust you, Shameeq."

He kissed her on the forehead.

"I gotta go. I'll hit you later."

She watched him walk out with the trust she prayed he'd never break.

CHAPTER 17

You down wit' OPP?!

Shameeq drove along Atlantic Avenue with the sounds of a new group called Naughty by Nature on 103 Jamz. He had to chuckle to himself at how the group had flipped a local saying into a national anthem. OPP really stood for Oval Park Posse, a crew in East Orange, New Jersey. At parties, they used to yell, "You down wit' OPP?!" Everyone would respond, "Yeah you know me!"

Naughty by Nature, who used to be called New Style, had changed it and made millions.

His car phone rang, and the system lowered itself.

"Peace," he spoke, picking up the phone.

"Hey, baby. How are you? I've been beepin' you all night. Are you okay?" Sherrie questioned.

"Yeah, I'm peace, love. I was just caught up, that's all," he replied, knowing he was fucking Nya when Sherrie was blowing up his pager.

"So when are you comin' home?" she probed.

"Soon."

"Oh."

Shameeq could tell she wanted to say more, but she wasn't raised to question her man. A strange thought went through his mind: the words "it's a thin line between love and hate." But he quickly brushed it off because he knew she didn't have the nerve to hurt him.

"Real soon, baby girl. And then we'll do something nice, a'ight? I promise."

Her voice brightened.

"Okay, baby, I love you," she sang.

"I know you do. Peace."

Shameeq hung up the phone, silently cursing himself. He knew he wasn't shit when it came to chicks, and Sherrie was a good girl.

Fuck it, it's a cold world. She gotta learn sometime, he thought to himself.

He arrived at YaYa's condo in the cut out in Chesapeake. He pulled his car into the back parking lot where YaYa parked his car so no one would know exactly where he lived. But he didn't see YaYa's Porsche. He got out anyway and took the back way to YaYa's apartment and knocked on the back door. Trello opened it.

"What up, B," Shameeq greeted with a gangsta's hug.

"Chillin'."

"Where Ya?"

"On the couch."

Shameeq walked in to find YaYa in a dope nod on the couch. "King of New York" played on the big screen, watching YaYa instead of the other way around.

Shameeq hit his leg, then sat in the armchair.

"Nigguh, get yo' dope-fiend ass up," Shameeq growled.

"Fuck you," YaYa hissed, raising his eyelids to half staff.

"Where your car?"

"Fuck you mean, where my car? Parked out front. Where else?" YaYa retorted.

"You slippin', B. Word to the mother, this shit bigger than dog food, God," Shameeq warned him.

"Ain't nobody slippin'," YaYa replied, scratching his leg. "Them muhfuckas ain't cut to bring it to the God," YaYa bragged.

"Fuck you mean?! They brought it to me!"

YaYa sucked his teeth and smirked.

"That's cause you getting soft, B! You on some pass the Grey Poupon shit!"

Shameeq snickered.

"Get the fuck outta here, B. Nigguh, don't forget *I'm* the live wire in the crew," Shameeq shot back. "Why you think them nigguhs started callin' us *Drama's* Squad?"

"You just the face nigguhs remember, I'm the shadow nigguhs fear," YaYa boasted, messing with his nose.

"Whatever, yo. What up wit' what you talkin' about?" Shameeq questioned.

YaYa sat up slowly and took a Newport out of the box on the table.

"Local nigguhs, B," he began, then lit his cigarette. "They was eatin' wit' Don, and now they ain't got a pot to piss in. Shit wasn't planned, that's why it was so sloppy. They just saw you and tried to nod you on the spot," YaYa explained.

Shameeq nodded, his temperature rising with the heat of revenge.

"So where they at?"

"Tonight they be at this pool room. Yo, Trel, what's the name of that shit?"

"Eight Ball," Trello answered, watching "King of New York."

"Yeah, yeah, Eight Ball. It's in Bad News."

"Then that's what is it then," Shameeq confirmed, ready to get it right then. "But you still slippin', God. We in a whole new tax bracket. We ain't usin' money machines no more; we just weighin' money—a million dollars in fifties is twenty pounds. Do the math! And we ain't got no room for errors! Do the knowledge, God, and you'll understand what I speak. Be right and exact," Shameeq told him.

"I'm all eye-seeing supreme being. I'm sharper sleep than most nigguhs wide awake!" YaYa barked, blowing smoke.

"You know why them Cali nigguhs call police 'one time'? 'Cause we can get away a thousand times, but it only takes them one time," Shameeq jeweled him.

"Whatever, B. We ain't in Cali," YaYa mumbled.

Shameeq just shook his head.

??????

Officially, the pool room closed at midnight. At 12:01, the after-hours gambling spot unofficially opened. The place was run by an old coon named Lester who always kept his ear to the street. He was the one who schooled Montez on who the guys were that tried to kill Drama. Montez, YaYa, Shameeq and Trello parked around the corner, then came to the back door all the gamblers used. Lester looked out the peephole, then let the four men in.

Inside, there were about eight dudes gathered around the pool table, using it as a defacto craps table. Short money was scattered about the table. The major gamblers only came on selected nights, and no one else was getting in at that time.

As soon as they entered, Lester let them know who they were looking for with a simple head nod. One was holding the dice. When the other one looked up and saw Shameeq, he went for his gun, but it was too late. Shameeq put three .40-caliber slugs in his chest, literally lifting dude onto the pool table behind him.

The rest of the crowd instantly put up their hands. Shameeq put the gun in the dude's face holding the dice and instantly remembered him as the dude he locked eyes with right before they tried to kill him.

"Remember me?" Shameeq sneered sinisterly.

The dude took the cigarette from his mouth and replied calmly, "Yeah, stic, you got the drop. Do what you came to do, 'cause I ain't beggin' nobody but Jesus."

Shameeq smiled.

"Least you ain't go out like no sucker. You shoulda just came and hollered at me. I coulda used a trooper like you," Shameeq remarked.

The dude took a long pull of his cigarette. "Fuck it, what's done is done."

"True."

Boom! Boom! The hollow points entered his forehead and blew the back of his head all over the mouth of the dude standing next to him. Luckily, the gruesome sight made him faint, therefore he didn't even feel the two Trello put in his temple as the whole crew opened fire, gunning all eight dudes down.

When Montez turned the gun on him, Lester hollered, "Young blood, don't do it! I'm on your side!"

"Nigguh, if you'll tell on them, you'll tell on us!" Montez spat coldly, punctuating his statement with three in Lester's chest, center mass.

The massacre spread through the seven cities like wildfire. Because the New York beef had been handled so quickly and quietly, nigguhs had to test the Drama Squad's gangster. The answer they received let the streets know that the Drama Squad wasn't to be fucked with.

??????

Present Day 1994

"See, nigguhs ain't know how we moved down here and laid our shit down so easy. All of a sudden, it was Drama Squad this and Drama Squad that. So a few muhfuckas got it in their head to see how we was cut," he explained. "But once they saw that our hammer game was real, nigguhs fell back. Of course, we had a few lil' beefs here and there, but nigguhs knew we played for keeps."

"I'm sure the Newport News police will be happy to finally close that case," Jacobs quipped.

"Tell me more about the operation in DC. We weren't aware that Drama Squad had a base there," McGrady inquired.

"Well, we did and we didn't," he answered, "because ultimately Tony handled DC."

"I thought you said the guy Lo was your man in DC," Mullins said.

He smiled.

"He was ... until Tony killed him. We didn't know it at the time, of course, but Tony was a C.I. with the feds. He got Lo out the way to get closer to us."

Jacobs' eyes got wide. He looked at McGrady, McGrady looked at Mullins, and Mullins glared at him.

"So the feds are already involved," Jacobs noted, looking at Mullins.

"And you're absolutely sure that Nya Braswell met with Tony?" Mullins wanted to know.

"I'm sure of everything I'm tellin' you," he assured.

"Where is this Tony?" Jacobs asked.

He shrugged.

"Your guess is as good as mine," he lied.

Mullins picked up a pen.

"Describe him."

"I don't know—he's dark skin, curly hair and has a fetish for fat women," he quipped.

Mullins put the pen down, frustrated.

"What's his last name?"

He leaned his elbows on the table and pulled the last cigarette from the pack. "Last name? I don't even know if Tony is his real *first* name."

Jacobs grunted, then Mullins turned to Jacobs and said, "Run the name Tony. I know, I know, you'll get a million Tonys. Check New York and DC and—"

"Don't forget Virginia," he quipped with a grin.

Mullins shot him a look.

Query New York, DC and Virginia. Cross-reference it," Mullins instructed McGrady. "That should narrow it down."

Jacobs nodded and walked out.

"Why the hell didn't you just tell us who the informant was when we asked earlier?" Jacobs asked, exasperated.

"Because if I did, then you'd want to know how we met him, where he came from and all that. Then I'd have told you the same story I've been tellin'," he snickered. "Besides, it isn't important—or is it?"

"Just keep talkin' and save the wise cracks," Mullins warned him. "Did Braswell ever directly supply Tony or in any way have any other dealings with him?"

He lit his cigarette, French-inhaled, then replied, "He did, but she didn't know it—not until it was too late. That's why we're sitting here now. Tony knew exactly who it is that Nya herself must answer to."

"Who?" Jacobs asked intently.

"Hold on tight 'cause this is where it gets deep," he told them, blowing the smoke in the air.

??????

1990

For the next eighteen months, the name Drama Squad spread throughout the Dirty South to Ohio in the Midwest to Delaware. Richard was pleased with how quickly they moved product and how organized the Drama Squad ran their operations. Drama and his main team no longer had to touch any weight, and by keeping their hands clean, they kept their connect clean too. They still stayed close to the streets through more legitimate means. YaYa opened up a chain of hair salons while Montez got into flipping houses.

Blue started promoting concerts and turned Peanut on to the music business, which was just becoming lucrative in urban America. Peanut also started moving Motorola flip phones, known as burnouts on the street because they chipped and turned on illegally. It was a time when nobody on the street really had cell phones, so there was opportunity everywhere. Egypt even put her brief college education to work by opening up a few clubs in North Carolina. Shameeq and Nya took a few more trips to Macau to snatch up prime real estate to prepare for the property boom about to hit the region.

Their relationship remained a power struggle between equals. They got closer despite being so much alike—manipulative and conniving. Their love-hate thing became the yin and yang of their relationship.

Everything was going smoothly for the Drama Squad except two things: Lo was killed at the Ibex in DC, and Lil' B's murder charge and subsequent trial. These seemingly isolated incidents would be woven together to help unravel the reign of the Drama Squad.

??????

"Yes, we have, your honor. We find Bernard Cross not guilty of all charges."

"Nooooo! He killed my baby!"

"Murderer!"

"Order! Order in the court!"

The judge banged his gavel as the family members of the deceased broke out in tears and anger. One of the young males even lunged at Lil' B and had to be restrained by a bailiff.

Lil' B was unfazed.

"Come on, playboy, don't do that in front of the police. You know exactly where to find me," Lil' B smiled and winked.

The only people there with Lil' B were his girl and his mother. Of course, Nya was his attorney.

"Relax, Bernard, you've won. Let them have their grief," Nya told him.

He hugged his mother, then tongue-kissed his girl. Then he turned and shook Nya's hand.

"Oh, what? I'm not family too?" Nya quipped with open arms.

"Hell, yeah," Lil' B replied, anxious to wrap his arms around the delicious vixen.

Nya whispered in his ear.

"Shameeq sends his love. He's arranged a big block party for you, so act surprised when we get there."

Lil' B pulled away and smiled.

"Then let's get outta here, so I can get out of this monkey suit," he commented as he loosened his tie and unbuttoned the jacket of his Armani suit.

They walked out as the grieving family members huddled in agony, praying for justice in the next life since it had been denied in this one.

Tidewater projects was alive with music pumping from the Buddha Brothers' gigantic sound system and the happy sounds of children. The Drama Squad had done it up big to celebrate the return of one of the crew's top bosses. They had eight grills going, keeping the food and drink flowing, and the Buddha Brothers had come to provide the sounds. They even had pony rides and a moon bounce for the kids. Sneakers and bikes were being given out like candy, as were cash prizes for the parents.

Lil' B, his mother and his girl pulled up in his Cadillac. Nya followed in the Jag. They all got out as Big B of the Buddha Brothers announced, "The man of the hour has arrived! Welcome home, B! I repeat, not guilty!" The crowd cheered his return as DJ Law threw on "Time for Sum Akshun" by Redman. The crew welcomed him home with hugs and pounds, glad to see their man free.

"What's up, my nigguh?!" Montez greeted, hugging Lil' B.

"What up, Tez?"

Montez looked at Nya and eyed her up and down.

"What's up, Miss Braswell? You a regular Perry Mason, huh? I hope I don't ever catch a charge, but if I do, will you get me off?" Montez quipped playfully, wiggling his eyebrows.

Nya snickered.

"Montez, you're too much," she said, looking around until she spotted Shameeq. He was standing near the pony ride, talking to three chicks. Montez followed her eyes and saw Shameeq. He started to call to him, but Nya covered his mouth.

"Uh-uh, you better not," she warned playfully. "I got this," she said as she strutted away.

Montez whistled admiringly. "Lawd ha' mercy! You damn sho' do!" he said, thickening his country grammar.

"Yeah?" Shameeq chuckled. "You can do all that? Well, check—" he began to say, but Nya stepped in front of him and put her tongue down his throat.

Three girls looked her up and down like, No, she didn't! Nya broke the kiss, arms still around Shameeq's neck, looked over her shoulder and said, "Run along, girls—Mommy's here."

She turned back to Shameeq as the three girls walked off, rolling their eyes and sucking their teeth.

"Damn, love, I was just about to put my mack down," Shameeq joked.

"Oh, really? Well put it on me," Nya flirted.

"A'ight, well, check—why don't we get up outta here and—"

"Sorry, not interested," Nya said, then started to walk away.

Shameeq grabbed her around the waist and picked her up. "Not interested? Girl, I'll take that pussy."

"Hmmmmm ... I like that," she replied as he kissed her again.

"You're beautiful, you know that?" Shameeq said, looking into her eyes. It was moments like this that Shameeq's and Nya's energy really connected, but they always seemed fleeting because they were always interrupted.

"Yo, Drama, your girl did it! She ate that shit!" Lil' B remarked as he approached.

Shameeq put Nya down and gave his man a hug and a pound.

"Did you ever doubt it? You think we would spend all this money to welcome you home if we wasn't sure?" Shameeq chuckled.

"No doubt, stic."

"But yo, you know the police gonna catch feelings 'cause you beat a body. So you might need to lay low," Shameeq suggested.

"Shit, I'm two steps ahead of you, playboy. Me and my girl 'bout to go on a long-ass vacation," Lil' B chuckled. "Barbados, Aruba, then we goin' to Cancun. My youngins can hold it down for a while," he told Shameeq.

Shameeq nodded.

"Well, if we don't get going, we'll miss our celebration vacation," Nya reminded Shameeq.

"I'm ready whenever you are," Shameeq told her.

He dapped Lil' B, then he and Nya headed for the Jag. She tossed him the keys as they neared the car.

"Ay, Yo! Montez!" Shameeq called out.

They both looked up. Shameeq smiled and gave them the finger.

"Yeah, fuck you too, nigguh! I hope your boat sink!" YaYa yelled back.

"And I hope you can't swim!" Montez added, laughing.

Shameeq laughed as he pulled off.

"I like that you guys are so close," Nya commented.

"Yeah, that's my family there. I'd die for them nigguhs," Shameeq told her sincerely.

"Wow. I've never had friends like that," Nya replied wistfully.

Shameeq looked at her.

"You do now."

Shameeq's cell phone rang. He reached in his pocket and flipped it open.

"Peace."

"Peace. What's the word on Lil' B?" Egypt asked as she drove down highway 85 North.

"What you think? He now God," he replied cryptically, using the supreme alphabet to answer her. Translation: not guilty—now meaning "not," and God meaning "guilty."

"Hell yeah! Where he at? Tell him I'm on my way," she replied.

"I just left. I'm 'bout to go on a cruise."

Egypt sucked her teeth.

"Damn, Meeq. I had somebody I wanted you to meet," Egypt whined.

"Who? Your man?" Shameeq asked with a scowl.

"No, stupid, this nigguh named Biggie Smalls."

"Biggie Smalls? Who the fuck is that?"

"Yo, Meeq, I'm tellin' you, dude is nice. He an emcee. That's why I'm late, 'cause he had a lil' crack charge, so I lifted him. I met him in Raleigh. He wit' me now," Egypt explained.

"An emcee? Fuck I wanna meet an emcee for?" Shameeq questioned.

"Yo, Biggie," Egypt said, "kick somethin' for my brother."

Egypt handed him the phone. "What up, God," Biggie said, breathing heavily.

"Peace. You God body?" Shameeq questioned.

"Naw, but I'm from Brooklyn, yo. That's close enough," Biggie replied.

Shameeq laughed. He like the dude's sense of humor.

"My sister said you nice," Shameeq said.

"The nicest. Check it," Biggie responded, then hit a freestyle.

"Yeah, B, I like that," Shameeq said, bobbing his head.

Egypt got back on the phone.

"What I tell you? He fuck wit' some kid named Puffy that fuck wit' Mary J. Blige and Jodeci. He 'bout to do his own thing. I'm tellin' you, God, the music business gonna be the next crack game," Egypt snickered.

"Maybe. I'ma hit you when I get back and we'll talk. Peace."

"Peace."

"Who was that?" Nya asked.

"Egypt."

Before she could reply, Shameeq's phone rang again.

"Peace."

"Shameeq," Sherrie sobbed, "I ... I—"

Shameeq sat up in the seat. "Sherrie, what up? What's wrong?"

Hearing Sherrie's name, Nya's ears perked up.

"It's my mother," Sherrie cried. "She ... she had a stroke." She broke down in tears.

"Just calm down, love. Where are you?" he asked intently.

Nya was boiling because Shameeq called Sherrie love, just like he did. To him, it was just an expression he used with females, but since Nya had only heard him use it with her, her temper flared.

"At work. I want to go to the hospital, but I can't drive. I'm shaking like a leaf. I don't know what to do."

Shameeq looked at his watch and sighed. He knew he should go to Sherrie, but he knew Nya would be pissed. They'd definitely miss the flight to Florida, from where the boat was leaving. He decided to go to Sherrie.

"A'ight look, I'll be there in a minute, okay? Just chill, love. I got you, okay?" he told her in his most comforting voice.

He hung up and could feel Nya looking at him.

"Yo, Nya, I—"

"No."

He looked at her.

"Ma, this shit is important," he stressed.

"I don't *care*, Shameeq. What we're doing is important too. Or have you forgot?" she shot back.

Shameeq sighed hard.

"Look, love, I—"

"*Don't*," Nya gritted, "call me that anymore."

"Okay, *Nya*, her mother is in the hospital. She had a stroke," Shameeq tried to explain.

"So? I don't care!"

"How you not gonna care about her mother?! That shit cold-blooded!"

"Because I don't know her mother, Shameeq! People die every day! I'm supposed to put *my* life on hold every time?" Nya ranted.

"You not makin' no sense right now, a'ight? Actin' like a fuckin' spoiled brat. I already gave shorty my word I was comin'," he replied.

"And you gave *me* your word that I wouldn't be second!" Nya accused.

"How is this puttin' you second? It's a fuckin' emergency! Fuck! I can't see the future!!" he barked.

"Why not? Aren't you supposed to be God?" she quipped sarcastically.

He glared at her.

"Don't play wit' me, Nya."

"You promised me, Shameeq!"

"I ain't puttin' you second!"

Then your word is meaningless because you *broke* it," she said, folding her arms across her chest and looking straight ahead.

"Fuck you mean, it's meaningless?! My shit is bond! I ain't puttin' you second, and you ain't gonna twist my words to fit your tantrum!" he huffed.

"Meaningless," she repeated, still not looking at him.

"Whatever."

When they got to Payless Shoe Source, where Sherrie worked as a manager, Shameeq hopped out of the car.

"I'll call you, a'ight," he said.

Nya slid over under the wheel.

"I won't be there. I got an itch to scratch," she smirked.

"Get yours, love," Shameeq smirked then walked away.

??????

CHAPTER 18

When he and Sherrie got to the hospital, she was allowed in the room, but he wasn't. He stayed in the waiting room until Sherrie came back out fifteen minutes later. Shameeq stood up.

"How is she?"

Sherrie sat down, so Shameeq did too.

"Not good," she replied, her eyes red and puffy. "She's resting. The doctor gave her a sedative."

"How are you?" he asked with concern, holding her hand.

"I don't know. It's just ... this is her third stroke."

"Third?" Shameeq echoed in shock.

Sherrie nodded.

"What is it? Is it her diet? Does it run in the family?" Shameeq probed.

Sherrie looked him in the eyes.

"It's my father. He and mama been married almost thirty years, and I don't think a year's gone by that he hasn't ... had somebody else," Sherrie explained

Shameeq shook his head but didn't speak. How could he? It would only be calling the kettle black.

"Don't get me wrong, he's a good provider for all his kids. I have six sisters and eight brothers, but only four are by my mother. I ... I don't hate my father; I just don't understand him. How can a man say he loves you and still hurt you so bad?" she asked.

He caressed her cheek.

"Baby girl, marriage is a deep commitment, a bond. If it was me, I would honor it, but it's not me, so I can't answer that."

"It's killing her, Shameeq," Sherrie said, tears streaking her cheeks. "Little by little, she's dying of a broken heart," she sobbed as Shameeq hugged her to his chest. "I don't want to be like that,

Shameeq. I don't want to be just another girl to you," Sherrie told him.

"You're my baby girl," he told her truthfully.

She sat up and looked in his eyes.

"No, you don't understand, Shameeq. I don't want to be just another girl to you because ... because I'm pregnant, Shameeq. I'm having our baby," she told, searching his eyes for his true reaction. She wasn't disappointed when she saw them light up.

"A baby?" he asked, smiling.

She nodded, watching him intently.

"Baby girl, sun, moon and star. You my moon and your radiance reflects the light of the sun," he jeweled her, pointing to himself. He touched her belly and added, "And together we give birth to the stars."

Sherrie had been around Shameeq long enough to understand his words. A woman (moon) reflected the light of her man (sun) if he was right and exact. The star (child) was a manifestation of the sun, which is only a star itself.

She threw her arms around him and whispered, "Thank you."

But the way she said it, he knew she wasn't talking to him.

The light in his eyes began to cloud as he thought about Nya's words. He had heard somewhere that when a child is born, someone dies. He hoped that the birth of his seed wouldn't be the demise of his run.

??????

When they got home, Shameeq ran Sherrie a hot bath, then he went in the kitchen and set about fixing her a steak dinner, with sautéed onions and mushrooms. Shameeq was a good cook even though he didn't do it that much. He just wanted to let Sherrie know how special she was, if only for one night.

After her bath, he toweled her off and rubbed her down in her favorite scented oil. While she ate, Shameeq massaged her feet while Jodeci played in the background.

So you're having my baby

And it means so much to me
It's nothing more precious
Than to raise a family

After she ate, Shameeq made a meal of her. He started at the ball of her foot and ran his tongue along the arch of her foot until he got to her toes. He nibbled her ankle until she began to purr her approval.

"Mmmm, baby, that feels so good," she moaned as he worked his way up to her inner thigh.

He cocked her legs back and let them rest on his shoulders. He pulled back the hood of her clit and sucked it gently, then applied more pressure. Her pussy was soaking wet, and her legs began to tremble.

"Sha—" she gasped, "I'm cummin', baby. Oohhhh!" she squealed as her milky juices ran out her pussy and coated his lips and tongue. He spread her pussy lips and began tongue fucking her until she came again.

"Please, baby, put it in. I need to feel you now," Sherrie panted, urging him inside of her.

Shameeq slid the head of his thick dick in her pussy, then pulled it out. He slid it in again, then pulled it out. Sherrie's pussy was on fire.

"Stop teasing me, baby, and give me that," she begged, but this feeling of being penetrated over and over again made her pussy twitch and explode. This time Shameeq slid all nine inches inside her in one thrust, taking her breath away.

"Wh--what are you doing to me?" she squealed as Shameeq long-stroked her and sucked and pulled her nipples with his lips.

"Anything you want me to," Shameeq crooned.

Sherrie wrapped her legs high around Shameeq's back, arched her back and met him thrust for thrust.

It felt so good tears of ecstasy ran down her cheeks. It felt like he was loving her forever. Shameeq gripped her under her ass, spreading her pussy with his fingers, dicking deeper and deeper into her wet, juicy pussy.

"Oh, I love you, I love you. I love you so much," she panted.

Shameeq sat up and put both her legs to one side.

"Show daddy you can take this dick," Shameeq grunted.

"I--I can--I can take it," Sherrie moaned, throwing the pussy at him harder.

Shameeq pounded her pussy until he came hard deep inside her.

While Sherrie slept, Shameeq flipped on the TV to check the Knicks' score. He and Blue had a bet on the Knicks-Bulls game. He turned on the news and heard, "A naval officer, John Denny, was arrested on six counts of child molestation and possession of child pornography. He was arrested in a small hotel outside of Nor—"

Shameeq turned the channel in disgust. "Punk muhfuckas. All them fuckin' faggots need to burn."

He flipped the channels until he found ESPN. His phone rang. He walked over to the table, keeping one eye on the screen as he grabbed the phone.

"Peace."

He heard the blare of music in the background.

"Yo," he shouted.

"Can you hear me? This is Tony!" Tony yelled back, heading for the bathroom. When he got inside, he asked, "Is that better?"

"Indeed. What up?" Shameeq replied as the sportscaster began to run highlights of the Knicks-Bulls game.

"Yo, Drama, you still wit' that chick? The lawyer?" Tony asked.

"Yeah, something like that," he mumbled watching Jordan slam over Starks.

"Yo, my man, I hate to tell you, but I just saw her! I'm at The Metro Club, and she's out on the floor with guys all over her."

Shameeq forgot all about the game.

"What you just say?"

"Two guys, mi amigo, and no disrespect, but she's acting like a real puta, know what I mean?" Tony told him.

Shameeq was heated. He couldn't stand the thought of another man touching Nya, let alone two!

"Yo, Drama, you still there, man?" Tony said.

"Yeah."

"You want me to do something?"

"Naw," Shameeq said. Then he thought about it. This was the perfect opportunity to show her how wide his net spread. Never mind it was just coincidence, he planned on using it to his advantage, like he knew her every move. "Yeah. Matter of fact, watch her. If she leaves wit' anybody, follow her. When they get where they're going ... "

He let his voice trail off, but his tone was unmistakable.

"Her too?" Tony probed, shocked.

"Naw, just the dude or dudes. Leave 'em at the go-go," he smirked, remembering Lo's expression for killing somebody.

"No problem, man. I take care of that for you," Tony assured him.

"And, Tony ... I won't forget it," Shameeq said, then hung up.

"I'm sure you won't," Tony smiled to himself.

He knew this was his opportunity to get even closer to Drama. He was already handling most of DC for him. He had Lo killed for that very reason. He knew taking care of this personal issue for Shameeq would endear him to his heart.

The moment he saw Nya, he was on her. She had on a brownish wig, but it didn't fool Tony. The eyes never changed. At first, he was going to push up on her, remembering how she had flirted with him, but when he saw how she approached the two men, he saw a golden opportunity.

He sat nursing his drink for the next fifteen minutes, until he saw how freaky the trio was getting. His dick was hard watching one dude with his hand up Nya's tiny mini skirt and the way she was gripping the other dude's dick. They made their way to the front door, and Tony was close behind them. He called Shameeq.

"Peace."

"You on it?"

"Like a blanket, amigo," Tony replied. "Hold up."

He watched as they neared Nya's limo. Apparently, her phone rang, because Nya went into her clutch to get it. Then she put it to her ear. Her body language changed. She looked around, then hung up. She turned to the two dudes and said something. They seemed to protest, but she got in the limo.

"Yo, she got a call and like—I don't know, she musta changed her mind, because she's leaving alone," Tony informed him.

"Follow her," Shameeq told him.

"Si."

Tony hurried to his car and followed the limo. He followed her down Missouri Avenue until she made a right on South Dakota Avenue, a right on Rhode Island Avenue and a left on 18th Street.

"She just stopped at an alley at Langdon Park," Tony told him.

"Langdon Park," Shameeq echoed. "Somebody in the limo wit' her or something?"

"Not that I can see. Nobody got in with her."

Nya pulled over in the parking area where a dark sedan was sitting near a streetlight. Tony pulled over and turned off his headlights.

"She just pulled over. There's a car ... hold up ... she just got out. The driver of the other car is getting out."

"Who is it?" Shameeq wanted to know. His street instincts were telling him she wasn't there to fuck in the park.

"It's ... mi dios, poppi, it's some white guy," Tony replied in confusion. "What's she doin' meetin' in the park for?"

"Can you—"

"Oh, shit! Drama!"

"What?!"

"He just smacked the shit out of her! He did it again! Now he's barkin' on her, and she's crying," Tony told him.

Shameeq's mind was on full alert.

"Can you see the license plate?"

"Yeah, sure, it's Kay, Larry, Cat, Alpha 6, 1—hold up ... 6, 1—I can't make out the last number," Tony squinted.

Shameeq wrote down KLCA-61.

"I'll try and get closer."

"Don't let 'em see you."

Tony let the car inch up without the headlights. Nya and the man were deep in their conversation, but the man looked up in Tony's direction.

"Oh, shit, he's lookin!"

Tony threw on his high beams, so the man couldn't see the car. As he drove past, Nya tried to look inside the car.

"Got it, poppi!" Tony said as he sped off. "It's a 9!"

Shameeq wrote it down.

KLCA-619

He smiled to himself, then said, "Okay, Tony, that's good lookin' out. Peace."

Nya apprehensively watched the car disappear. She didn't know who it was, but she could see clearly that it was a BMW. Just the expensive type of car drug dealers drove. Dealers like the Drama Squad.

??????

The next morning Nya called Shameeq bright and early.

"We have to talk."

"About?" Shameeq questioned, half sleep, but on point.

"Meet me at the pier in one hour."

Click.

??????

He drove to Virginia Beach and arrived at the pier where they always met. The sky was overcast, and the waves were crashing with the fury of a pending storm. He saw Nya was standing at the end of the pier with her back to him. She was leaning on the rail and looking at the ocean.

As he approached, he studied her figure, wondering how someone so beautiful could be so dirty. People are never who they seem. When he heard her, she turned around. She was wearing Chanel sunglasses, a simple jogging suit and no makeup.

"You have to kill Richard," she told him, stone-faced.

Shameeq just looked at her, then replied, "Come here."

"What? Shameeq, this is no time for—"

He cut her off by gently pulling her to him and wrapping his arms around her. At first, she thought he was huggin' her, and she started to protest, but then she realized it wasn't a hug at all—he was searching her for a wire.

"Shameeq, what are you doing?

"Shhh," he said softly, but the coldness in his eyes never left her face.

He felt under her breasts and slid his hands in her jogging pants and felt around her ass and thighs.

He had to smile to himself because he felt how wet his touch made her.

When he concluded the search, he stepped back and said, "Okay, let's walk."

"Shameeq, do you really think I'd set you up?" Nya asked.

"Yeah, I do. Now walk," he told her as he grabbed her arm.

As they walked, he asked, "Now what the hell are you talkin' about?"

"Richard has to go. Something's happened, so long as he lives, we're all in danger," she replied.

They walked down onto the beach. There were a few people there, so they walked a little farther down.

"Now tell me, what's going on?" Shameeq wanted to know.

"I just did."

"No, *what* happened?"

Nya sighed.

"A guy got busted yesterday, some kind of child porn ring. A Navy guy," Nya began as Shameeq remembered the story from the news. "The guy is Richard's boyfriend."

"Boyfriend?" Shameeq echoed. "Richard's a faggot?"

Nya nodded.

"Yes, he's gay."

"I still don't see the connection."

Nya sighed.

"Richard was bringing it down through the shipyards. His boyfriend was a Navy officer that had access and could get clearance to make sure it got off the boat and into Richard's hands. Now, with this porn thing hanging over his head—that'll look like peanuts compared to this," Nya informed him.

The picture was becoming clearer to Shameeq. All the pieces were starting to fit together.

"So it's over. The connect is dead either way, huh?" Shameeq surmised.

Nya nodded.

"I told you the game doesn't last forever."

"What about the Navy cat? Red rum? Him too?" Shameeq probed.

"Rather be safe than sorry," Nya replied.

Shameeq thought about the situation and came to the same conclusion. If the Navy cat rolled over on Richard, Richard would roll over on Shameeq. That was how the dominos were designed to fall. He may've been the low man on the totem pole, but he was still on the pole nonetheless.

"I thought you were just his lawyer?" Shameeq probed.

"I laundered his money. Same thing I do for you," she reminded him, still not telling him the full story.

"Okay, cool. Where Richard rest? What's his routine? I'll send a team at him today," Shameeq suggested.

Nya chuckled.

"The man's ex-military, and he moves hundreds of kilos a week. You think he's just a sitting duck? No, it has to be more personal, more intimate. He's still teaching you how to drive the boat, right?"

"Yeah."

"You can do it then. He trusts you. He won't see it coming," Nya surmised.

Shameeq shook his head.

"It's always the one you trust, huh? Makes you wonder whether you should trust anybody anymore," Shameeq commented.

Nya looked out at the crashing waves.

"Maybe it's easier that way."

"What happened to your face?" Shameeq asked as if he didn't already know.

She touched her reddened cheek and looked at him.

"I told you, I had an itch to scratch. It just got a little rough," she grinned.

"Was it good?" he quipped.

"The best," she retorted.

"Better than this?" he asked, pulling her to him and sliding his tongue into her mouth.

She resisted at first, but the waves of pleasure drowned her objections as Shameeq's tongue caressed hers. She loved the way Shameeq held her, like she belonged to him and only him, no matter what she did.

He pulled away and asked, "Well?"

"You don't even come close," she lied.

Shameeq laughed, "Yeah? That ain't what your body sayin'."

She narrowed her eyes to slits.

I hate you," she hissed.

"Then I guess I'm that nigguh you love to hate!" he quipped with a chuckle, making Nya smile as well. She hated that he knew her so well. She could hide everything from him except her true emotions.

For Shameeq's part, he knew killing Richard was only the beginning of the end. Once Richard was gone, Shameeq would be another loose end, but he didn't intend to be clipped. He knew the hand that reddened Nya's cheek would be the hand coming for his throat. Shameeq was in bed with the enemy, but he had to keep her close in order to figure out a way to get them before they got him.

??????

Yeah, B, that's deep right there," YaYa commented as they rode through Portsmouth. He took a deep pull of the Newport, then thunked the ashes in the ashtray. "So," he said, blowing out the smoke, "it's all over, huh?"

"Yeah," Shameeq replied as they drove through the night, "for the connect it is, but the game is just beginning. Somebody cleanin' shop, and ain't no doubt in my mind we on the list."

"So fuck it, if we dead the bitch, we cut all ties and be out," YaYa surmised.

"Naw, God, I told you about the cracka in the park. I *know* he know who we are, but we don't know who he is. We got an invisible enemy, and Nya our only way to solve the equation of who he is," Shameeq explained.

"True. So what we gonna do? Ain't no way we just gonna sit and wait for them to move," YaYa said, thunking his cigarette out the window.

"Hell no. We gonna move first. Startin' wit' Richard. He gonna tell us what we need to know," Shameeq nodded.

"Why he gonna talk? He a dead man walkin'. How you gonna get him to talk? You 'posed to dead him, so it ain't like you can threaten to kill him," YaYa responded.

"Indeed, but he want his lil' boyfriend to live. That I know. Faggot muhfucka gonna sing like Liberace if I tell him I'll give his man a pass," Shameeq grinned.

"But," YaYa interjected, "what if it's all a setup? What if shorty sendin' *you* into a death trap and *you* really the hit?" he reasoned.

Shameeq shrugged.

"Could be, but it's a chance we gotta take. Richard is the only one that can give us answers."

"Naw, shorty could too. Snatch her ass up and *make* her talk," YaYa growled.

"Naw, Ya, that won't' work. She fear the truth more than she fear death," he replied, remembering the look in her eyes on the balcony before he scooped her up. She was ready to let go.

"You sure?" YaYa asked.

"Of course, I'm sure. I saw it."

"Naw, God, I mean, are you sure that's the real reason you don't want to dead her?" YaYa smirked. "Or is it 'cause you open on her?"

Shameeq looked at him and frowned.

"Fuck you mean, open?"

YaYa laughed.

"Nigguh, don't gimme that gorilla shit. I know you, Meeq. This chick ain't like the rest. You can't break her like you want, and you stuck."

Shameeq hissed.

"Fuck outta here."

"A'ight, if you say so," YaYa shrugged. "Just put your bond on it, that if we gotta dead her, you'll pull the trigger."

Shameeq looked at him again, steel in his eyes.

"Word is bond, if it come to that, she dead," he vowed, hoping in his heart it wouldn't come to that.

CHAPTER 19

Two days later, Shameeq went to the docks for his weekly boating lesson. He had fallen in love with Richard's yacht and wanted one himself, so Richard took him under his wing. Shameeq had come to enjoy the little conversations they had each week because Richard had been around the world in the Navy and had a worldly wisdom Shameeq respected. But Shameeq never suspected him of being a closet homosexual.

"Mornin', Shameeq," Richard greeted, the morning mist hovering over the water.

Shameeq saw he wasn't his usual relaxed self. It was only a little after six in the morning, but by that time, Richard would already be a little tipsy. Today, he was stone sober and aloof. Shameeq thought about what YaYa's said: What if it's all a setup?

That thought put Shameeq's senses on point as he boarded the yacht.

"What up, Rich? No drinks this mornin'? What, you been to an AA meetin' or somethin?" Shameeq joked, trying to feel Richard out.

Richard grinned half-heartedly and replied, "Just been a long time since I've really seen an ocean morning, you know? I used to really enjoy them. I guess I'm feelin' a little nostalgic. You want to do the honors?" Richard offered, referring to the operation console of the boat.

"Naw," Shameeq replied casually, keeping a close eye on Richard. "You take the first leg."

Richard shrugged and cast off. The engine roared to life as he guided the boat out the docks.

I've been thinking about what you said concerning the nation of Gods and earth vision of creation," Richard said over his shoulder.

"Yeah?"

"Yes, and I find it very similar to a philosophy called existentialism. Have you ever heard of it?"

"Naw, can't say that I have. Add on, though," Shameeq answered, easing his gun from his waist and concealing it behind his leg.

"It was espoused by a French philosopher—Satre was his name—and it basically says that man wasn't created for a purpose. He must find that himself, find his own reason for existence, and basically create himself," Richard explained.

"I agree with that," Shameeq nodded. "I, self-lord and master, am the master of my own destiny."

"Are you?" Richard smirked and turned to Shameeq.

They were out in the middle of the Atlantic, a breathtaking panorama all around them. "Is man truly in control?"

"The wise and intelligent are," Shameeq answered.

"A man, any man, even one wise and intelligent, decides to go to the store. Three other men, equally wise, decide to do the same. They each get into their cars and head for the same store from different directions—north, south, east and west. The traffic light at this intersection is broken, so they all see green. Thinking they all have the right of way, they proceed into a four-car, head-on collision. Now," Richard smirked, "were they masters of their destiny or simply the victim of someone else's?"

Shameeq thought about the question, but from the look in Richard's eyes, he was using the story as a metaphor for the current situation.

"A man can't think for others," Shameeq replied.

"No," Richard admitted, looking down wistfully, "and that's a shame because the decisions of others affect us directly. It's the butterfly effect. It's why we are here right now: to do what has to be done."

Shameeq rested his gun on his side so Richard could see it. From the way he talked, he knew Richard had seen it coming, so Shameeq prepared himself for any sudden moves.

"I assume you've talked to Nya?" Richard asked.

"Yeah, Rich, we talked."

Richard nodded, then looked out at the sea he loved so much. "It was stupid. I told him ... told him too much was at stake. But like you said, you can't think for others." He looked at Shameeq and smiled, "You've come a long way since we first met, and I've grown to like you. You're smart, I'll give you that. But so far, Nya's smarter."

"How you figure that?" Shameeq asked, his pride slightly bruised.

"Don't be offended, Shameeq, Nya's smarter than a lot of people, including me. You see, I knew this was coming. I didn't run or hide because a captain always goes down with his ship. It went bad under my watch. I take responsibility, but I also knew it would be you to do it."

"Why? I dead you, Nya dead me? It ain't gonna happen," Shameeq gritted.

"Maybe. Or maybe she's got the sheriff waiting at the docks for your return. Then she's killed two birds with one stone," Richard surmised.

"I'd rather go out guns blazin' for some shit I did instead of being caught in a maze I ain't create. I like choices, Rich, and I have one for you."

"Which is?"

"John."

Richard stared at him intently.

"He knows no one but me," Richard stressed. "If he rolls over, it'll only be on my grave, no one else's, so you're safe."

Shameeq could tell Richard wanted to save John, just like Shameeq knew he would.

"But I'd rather be *safer* than sorry. Nya wants him dead too. Do you love him, Rich?"

"Yes. Yes, I do," Richard said, his eyes pleading.

"My word is bond. Tell me what you know, and John gets a pass," Shameeq offered.

Richard searched Shameeq's eyes for deceit, then looked down at the floor. Finally, he looked at the slight drizzle that was beginning to fall.

"In 1981, Omar Torrijos's plane crashed. He was the dictator of Panama. The official report was engine failure, but the truth was," he said, shaking his head, "America wanted Norega to take over Panama. It was all Cold War shit. It was a dance with the devil based on good intentions. They used the Navy to get the drugs in. I got caught up in it."

"So where does Nya fit in?" Shameeq asked. "She CIA? Fed?"

"No, neither. And as to where she fits in, right at the top. I work for Nya," Richard told him.

Shameeq's mind was on topspin. All this time she had him thinking it was Richard, but the whole time Shameeq had really been working for her! He had to give her props, but he was determined to beat her even if he couldn't break her.

"I saw Nya meeting some white dude in DC, in Langdon Park. Who is he?" Shameeq said as lightening flashed overhead, followed by a boom of thunder.

"That, my friend, I can't tell you," Richard answered.

"Then you won't be holding your end of the deal," Shameeq warned.

"You asked me to tell you what I know. Nya in the park is something I *don't*," Richard reminded.

"Answer the question."

"You gave your word, Shameeq! I've told all I can. Not even John's life is worth the rest."

"You love him, remember? His fate is in my hands," Shameeq retorted.

"Yes, I do. But there's something I cherish more: my secrets. If I expose them, they'll expose me, dead or alive. That is my own priority," Richard told him defiantly. "You're smart, Shameeq. The answer is right in front of your face."

"Enlighten me."

"I've already told you. I was the one taking it off the ships. Ask yourself who puts it on," Richard grinned, then looked out at the ocean. "I'd like to ... smell the sea air once more, if I may."

Shameeq followed Richard out to the aft of the boat. Richard stood at the rail and took a deep breath. The rain drenched them as Shameeq raised the gun.

"Shameeq?"

"Yeah?"

Shameeq cocked the hammer.

"When you talk to Nya ... tell her I'll see her in hell."

Boom!

The blast of the gun rippled through the air and blended with the boom of the thunder. Richard's body fell to the deck, lifeless.

Shameeq quickly weighted the body, then dumped the corpse overboard. He took control of the vessel and guided it to the dock in Elizabeth City, ready for any surprises. His team awaited him as he got off, and they set fire to the yacht.

As he drove away, his mind was reeling. He was definitely trapped in a maze, one that meant freedom or death, and his mind was focused on finding a way out.

??????

Laborfest was to Virginia Beach what spring break was to Daytona Beach. It was the place to be. College kids, hustlers, entertainers, sack chasers and wannabes flocked to VA Beach every year to be a part of the orgy of sex, music, drugs, and money. If you came to stunt and floss, you'd better come correct, because Atlantic Avenue looks like a fashion and car show.

The Drama Squad had Laborfest on lock. Everywhere you looked, the crew was out in full force. In the years they had Virginia, the Squad had grown from five to more than five hundred. Everybody wanted to rep Drama Squad.

"Yo! What the fuck?! Yo, Trello, look at your man!" Montez laughed, pointing.

Trello looked to see what Montez was laughing at. He saw big Blue, shirtless, with two big-ass Cuban links around his neck and a girl under each arm rubbing his belly.

"Yo, Blue! You lookin' just like a goddamn beached whale!" Montez called out, laughing.

"You ain't heard?!" Blue called back. "Biggie put us fat black nigguhs in! Baby baby!"

While Montez was joking, Egypt, Sherrie and two chicks from Elizabeth City sat in beach chairs, chilling. Egypt was getting her flirt on.

"What's up wit' him? Sherrie, you ain't gonna tell me he ain't fine," Egypt remarked and her two yes-girls agreed.

"He okay. Just not fine as my baby," Sherrie replied.

"Girl, stop it. Just 'cause you wit' my brother, I ain't gonna tell shit. Everybody got eyes. What's up, daddy? How you?" Egypt called out to a cinnabrown dude with curly hair and hazel eyes.

He came over, smiling.

"What's your name, cutie?" Egypt flirted.

"M--m--m--my n--n--name is—" the dude stuttered.

"Huh? Oh, hell no! Keep it movin'," Egypt said as she and her girls laughed.

"B--b--b—"

"No, l--l--l--later," Egypt mimicked him.

"F--f--f--fuck you, b--b--b—"

"Yeah, whatever, write it down next time," Egypt said, waving him off.

The dude wanted to spaz, but Shameeq walked up, so he kept it moving.

"Now that's what I'm talkin' about," Sherrie remarked, looking him up and down. "What's your name?"

"Him? Please, girl, he ain't all that," Egypt joked.

"Hey, Drama," the two girls said in broken unison, eyeing him hard in his wife beater and jean shorts, showing off his chiseled his frame and bow legs.

"Peace," he replied, not even looking at the two girls he had already run through. He was focused on Sherrie.

"How you, baby girl? It ain't too hot out here for you, is it?" Shameeq asked with concern, squatting down beside her.

"No, I'm fine," Sherrie answered.

"You sure?"

"Damn, Meeq, she ain't made of glass; she ain't gonna break. Now, breeze. You're scaring the nigguhs away," Egypt huffed, shooing him with her hand.

A dude walked by looking at Egypt. Shameeq turned to him. "Don't fuck wit' that, B. She really a man."

Egypt tried to kick Shameeq in his nuts, but he backed up, laughing.

"It's big as mine!" he yelled.

Egypt got up and swung on him, but he weaved and jogged off.

"I hate your stupid ass, Shameeq! Get on my damn nerves. I'ma fuck you up when I catch you!" Egypt yelled.

"Yo, Shameeq! Shameeq!"

Shameeq turned in the direction of the voice and saw Sincere approaching him. When they met, he gave him a gangsta hug and a pound.

"Peace, God," Sincere greeted.

"Peace, peace," Shameeq replied. "I'm glad you made it."

"Shit, ain't no way I'ma miss a gatherin' of the power u!" he joked, the letter "u" meaning pussy.

Shameeq laughed.

Over the years, he and Sincere had built a respectable rapport. They weren't friends, but they were friendly. Their bond was based on money. Sincere saw more money with Shameeq than he had ever seen with Don, and in return, he made Shameeq richer. Fair exchange ain't no robbery.

"Word to mother God, I brought some shit down here that be havin' the chicks on fire," Sincere exclaimed.

"Word?"

Sincere nodded.

"X."

"X?"

"Ecstasy pills, yo. Muhfuckas in the hood ain't up on 'em yet, but I'm tellin' you, that shit have 'em all touchy feely and shit. I got my coat pulled to the shit by them freaky-ass college girls in Ohio. They turned me on to the connect outta Canada. X go for like fifteen, twenty a pill, and I get 'em for seven," Sincere chuckled. "I'm killin' them crackas!"

Shameeq laughed. "Word? I might hafta check that shit out."

"Indeed. I'm 'bout ready to come see you on that too," Sincere said.

Shameeq hadn't told anybody that the well had run dry. Once he ran out, the team was closing up shop.

"Whenever you ready."

"Poppi! Como estas, huh?" Tony called out as he approached with a couple of bad-ass Latina chicks in string bikinis. Ass and titties everywhere.

Shameeq turned to him and shook his hand.

"Peace, Tony. I would ask how you doin', but I see—better than me!" Shameeq joked, referring to the chicks.

"What's this? Te gusta? You like? Pick one," Tony offered.

"Naw, I'm good. Enjoy yourself."

"You sure? Just say the word. Anything for you, my friend," Tony replied.

"Maybe later, B," Shameeq humored him.

"Cool, cool. But check it, I need to speak with you real soon," Tony said, and Shameeq knew what he was talking about.

"I'll hit you before I leave."

Tony nodded, then looked from chick to chick. "Let's go."

Sincere watched Tony as he walked away. He had been scrutinizing Tony the whole time he was standing there. Tony didn't notice, but Shameeq did.

"Yo, God, what you say his name was?"

"Tony. Why? What up?"

Sincere scowled.

"Where you meet em?"

"DC. Why, you know him?" Shameeq questioned.

"I don't know," Sincere said slowly, "but my man Mark was fuckin' with a Puerto Rican Tony in Richmond when he got knocked. I mean, Tony is a common name, but it's a small world, you know? You might need a nigguh to pour you a drink about son," Sincere suggested.

A couple of girls in bikinis sashayed by, flirting with their eyes. One had a camera.

"Pardon me, love, is that your camera?" Shameeq inquired smoothly.

"Yes," she chimed.

Shameeq pulled out a knot of money and peeled off five hundred-dollar bills. "Is it for sale?" he smiled.

"It is now," the girl greedily replied.

They exchange money for the camera, then she asked, "You need anything else?"

"Naw," Shameeq replied dismissively, without looking at her.

"'Preciate the camera, though. Yo, Tony! Tony!"

Tony looked back. Shameeq and Sincere caught up with him.

"What's up, poppi?"

"Yo, seein' these chicks from the back, goddamn! I know my man in the joint would love this shit," Shameeq gamed.

"No problem, Drama."

Shameeq handed the camera to Sincere, and the girls stood with their asses to the camera around Shameeq. "Naw, yo, take it wit' me."

"I ain't really the picture type," Tony replied.

"Come on, amigo, for me," Shameeq winked.

Tony relented and got in the picture reluctantly. Sincere snapped the picture, then Tony and the girls walked away. Sincere handed him back the camera.

"Good lookin' on that, God," Shameeq said.

"Nigguhs got the game fucked up. You just never know," Sincere shrugged.

"But about that X connect, I'm tellin' you, yo, it's the fuckin' future. Let me know, and we'll set something up."

"Let me think about it, and we'll holler later," Shameeq replied.

But later would never come. Sincere went back to Ohio the next day. Two weeks later, he was gunned down in Brooklyn.

??????

Shameeq called Peanut and found out where he was. When Shameeq got there, Peanut was redlining on his green and black Honda CBR 900. Shameeq watched and smiled. Peanut had come a long way. He was the baby of the Squad, but he had his head on right, putting his dope money into the music game.

When Shameeq walked up, chicks were all around Peanut. One dude stood with him. Shameeq gave him dap.

"What up, Lil' Nut. What's the science?" Shameeq greeted.

"Bullshittin', kickin' it wit' my man. Meet the next Teddy Riley, my nigguh Timbaland. Tim, this Drama," Peanut introduced.

"What up, B? How you?" Shameeq said, shaking his hand.

"What up, Drama? I heard a lot about you," Timbaland replied.

"Word, stic, this my secret weapon," Peanut boasted. "He gonna make me the next Russell Simmons!"

Shameeq laughed.

"Do your thing, God. But yo, I need to holla at you."

Peanut climbed off the bike, then he and Drama walked out of earshot.

"What up, stic?"

"You still fuck wit' them Richmond nigguhs?" Shameeq asked.

"Yeah and no. I got a studio up there now, so I let my man get his hands dirty mostly," Peanut answered.

Shameeq handed him the camera.

"A'ight, look, it's a flick in here of me and this Spanish cat named Tony. Take it up there and let nigguhs see it. Let me know how muhfuckas respond," Shameeq explained.

"When you need it?"

"ASAP!"

"I'm on it today then, stic. What up wit' this Tony nigguh?" Peanut asked.

"That's what I need to know," Shameeq replied.

"Let me drop my bike off, and I'll shoot up there now."

Two days later, the results were in. Tony had indeed been hustling in Richmond a few years ago, and the two dudes he messed with had both gotten popped by the feds. No one knew for sure, but Shameeq smelled a rat.

"Yo, Drama."

"What up?"

"Yeah, stic. The muhfucka sour, straight up. He fucked wit' some cat named Chill and another nigguh named Mark. Both of 'em got busted and doin' dinosaur numbers. Tony disappeared without a trace."

"Good look, Nut. Peace."

Click.

All the pieces of the puzzle swirled around in his head, unconnected. He thought about what Richard had told him, Nya in the park with that guy and how Tony was probably informant. Shameeq didn't know what was going on, but he knew he had to figure it out, and he had to move first, before he got moved on.

With that phone call, Shameeq began to formulate his next move, and he knew exactly where to start: with Nya.

??????

Shameeq knocked on Nya's office door.

"Come in," he heard.

He entered to find Nya with a lit white candle on her desk. The candle holder was an ivory angel. She was blankly looking at the flickering flame and the melting wax.

"You okay, love?" Shameeq asked.

She nodded, then without looking at him, replied "This is the day my mother died. She was a devout Catholic, so I do this for her."

Shameeq studied her for a moment.

"You miss her a lot, don't you?"

Nya looked at him.

"Yes, I do," she answered honestly.

She got up and set the candle in the window, carefully. She turned back to Shameeq. He coughed into his hand and sniffed.

"Flu season," he commented. "I'm out, Nya. I just came to say, good-bye."

"I see," Nya replied, holding back her emotions. "Just like that? Why so sudden?"

She couldn't just let him leave. Regardless of how she felt for him, there was too much at stake. He had to be dealt with.

"All good things must come to an end. I guess this the end," Shameeq shrugged nonchalantly.

"Are you talking about us or the situation?" Nya probed.

Shameeq chuckled.

"Come on, Nya, you know like I do that we were never good for each other. I couldn't break you, and you can't break me. I give you your props, though."

"So I'll never see you again?"

"Maybe, in Macau," he winked, referring to the location of his real estate investments, "beyond the golden key."

Nya lowered her eyes and laughed lightly while silently cursing fate. Why did it have to end like this? She was preparing to drop a dime on him for Richard's death, so she knew he might run, but he couldn't hide once he was convicted, and then her problems would be solved. But why? He was right—he couldn't break her because she had long been broken. Her ability to separate feeling from emotion had desensitized her totally. But the fact remained, Shameeq was the only man who could handle her, and maybe in some disconnected way, even love her. But now, it would end before it ever really started.

He coughed again, harder.

"Besides," he began, "it's getting too hot around here."

"Hot?" she echoed.

He nodded.

"We got a problem: a member of the team is snitchin'," he told her.

"Who? Are you sure?" she asked, attention undivided.

"There was an incident in DC recently, right after the club," Shameeq explained.

Nya listened, totally unaware of what was coming next.

"They were followed into Langdon Park, where they met with some old white muhfucka," Shameeq told her, never losing eye contact. Nya didn't blink, but her heart began to beat faster. Her mind raced with thoughts. She flashed back to the park, the headlights, the car that sped by. Inside, she stressed, but her composure stayed calm.

Shameeq just eyed her, admiring how good a poker face she had. He waited for her reply, but when she didn't say anything, he said, "You gonna tell me who you were talkin' to that night, Nya?"

"Me?!" she echoed, feigning Oscar-worthy shock. "What the hell are you talkin' about?! I'm a snitch?!" she laughed in his face. He patiently waited for her laughter to die down because he knew he was holding all the cards, and that would force her to show her hand.

Shameeq shrugged.

"I don't expect you to be honest, Nya. That's why I got the license plate and had it run. You know what came back, don't you, love?" Shameeq grinned, toying with her.

"No, why don't you tell me ... love," Nya quipped.

He left her dangling and didn't answer the question. Instead, he said, "But you ain't know who I was talkin' about when I said someone was snitchin'. It's one of three people, and the problem is they were all together the night they seen you," Shameeq lied, baiting her. "And that's a problem—not for me, though, for you."

"You're in this just as deep as I am, Shameeq!" Nya shot back, her facade of total detachment cracking ever so slightly.

Now it was Shameeq's turn to laugh.

"That's not what Richard says, boss," he winked, trying to totally push her buttons. "Richard's dead because *that* was my problem as much as yours, but John? To me, he's not a threat. So me and Richard made a deal. I keep John alive, and he'd tell me the *whole* story!" Shameeq told her truthfully.

He had kept his word and gave John a pass, but he had John tucked away so Nya couldn't send someone else at him.

"You're a fool, Shameeq. You don't think John knows who you are, what you do?"

"From what Richard told me, I'm small, peanuts compared to Panama. The Navy and tons of Panamanian coca," Shameeq replied. He leaned on her desk and looked her in the eyes. "So I figure if the snitch saw you, and we both know he did, then he can identify who it was with you. Then, if I tell him what Rich told me, and give him John?" Shameeq paused for effect, then whistled. "Soon they'll have a come up wit' a new charge for a queenpin."

"Then you're a snitch too, a *rat*," she hissed.

He shrugged.

"Call it what you want, but I'm on my way to meet all three now. I'll know the snitch because he'll be the one wearin' a wire. So the next move's on you, Nya. If I go down, you goin' too."

He slowly straightened up. "But if it wasn't you in the park and Rich lied, then you won, and you ain't got nothin' to worry about, right?" he smirked.

Shameeq turned for the door.

"Shameeq."

He looked back.

"If I were you, I'd forget what I *think* I know and forget about Virginia. I can guarantee Virginia will forget about you," Nya said with a solemn expression on her face.

"Why? So you can play your trump card whenever you get ready? Naw, love, you may have a helluva poker face, but I'm callin' your bluff. I'm getting out this game, period, or we all gonna do a very long time in the box. I can handle mine. Can you?" Shameeq taunted. He held his gaze a moment longer, then walked out.

He called YaYa as he walked down the hallway. "You there yet?" he said as he walked past the secretary. "Naw, Ya, I said the Thomas Café, downtown Norfolk. We on our way now. Peace."

He hung up and exited the office.

A few moments later, Nya came out, putting on her sunglasses.

"Hold all my calls," Nya told her.

"But, Ms. Braswell, you're due in court at—"

Nya cut her off sternly.

"I said hold my calls. I have something to take care of."

"Can you be reached via the Thomas Café or by cell?" the secretary asked innocently.

Nya stopped short.

"Where?"

"The Thomas Café in Norfolk. You are meeting Jamal there, right? He told someone on the phone that he was on his way," she said.

A smile spread across Nya's face.

"Just hold my calls."

As she walked out, she made a call of her own.

"We had a problem, but it just solved itself," she smiled.

CHAPTER 20

When Shameeq arrived at the restaurant, he saw Blue's Blazer parked outside. He had already told Blue and YaYa to go to DC and pick up Tony. They were to arrive unexpected and tell him it's urgent and make sure he made no phone calls. En route, Shameeq had called Tony and told him, "Shit is about to blow, yo, it's deep! Fuckin' shit was comin' in through the Navy! I'll school you when you get here!"

He wanted to pique Tony's interest but keep him isolated so he couldn't contact the feds. Shameeq needed a three-man decoy, so he chose YaYa and Blue, the two that were closest to him in rank and stature. He had to make the deal look sweet.

Shameeq walked in and greeted all three of them at the table, one by one as they stood. When he got to YaYa, he gave him a gangsta hug just as he did the other two, but he whispered, "I love you, nigguh."

YaYa seemed a little perplexed by the timing of the statement, almost like Shameeq was saying good-bye.

"I gotta go to the bathroom," Shameeq told them. "Y'all nigguhs order me some fish, rice and cabbage. Make sure it ain't cooked in pork," he said, as he walked away.

"Stic, this the South! Ery'thing pork!" Blue chuckled.

"Everything except what's on my plate!" Shameeq yelled back.

YaYa curiously watched Shameeq walk away. He could sense something was up.

Shameeq turned the corner and saw the bathroom doors and the kitchen door. He walked right past the bathrooms and entered the kitchen. The chefs and preps looked up, their eyes wide. Shameeq tossed a hundred-dollar bill on the table.

"Just chill, I'm just lookin' for the back door," Shameeq said.

Both cooks pointed.

"Good look," Shameeq replied, then he was out.

Shameeq had parked down the street, so he took the back block, then rounded the corner to his car. As he got in, he saw the two unmarked cars skid up in front of the restaurant. A few minutes later, three agents, all with D.E.A. across the back of their jackets, walk YaYa, Blue and Tony out in handcuffs. He saw YaYa's scowl as he looked up and down for him. As they pulled off, Shameeq smiled to himself as he headed the other way.

Shameeq went out to Elizabeth City to see Egypt. He found her posted up at a basketball court with her girls. Casper was on the court balling. Egypt was sitting on the hood of her brand-new white Acura Legend. When Shameeq approached, the three girls walked off to let them talk. He tried to kiss Egypt, but she moved. "Don't be kissin' on me, boy. You already got me sick," she sniffed.

"Shit, YaYa gave it to me. But peep the science and let me pour you a drink on some shit," Shameeq replied.

Shameeq explained the whole situation to Egypt, leaving out nothing from the day they set foot in Virginia, so she could understand his reasons for doing what he intended to do.

"Do what?! Shameeq, that's crazy! Don't!" Egypt exclaimed, totally shocked to hear what he was saying.

"Egypt, this the only way," Shameeq replied. "Shit is deep, so we *gotta* go to 'em."

Egypt shook her head. "This is crazy. Shameeq, you know how muhfuckas gonna look at it. They gonna look at it like—"

He cut her off firmly.

"You think I give a fuck about how it look?! I told you, I don't give a fuck about being a legend or nothin' else, all I care about is surviving'! I got a seed on the way, and I'ma be there for him no matter what! The God gonna look out for his!" he vowed.

Egypt sighed.

"Shameeq, you're my brother and I love you. You know I'ma hold you down regardless. I'm just sayin', what if you're wrong?"

He smirked.

"I'm not."

Egypt looked at the court, at the glistening bodies of black men at play.

"What about Casper?"

"Nobody needs to know besides me and you. You hold your end down. You understand the whole situation, so you equipped. Don't worry about my end. I'll handle the dirty work," he winked.

Egypt hugged his neck tightly.

"I love you, boy. I got you. Win or lose, I got you," Egypt vowed.

Shameeq kissed her cheek, then walked away.

??????

"Peace, queen."

"Peace, king. What's wrong? I can hear it in your voice."

"I'm good, Sherrie. I need you to empty the stash and meet my peoples in Elizabeth City.

"Shameeq, what's going on?"

"Ma, don't ask questions. Just do as I say, okay? I'll get at you as soon as I can.

"O-okay, Shameeq, I will. I love you."

"I know."

Click.

??????

CHAPTER 21

Two hours later, Drama pulled up in front of the federal MCI building in Norfolk and parked. Drama looked up at the dull gray building as he got out, then broke into a fit of coughs that made him spit a glob of mucous on the sidewalk. Drama really wanted to throw up, not being able to stomach what had to be done.

Drama walked inside, approached the registration desk and said, "I'm Drama. I'm here to see the D.E.A. about the Drama Squad."

The thing about jail is, somehow, some way, word of anything big spreads like wildfire. No matter what happens, an inmate knows. In this case, it was a trustee janitor who saw Drama being escorted into an interrogation room, uncuffed. The janitor knew his face. He also knew that if he was uncuffed, he hadn't been arrested; therefore, he had come on his own, voluntarily. That could only mean one thing. The janitor told another employee who worked in the kitchen, who told another janitor from another floor, who told the run man in YaYa and Blue's pod. The run man spread the word throughout the pod, until it reached the ears of a dude who knew and respected Blue. The dude headed to Blue's cell, where he and YaYa were talking.

When he came to the door, they both looked up. "Yo," the dude began slowly, "I don't know how to tell you this, stic, but the word is that the nigguh downstairs talkin' to the D.E.A. is ... Drama."

YaYa shot to his feet.

"What?!" he snapped.

The dude held up his hands in a don't-shoot-the-messenger tone said, "Yo, I'm just tellin' you what muhfuckas sayin'."

"Who's sayin'? How they know?" Blue asked.

"Somebody downstairs seen him come in uncuffed and goin' in the back wit' three agents," the dude explained.

"That's bullshit!" YaYa barked. "Who the fuck said they seen my man!"

He walked out and looked around the dorm. He looked at all the sly smirks and whispers. He turned back to Blue. "Gimme the bangas!" he said.

"Yo, Ya, let that go. These muhfuckas don't know what they talkin' about. Fuckin' prison rumors," Blue answered calmly.

"Gimme the goddamn bangas," YaYa gritted.

Blue sighed and shook his head, then went under his mattress and handed YaYa a short ice-pick like weapon made of sharpened steel.

"Gimme two," YaYa hissed.

"Ya, what the fuck you tryin' to do, get a murder beef too?! The D.E.A. ain't got shit! Son, chill!' Blue huffed.

"Blue!"

Blue reached back under the mattress and handed YaYa a second shank, almost identical to the first. Blue grabbed a shank wrapped with electrical tape and a wickedly jagged piece of steel." I'ma get the chair fuckin' wit' you," Blue growled.

YaYa stepped in the middle of the pod, shanks in both hands and barked, "The next muhfucka I hear speakin' blasphemy against the God gonna die where he stand! Who want it?! Who?! Bitch-ass nigguhs, talk now!"

A few dudes diverted their eyes and a few even went in their cells and locked themselves in. No one picked up the challenge. The real gangstas didn't feel offended because they weren't the type to gossip. Those who did were pussy anyway. YaYa looked at a group of four dudes grilling him. He stepped to them.

"Fuck you, fuck you, fuck you and fuck you!" YaYa spat, then dropped one of the shanks at their feet and stepped back. "There you go, get it off your chest.

"Yo, God, I don't want no problem," one said.

"YaYa looked from face to face and none dared to meet his stare. Satisfied, he slowly scooped the shank off the floor and walked away. Blue stayed in position, grilling the dorm as Ya went in his cell and slammed the door.

He tucked both shanks in his waistline and braced himself against the wall with his hands on either side of the mirror as he looked in it.

"It ain't no way ... ain't no fuckin' way," he mumbled to himself, looking into his own eyes.

But his mind was saying something else. His mind was remembering Shameeq's words at the restaurant. "I love you, nigguh." Why did he say that then? In that tone? And where did he go when the D.E.A. came in? How did they know they were there? Because Shameeq told you to meet him there, his mind answered.

"Naw," he said, shaking his head, turning away from his own reflection. He sat on the bed with his head in his hands. His anger formed a picture of Nya in his mind. He knew Shameeq was open on her, without doubt. Had she turned him? Had he chosen her over nigguhs he bled, sweated and pissed tears with?

YaYa stood up and paced the room. He had known Shameeq since they were ditty-bopping through Mary Mcleod Bethune Middle School. They went so far back that if it wasn't for Shameeq, he'd still be on heroin. The thought of how he kicked it brought a smile to his face.

Shameeq had been telling YaYa he was slipping. Now that YaYa was getting more money, he was sniffing more and more. He claimed he could handle it, until one day he got caught slipping at a traffic light. He was boxed in between two vehicles, a van in the front and a car in the back. The masked gunmen snatched his door open and put the gauge up to his cheek.

"Breathe too deep, you die," the one holding the twelve-gauge hissed.

They snatched YaYa out of his car and tossed him in the back of the van. They took him way out in the country, and the next thing YaYa knew, he was being taken inside a small home. They put him down in a small, airy, damp basement. The only thing in the room besides card boxes and the sound of rats scurrying to and fro was him.

"Your man got twenty-four hours to make the deal or you a dead man," one gunman hissed, then they left and dead-bolted the door. YaYa searched the room top to bottom for some type of opening—a window, a small door or even a large crack— to no avail. He was trapped in every sense of the word.

Twenty-four hours turned into forty-eight, and he was still in the basement. They tried to feed him, but he refused, not only because he didn't trust them but because he couldn't keep anything on his stomach. Withdrawals were kicking his ass. He threw up everything he had eaten recently until he dry heaved. He was sweating and suffering from cold chills, sending waves through his body. He shook uncontrollably. He had no sense of time, but he knew it had been longer than twenty-four hours. Where was the Squad? Had they decided not to pay the ransom? Had they left him for dead? The thought made him angry, and his anger strengthened him. He refused to show weakness. When his captors offered him food, he spat at them. "Fuck you, pussy-ass nigguhs! You better kill me now, or I'ma kill your goddamn mothers and gut your fuckin' kids!" he told them.

Physically, he was weak, but his spirit was strong.

As time passed, his withdrawal receded, and he passed the time by reciting the 120, 120 Lessons of the Nation of The Gods and Earth that Originated with the Nation of Islam.

"Who is the original man? The original man is the Asiatic black man. The maker, the owner, the cream of the planet Earth, father of the civil Nation, God of the Universe," he read. "Who is the colored man? The colored man is the Caucasian (white man) or Yacub's grafted devil of the planet Earth. Then why did God make the devil?"

After seven days, one gunman came in and stood over YaYa's listless body. He lay on the floor peacefully. He had only drunk water and eaten very little food, so he was physically weak, but his mind was still sharp.

"It's time," the gunman said.

"Then get it over with," YaYa hissed with no fear of death.

The gunman walked out, and Shameeq walked in. The stench hit him in the face and almost made him throw up.

YaYa shielded his eyes from the light emanating through the open door and squinted at the figure before him. He thought he was seeing things.

"Shameeq?"

"Indeed, God. How you?"

"Yo? How the fuck? That nigguh that just walked out ... he—"

"I know. I told him to."

"What?!" YaYa barked weakly.

"What's the number of God?"

"Seven." This is the seventh day you been here, underground. Like a coffin," Shameeq explained. "What's the science of physical death?"

"One returns to the essence."

"Then what is the true resurrection?""

"A mental resurrection, from the way of the savage, the deaf, dumb and blind, to the realization of your true self that we be divine."

"And who are you?"

"The maker, the owner, the cream of the planet earth, the father of civilization, God of the universe."

"Show and prove."

And then, YaYa knew what it had all been about. No one can save us but ourselves, so Shameeq had pushed YaYa into a situation where he had to do just that.

YaYa struggled to his feet. Shameeq made no attempt to help him until YaYa, almost erect, stumbled. Shameeq caught him.

"You look like shit, Ya," Shameeq chuckled.

"Fuck you," YaYa grinned. "I respect what you did, but when I get my weight back up, I'ma beat yo' ass!"

Shameeq laughed as he helped YaYa upstairs to the shower.

The memory made YaYa smile to himself as he leaned against the cell wall. "Damn, Shameeq," he whispered. "It can't be."

It was something he refused to believe, but he also knew every man had his breaking point and even love had its limits.

??????

"That is a hell of a story, Drama," McGrady smirked. "After all those murders, the money, the fear you instilled in the streets ... after all that, here you are, broken, begging for us to save you," McGrady gloated. "You're fuckin' pathetic."

"Sometimes you gotta do what you gotta do," Drama shrugged, expressionless.

"But your own *sister*? You told on your own sister? Christ, do you people have any loyalty?! You'd probably tell on your own mother to save your ass!" McGrady laughed.

He struck a nerve with that comment. Drama lunged at him, but McGrady pulled his gun and took aim.

"Come on! Gimme a reason!" McGrady barked nervously.

Mullins stood and pointed at Drama.

"You! Sit the fuck *down*! And, McGrady, enough of the taunts! Holster your weapon!"

McGrady and Drama eye-boxed a moment longer.

"I said, holster your weapon!" Mullins repeated.

Slowly, both men complied.

"Now, Drama, I understand everything you've told us. Every piece checks out, but the Navy yards? Panama? You expect me to believe the military facilitated the smuggling of cocaine?" Mullins shook his head. "You have no proof."

Drama smiled.

"I do."

"What?"

"John, Richard's lover," Drama smirked.

"But I thought you said you were ordered by Nya to kill John," McGrady said.

"I was, but I didn't. I tucked him away. Call it ... insurance," Drama snickered.

"Where is he?" Mullins asked.

"Around," Drama replied vaguely, "and eager to get out of that porn charge he's under."

"You want this deal, you tell us *where*," Mullins demanded.

"Hold on. Because there's one thing I forgot to tell you," Drama began, leaning forward and folding his hands. "I told you Tony was a federal informant, but what I didn't tell you is he followed Nya one night. To Langdon Park in DC. You know the place, McGrady?"

"Can't say that I do," McGrady sneered.

"Anyway, he saw her talking to an older white guy out there. He must've been upset because he slapped her around a couple of times. I was on the phone, and I'm thinking, Who could that be? So I ran the plates, and guess what I found out," Drama teased.

"What?" Mullins replied.

"It was registered to the government, which really didn't tell me much because it could have been police or a politician," Drama said.

"Or a jealous lover. Maybe she was just fuckin' around behind your back," McGrady opined.

"But why be so hush-hush about it? Anyway, something told me his identity would answer all my questions, so earlier today I went to see Nya, and I told her what I'm telling you. Of course, she denied it, but I let it slip where I was meeting the snitch, in front of her secretary," Drama said. He smiled as he prepared to put the board in check, pawn for pawn. "Let me ask you something: How did you know where to find my peoples?"

Mullins looked at Jacobs, and Jacobs looked at Mullins.

"Don't rack your brains. I'll tell you," Drama said. "Nya told you, only she was so anxious to stop me, she didn't tell you *how* she knew what she knew. And you just accepted it because you figured she was just doin' her job. But she was the *only* one to know besides me and my peoples. I didn't tell you, nor did my peoples, so she *had* to tell you, and you came to snatch up the snitch, but you don't know which one it is, do you?" Drama taunted.

Check.

"You're fuckin' crazy," McGrady hissed. "Are you implying that—"

"I'm not implying anything. It's actual *fact* this ain't about Drama Squad. This about finding the snitch and eliminatin' him so the feds won't find out that one of you is really the connect," Drama concluded. "Matter of fact, I'm done talkin' to you. I wanna speak to the feds."

Jacobs laughed in his face.

"You wasted four fuckin' hours on *that?!* You come in here talking about a deal and try to tell us *we're* the suppliers?!" he said, laughing harder. "What are you, some kind of conspiracy theorist?!"

Drama looked at him stone-faced.

Okay, you wanna play games?" Mullins growled, then turned to McGrady. "Go prepare a cell for our notorious friend here. Make sure they know he's been talking to *us*," Mullins leered.

McGrady nodded and walked out.

Mullins and Drama stared each other down.

Drama broke the silence. "Yeah, I like that. I like how you got McGrady out the room. I guess he's not a part of this, huh? Now you can really ask what you want to know: Where is Tony?, Where is Tony, la-la-la," Drama sang derisively.

"Why would I care about a federal snitch when I got my own right here?" Mullins shot back.

"Because he can identify you," Drama replied, leaning into the conversation.

Mullins chuckled.

"You think you got it all figured out, huh? Well, I've got news for you: You're wrong!" Mullins spat. "You want the truth, huh? Do you? Yes, it was me at Langdon Park that night, but you know why? Because Nya works for the D.E.A., setting up punks like you!" Mullins told him. "She's my C.I., you see? We were working the Drama Squad from the beginning, and Nya helped us set the trap."

Drama just sat back and smiled at him.

"Now, don't you feel really stupid?" Mullins quipped.

"Was she good?" Drama asked.

"The best."

"No, I mean in bed. Was her pussy good?"

Mullins smiled. "Like I said, the best."

"Better than her mother's?"

"I wouldn't know. I didn't know the cunt had a mother."

"Of course you did. You should know your own daughter's mother," Drama jabbed.

"Daughter?" Mullins echoed. "I don't have a daughter."

"No? I guess not. I mean, what father wants to openly acknowledge the fact that he's fuckin' his own seed. That is, unless you're from West Virginia. You from West Virginia, Mullins?" Drama probed.

"You're delusional. This conversation is over. *No deal*," Mullins growled.

"What were you, late teens, early twenties? Probably from a place that didn't have many black women. Midwest? Probably would've married the girl next door, until you joined the Navy. That's when your eyes were opened and you wondered, fantasized."

Mullins busied himself with the paperwork, ignoring Drama.

"Yeah, you wondered, and then you met—what was her name? Never mind. Her name didn't matter to you. All you saw was this black goddess in physical form, but she wasn't nigguh black. No, that would never do. She was Creole, exotic. You could pretend, huh?" Drama smirked, and Mullins looked at him.

"In prison, you'll be somebody's goddess ... nigger," Mullins hissed.

"At first, it was just a fling, right? A chance to taste the nectar. But the black woman is powerful, seductive, and before you knew it, she was all you thought about. But you couldn't tame her. You weren't ... *man* enough to handle her." Mullins stood up.

"McGrady's taking too long. Let's go. I'll take you myself."

He snatched Drama by the arm and started for the door

"The day you caught her, you watched, didn't you? You stood there and listened to the moans you couldn't make her sing, the way she gave her body up to the black God between her legs.

You watched, heartbroken, but you were turned on by how he beat that pussy. That big black dick was creamin' her walls, and in the back of your mind you wondered how that big black dick would feel in your a—"

Mullins grabbed Drama by the collar and slammed him against the wall.

"The bitch was a whore! A goddamn whore! She deserved what she got! I watched her die slow, and I made that bitch suffer every goddamn day she lived!" Mullins seethed, his face reddened, and the veins in his neck bulged.

"Tony knows. He can identify you. You send me upstairs and I'll make sure he knows *everything*," Drama hissed.

"You think I'd put you in the same pod?" Mullins cackled.

"You think I'd be stupid enough to send him into a setup?" Drama shot back. "Tony isn't one of the three."

"You're lying."

"You wanna take that chance? Send me upstairs," Drama challenged him.

McGrady walked in and looked perplexed by the way Mullins had drama pinned to the wall.

"Uhhhh, Bill ... is everything okay?" McGrady asked. "The cell's ready."

Mullins looked at Drama, and Drama's eyes dared him to follow through.

"Okay," Mullins said, "just gimme a few more minutes. Go see what's taking Jacobs so long with the identity check."

McGrady left back out.

"Where is he?" Mullins demanded.

"Here's the deal," Drama began, "you want Tony, you let all three of my peoples go. We'll handle him ourselves."

Mullins let him go and stepped back.

"Let the Drama Squad go? No deal."

"Look, YaYa, Blue and Rivera ain't got nothing to do wit' this. I'm goin' to prison regardless. Let them go, you get the snitch, and I'll take the weight," Drama proposed.

"You?" Mullins smirked.

"I'm the boss. It's *Drama's* Squad, remember? That's the deal; take it or leave it. Either way, I go to prison. The only question is whether you and I will be cellies," Drama grinned.

Mullins eyed Drama closely, then said, "I think you're bluffing. This Tony guy is just as much a problem to you, so you couldn't let him run loose. So you made sure he was on ice until you could try and carry out this hair-brained scheme of yours. Who is it, huh? YaYa?"

He watched Drama's reaction, but he got nothing.

"Or maybe Blue?"

Nothing.

"No, no. It's Rivera, right? Am I right?" Mullins toyed with him but still got nothing.

"We got a deal or not?" Drama replied, then coughed hard.

Mullins sat on the desk and looked at Drama curiously.

"What is it? Some kind of honor thing? You supposed to be the noble knight willing to fall on his sword for the good of the whole? Why? Those guys are gonna get out and do the same damn thing. Maybe not this year, maybe not next year, but they will join you soon. You know why?"

"Why?"

Mullins approached him.

"Because you're *niggers*. Ignorant niggers. When will you get it? We push the shit to you and use the money to take over the world while all you get is Saturday visits and an asshole full of time. You're not even a cog in the machine; you're just the greasy shit that makes it squeak," Mullins snickered, shaking his head. "You wanna wear it? Fine, but I want *proof* that this is really the guy."

"We want him out the way as bad as you do. If it's a deal, then he's good as dead," Drama assured him.

Mullins flipped open his phone and hit speed dial. "Jacobs? Yeah, the three guys that were arrested earlier," Mullins said, looking at Drama, "let 'em go. You heard me. They're free to go. We got who we need right here."

Mullins hung up.

"Those three are the ones that's gonna handle it. My most trusted," Drama replied.

"I hope they're worth your life because with everything we got, you'll get the federal death penalty, *guaranteed,*" Mullins stressed.

Drama shrugged. "We all gotta die for something."

??????

CHAPTER 22

YaYa Mitchell! Dorrin McCoy! Pack up! You're outta here!" the marshal exclaimed.

YaYa was sitting on his bunk when he heard it. His ears perked up, and he came out into the dorm. Who?"

"You heard me. You. McCoy."

"Naw, that's me," Blue said loudly.

"I'm Mitchell," YaYa said.

"Both of you, roll your mat!"

YaYa looked at Blue, confused. They both headed for the front gate. If the agents had made a mistake, they weren't gonna waste time and let them correct it.

"Rivera," the marshal said, knocking on the door of the lockup cell. He knocked harder to wake Rivera up.

"Hey, Rivera! Rise and shine, you're being released!"

Rivera sat up quickly.

"It's about time," he huffed, thinking the feds had pulled the necessary strings to get him out quietly. He was in for a surprise.

??????

The sky was a curious purple as the sun set over Norfolk. YaYa and Blue walked out. Rivera walked out a few minutes later. Rivera was looking around, so he didn't even notice YaYa and Blue.

"Yo, Tony! Tony! What up, baby! I don't know how we did it, but we free!" YaYa exclaimed.

Tony's eyes got big as plates. What the hell were they doing out? Surely the feds didn't get them out too. Tony played it off and went over and gave them dap.

"I knew they couldn't hold us. Fuck they charge us with, having lunch?" Tony joked as he scanned his surroundings through his peripheral.

A black van pulled up, and Montez stuck his head out the driver's window. "Yo, let's go!"

YaYa and Blue walked over. Rivera followed reluctantly. When they opened the sliding door, YaYa exclaimed, "Yo?!"

"Just get the fuck in," Montez hissed.

YaYa and Blue climbed in. Tony hesitated.

"I'ma ... I'ma wait for my girl," Tony said.

"We got somethin' to handle. Get in!"

Tony knew he couldn't say no. He climbed in, and the van pulled off.

??????

"Yo, you tryin' to tell me this nigguh a snitch, God?!" YaYa scowled.

"And he fuckin' killed my muhfuckin cousin," Montez spat, then hooked Tony hard, knocking him to the ground.

They had him in the middle of the woods, scared and bloody.

"Please man, don't do this!" Tony begged the four of them.

His answer was a swift kick in the mouth, knocking out his two front teeth.

Montez raised the gun.

"Wait. Make the call."

Drama's phone rang.

"Yo."

"Peace."

Drama put his phone on speaker. Mullins heard the dull thud of blows to a human body, accompanied with the pleas for mercy.

"Please!"

"Tell 'em!"

"Okay, okay!"

Smack!

"Okay, I do, man, I do. I'm a federal informant! I'm the guy who got Mark busted in Richmond," Tony admitted.

Mullins listened intently.

"Ask him what his code name is. What's his code name? What does his handler call him?" Mullins wanted to know.

"What's your code name?" Drama repeated.

"Bobbito! They call me Bobbito!" Tony groaned in agony.

"Satisfied?" Drama smirked.

Mullins nodded.

"Slump 'em," Drama said into the phone.

"Nooooo!" Tony cried.

Loud gunshots rang out.

Drama flipped the phone closed and pocketed it. "I told you Drama always keeps his word," he quipped.

Mullins flipped open his cell and speed-dialed Jacobs.

"Yeah, forget that other query. I need you to run another deep cover, but be discrete. Federal C.I., code name Bobbito," Mullins told him, then hung up.

Drama looked at him.

"What's gonna happen to Nya?"

Mullins didn't respond. He just began gathering the files on the table.

"You're gonna kill her, ain't you? Operation's over, so now it's time to tie up all the loose ends," Drama surmised. "Your own daughter, huh?"

Mullins looked at Drama. "The bitch is her mother's daughter."

Mullins' phone rang.

"Yeah."

"Bill, you're not going to believe this! Bobbito is definitely C.I.! He's been active in Richmond and DC. And get this, his real name is Richardo Rivera! He's one of the guys we let go!" Jacobs told him.

Mullins grimaced.

"Fuck! Okay, just get that cell ready. We're done here," Mullins said, then hung up. He sneered at Drama. "You son of a bitch. I was right! Rivera was Bobbito!"

Drama shrugged.

"Shoulda called my bluff then."

Mullins chuckled.

"Doesn't matter. A small victory for the condemned. Savor it on your way to the electric chair," Mullins spat, taking his arm. "Let's go."

He walked Drama out into the hallway and got the attention of a passing marshal.

"Dress this one out. Take him to the penthouse."

"Yes, sir," the marshal replied.

"Hey, Mullins," Drama said as Mullins walked away.

Mullins turned around.

"Tell Nya we even now," Drama winked as he was led away.

Mullins shook his head as he headed back to interrogation room. He had to admit, Drama wasn't your average street dude. He had played his hand to a tee. It just happened to be a losing hand from the beginning. Drama also stirred up feelings Mullins had never recovered from. Every time he thought about Nya his insides boiled and his loins heated up. He wished he had Nya there right then so he could pound his pain away into her womb, until his anger and sick need were both spent. In his twisted mind, Nya wasn't his daughter, she was the reincarnation of the black whore he wanted to punish over and over. Too bad he would have to kill her, but she had to go. Self-preservation was the first law of nature, and she was the last person who could link him to the operation. He would fuck her one last time and then take her out.

"Agent Mullins!" the marshal huffed, out of breath. "The inmate—"

That's all Mullins had to hear. He drew his gun and ran behind the marshal.

He envisioned Drama having his people trying to break him out of the jail by force. He knew the Drama Squad had the balls to do just that, so he prepared himself for a gun fight and expected to hear gunshots at any moment.

They rounded the corner to the receiving room, where inmates are strip searched and issued a county jumpsuit. He heard no gunfire, nor was there any frantic movement. The room was empty except for another marshal and Drama, who stood with a blanket draped over him.

"Agent," the marshal who came to get him began, "he's ... he's ..."

Drama didn't give him a chance to explain. Drama tossed the blankets aside.

Mullins' eyes widened in shock.

"Oh, my God!" he gasped.

"No, God*dess*," Egypt quipped. "I'm Egypt. You still want to serve that warrant?"

??????

Shameeq, YaYa, Blue and Montez were at Blue's stash house out in the country. The same place they had taken YaYa for the fake kidnapping. Shameeq sat slouched on the couch, a lit blunt in his mouth, explaining the situation. How he had Egypt impersonate him long enough to free them and find out who the connect was.

"You did what?!" YaYa laughed. "Yo, God, you a mastermind! I knew in my heart you wouldn't flip on family."

"Yo, stic, I thought I was gonna have to catch a body behind this nigguh," Blue laughed. "Yo! Any muhfucka say my man snitchin', say it now!" Blue said, mocking YaYa. "He in there *giving* muhfuckas shanks, stic!"

YaYa shrugged.

"I wanted it to be a fair fight. I just hate that bitch-ass whisperin' shit, B, word to mother," YaYa said, then turned to Shameeq.

"You got that off, Meeq, but why the fuck you keep us in the dark?"

Shameeq passed the blunt to Montez.

"'Cause I know how you rock. Them snitch-ass nigguhs is like fuckin' antennae—they pick up any hostility. Ya, you mighta gave dude a pass, but you ain't got no poker face, B! You woulda made that cocksucker uncomfortable as fuck, and he woulda known somethin' was up!" Shameeq chuckled.

"Indeed," YaYa nodded in agreement.

"What about Egypt? She good?" Montez asked.

Shameeq looked at him like he was crazy.

"Yo, that's my heart, B. I woulda never got her involved if I ain't know the shit was right and exact."

"Yeah, but if you wrong, we goin' in there and bust her the fuck out!" Montez stressed.

"You goddamn right," Shameeq replied, giving him dap.

His phone rang.

Egypt speed-dialed Shameeq and extended the ringing cell to Mullins.

"Somebody wanna talk to you," she smirked.

Mullins snatched the phone and put it to his ear just as Shameeq answered. "Speak to the God."

"You fuckin' black piece of shit! You'll never get away with this! Do you hear me?!" Mullins yelled into the phone.

"I already did," Shameeq shot back calmly.

"I'll hunt you down like a *dog*, nigger! And your sister? I'm gonna hang her high for the whole goddamn show!" Mullins yelled, his body trembling with anger.

Shameeq laughed. "How? I'm sure she signed Miranda as *Shameeq* Stevens, and we both know she's not Shameeq Stevens, so what you gonna charge her wit'? Obstruction of justice?"

"You son of a bitch, I'll—"

"Yo, calm down, officer, " Shameeq taunted him. "I got somebody wanna talk to you."

"Who?!"

"Yourself," Shameeq replied, then pressed play on the recorder and put it to the phone.

"The bitch was a whore! A goddamn whore!" Mullins heard himself say on the tape.

"Sound familiar?" Shameeq teased.

He had heard Mullins' whole confession. Eqypt had her phone in her pocket on speaker from the minute she walked in the office. She had recorded every word.

Mullins laughed.

"You stupid bastard! What do you think you got?! The tape was illegally obtained. It would never be admissible in court," Mullins gloated.

"Court?" Shameeq echoed. "Who said anything about court? *This* was for daddy's little girl."

Shameeq played the end of the tape.

"What's gonna happen to Nya?"

Silence.

"You're gonna kill her, ain't you? Operation's over. Now it's time to tie up all the loose ends. Your own daughter, huh?"

"The bitch is her mother's daughter."

Shameeq stopped the tape.

"Nya's a sharp chick, yo. You think she'll be able to read between the lines? And if she does, what do you think she'll do?" Shameeq quipped.

"She won't believe you," Mullins countered weakly.

She already does," Shameeq answered. "She's already heard the tape. You should be expecting a visit from the feds real soon."

Mullins' mind was racing. If Nya thought he was going to kill her, she'd have no choice but to run to the feds. He had to get to Nya. Mullins smashed the cell on the floor in frustration, then said to the marshal, "Lock her up!"

"Yes, sir," the marshal replied.

Jacobs and McGrady came into the room. McGrady looked at Egypt strangely, standing there draped in a blanket. He didn't know what happened.

"Bill, there's a couple of federal agents out here that want to talk to you," Jacobs informed him.

It seemed like everything was coming down on him all at once.

"Fuck," he barked.

"Ay, McGrady," Egypt called out.

He looked at her, and she blew him a kiss.

"Fuckin' faggot," McGrady mumbled.

Egypt was smiling, but her eyes were granite. She had blown him the kiss of death. He could hear her laughter fade as he exited the room.

??????

CHAPTER 23

Six months later

The sky over South Beach in Miami was bright and sunny as the Drama Squad relaxed on the deck of Shameeq's new 35-foot yacht called 120 Degrees. The whole crew was there: Peanut, Trello, Casper, Blue, Lil' B, Montez, YaYa, Egypt, Sherrie and Shameeq, along with a crew of bikini-clad cuties to decorate the deck.

Shameeq held up *The Washington Post* newspaper. The cover story headline caught his eye: "D.E.A. Agent Indicted in Million-Dollar Drug Ring."

The story told it all, courtesy of the government's chief witness, Nya Braswell. After she heard the tape, Nya knew her life was in danger. She also knew this was the only chance of getting out of her father's grasp. The FBI had already traced the cocaine pipeline back to the shipyards. Nya only needed to provide the details. She gave it all up, except one thing: The Drama Squad.

Anytime they were mentioned, Nya would deny their existence.

"I've never heard that name before," she smirked, "unless Don Baron's organization was known by that name and I wasn't aware of it."

The noose had tightened, but the Drama Squad had slipped through the cracks. The only mention of them in the article was the murder of the D.E.A. agent Timothy McGrady and his entire family, even his six-year-old son. Of course, they weren't mentioned by name. Egypt didn't forget or forgive. McGrady had violated her rules, so he had to pay with the lives of his family.

Egypt rubbed her ultra-short hair in anguish. "It's gonna take forever for my hair to grow back, Shameeq. You owe me! I want a brand-new car, breakfast in bed for a year, a six-month cruise " she went on and on as the rest of the crew laughed.

"Yo," Trello said, a bottle of Don in each hand and a chick sitting on each leg, "we beat the feds and the fuckin' D.E.A We should change our name to the fuckin' untouchables!"

Shameeq's cell phone rang.

"Peace."

"Hello, Shameeq."

He smiled because he recognized the voice immediately. It was Nya. She was calling him on the three way, through her lawyer. Shameeq walked away from the ruckus of the celebration so he could hear and not be heard.

"Shameeq? Are you there?"

"Yeah, I'm here. How you, love?" he replied with his finger in his other ear so he could hear her.

"Congratulations. You won," Nya said, smiling. "I just called to tell you that ... and to apologize."

"No need to apologize, Nya. We playin' a dirty game, and I ain't holdin' nothin' against you. Besides, you held us down in the end. I appreciate that," Shameeq replied.

"No, Shameeq, I do have to apologize. I told you a lot about, you know, what my father did to me, but I didn't tell you everything, and now that I'm finally away from his control ... "

Her voice trailed off momentarily, then she added, "I know it sounds sick, but I needed my father's approval. I needed him to love me because he was all that I had ... until I met you."

"Naw, it ain't sick, ma. If that's the only love you knew, then you did what you had to do to keep it," Shameeq answered. He could hear that same little girl he had glimpsed in Macau.

Nya sniffed, so he could tell she was fighting back tears.

"I wish we could've met somewhere else, in a different way, you know?"

"Me too. I guess the timing was off."

"Yeah, time. I'll have plenty of that. My lawyer said I'll probably get ten, maybe be home in seven if I'm a good girl," she giggled. "Despite the years, I know you can't see the future, and tomorrow could look different than today, but do you think that after this we can be friends?"

Shameeq smiled.

"Of course, love. We friends now."

"Thank you, Shameeq. Uhhh … I don't have too much longer on this phone, but I need a favor," she said.

"What's the favor?"

"I left all my deeds to my real interest in my safety-deposit box. I don't have anybody I can trust, so I was wondering if you could look after it for me? I know I can trust you, Shameeq, because I know now you're a man of your word," Nya told him.

Shameeq smiled.

"I've got a few buyers lined up, so if we sell, we'll split it 50/50," she offered.

"Naw, love, that's your money. But I got you," Shameeq assured her.

"Oh, and the golden key's in there too," she chuckled. "Don't do anything I wouldn't do."

Shameeq laughed.

"Well, I guess that's it," Nya said as if she didn't want to hang up.

"Take care of yourself, Nya."

"You too, Shameeq." She paused. "I love you," she admitted.

I love you too, he thought, but he said, "I know you do, love. Peace."

He hung up and looked out at the setting sun. He was barely 25 and he had been given a second chance. He had ducked the fate of so many black brothers who ended up doing long sentences in the penitentiary. He didn't plan on trying his luck twice.

He walked back over and watched his family celebrating.

His eyes fell on Sherrie, eight months pregnant and glowing. His mind flashed back to the day in Macau when he looked at himself in the mirror. He had chuckled because he saw his father in himself. His mother killed his father because of his womanizing ways, and Sherrie reminded him of his mother, sweet and dedicated to her man. He knew he would be a good father, but he knew he wasn't ready to be a one-woman man. In the back of his mind, he could see Sherrie doing to him what his mother had done to his father. If she did, Shameeq accepted it because he believed in justice. Still, he was going to be him regardless.

"Yo, Meeq! Meeq! Fuck is you, deaf?" Egypt quipped, breaking his chain of thought. "I hear the Midwest is jumpin'! Iowa, Minnesota ... they even eatin' in Nebraska," Egypt said. "Let's make it happen!"

Shameeq shook his head.

"Naw, yo, the Drama Squad is officially retired. We going into the casino business," he announced.

YaYa stood up and held up his bottle of Don.

"To the future, God!" he said.

"To the Drama Squad!" Egypt boasted, and everybody raised their bottles to the sky.

"To the Drama Squad!" they all toasted in unison.

And if you don't know, now you know!

Dutch

Hailing from Newark, New Jersey, Kwame Teague is the award winning, critically acclaimed, and Essence #1 bestselling author of the street classic Dutch trilogy. His other novels include *The Adventures of Ghetto Sam, The Glory of My Demise, Thug Politics, and Dynasty- Dynasty 2, under the Pseudonym Dutch.*

Reviews are so important to authors, please feel free to leave a review and help us spread the word!

Thank you for taking the time to read Author Dutch and supporting DC Boodiva Publications!

Be sure to check out our other titles, just search DC Bookdiva on your e-readers for more details!

Befriend us on facebook and twitter, we would love to hear from you!

www.facebook.com/thedcbookdiva

www.twitter.com/dcbookdiva

Order Form

DC Bookdiva Publications
#245 4401-A Connecticut Avenue, NW
Washington, DC 20008
dcbookdiva.com

Name: __________ ______________________________
InmateID: ____ _________________________________
Address: ____
City/State: _____________________________ Zip: ________

QUANTITY	TITLES	PRICE	TOTAL
	Up The Way, Ben	15.00	
	Dynasty By Dutch	15.00	
	Dynasty 2 By Dutch	15.00	
	Trina, Darrell Debrew	15.00	
	A Killer'z Ambition, Nathan Welch	15.00	
	Lorton Legends, Eyone Williams	15.00	
	The Hustle. Frazier Boy	15.00	
	A Beautiful Satan, RJ Champ	15.00	
	Secrets Never Die, Eyone Williams	15.00	
	Q, Dutch	15.00	

QUANTITY	TITLES	PRICE	TOTAL
	-Coming Soon-		
	Dynasty 3, Dutch	15.00	
	A Killer'z Ambition 2, Nathan Welch	15.00	
	A Beautiful Satan 2, RJ Champ	15.00	
	A Hustler's Daughter, Pinky Dior	15.00	
	Tina, Darrell Debrew	15.00	

Sub-Total $__________

Shipping/Handling (Via US Media Mail) $3.95 1-2 Books, $7.95 1-3 Books, 4 or more titles-Free Shipping

Shipping $____ ______

Total Enclosed $__________

Certified or government issued checks and money orders, all mail in orders take 5-7 Business days to be delivered. Books can also be purchased on our website at dcbookdiva.com and by credit card at 1866-928-9990. Incarcerated readers receive 25% discount. Please pay $11.25 per book and apply the same shipping terms as stated above.

FICTION TEAGUE

Teague, Kwame.
[Question mark]

ALPH

R4001017521

ALPHARETTA
Atlanta-Fulton Public Library